CHERUB

THE DEALER

ALSO BY ROBERT MUCHAMORE

THE RECRUIT

MISSION 2

THE DEALER

ROBERT MUCHAMORE

Simon Pulse

New York London Toronto Sydney

This book is a work of fiction. Any references to historical events, real people, or real locales are used fictitiously. Other names, characters, places, and incidents are the product of the author's imagination, and any resemblance to actual events or locales or persons, living or dead, is entirely coincidental.

SIMON PULSE
An imprint of Simon & Schuster Children's Publishing Division
1230 Avenue of the Americas, New York, NY 10020
This Simon Pulse paperback edition August 2011

Originally published in Great Britain in 2004 by Hodder Children's Books as *Class A*
Published by arrangement with Hodder and Stoughton Limited

Also available in a Simon Pulse hardcover edition.
For information about special discounts for bulk purchases, please contact
Simon & Schuster Special Sales at 1-866-506-1949
or business@simonandschuster.com.
The Simon & Schuster Speakers Bureau can bring authors to your live event.
For more information or to book an event contact the Simon & Schuster
Speakers Bureau at 1-866-248-3049 or visit our website at www.simonspeakers.com.
Designed by Mike Rosamilia
The text of this book was set in Apollo MT.
Manufactured in the United States of America
2 4 6 8 10 9 7 5 3 1
Library of Congress Control Number 2004118122
ISBN 978-1-4169-9941-6 (hc)
ISBN 978-1-4424-1361-0 (pbk)

CHERUB

THE DEALER

WHAT IS CHERUB?

CHERUB is a branch of British Intelligence. Its agents are aged between ten and seventeen years. Cherubs are all orphans who have been taken out of care homes and trained to work undercover. They live on CHERUB campus, a secret facility hidden in the English countryside.

WHAT USE ARE KIDS?

Quite a lot. Nobody realizes kids do undercover missions, which means they can get away with all kinds of stuff that adults can't.

WHO ARE THEY?

About three hundred children live on CHERUB campus. JAMES ADAMS is our twelve-year-old hero. He's basically a good kid, but he has a habit of getting himself in trouble. There's also his younger sister, LAUREN. KERRY CHANG is a Hong Kong–born karate champion. GABRIELLE O'BRIEN is Kerry's best friend. BRUCE NORRIS, another karate champion, likes to think of himself as a hard man but still sleeps with a blue teddy under his chin. KYLE BLUEMAN is a more experienced CHERUB agent. He's two years older than James, but still a good mate.

AND THE T-SHIRTS?

Cherubs are ranked according to the colour of the T-shirts they wear on campus. ORANGE is for visitors. RED is for kids who live at CHERUB campus, but are too young to qualify as agents. BLUE is for kids undergoing CHERUB's tough 100-day training regime. A GRAY T-shirt means you're qualified for missions. NAVY is a reward for outstanding performance on a mission. If you do well, you'll end your CHERUB career wearing a BLACK T-shirt, the ultimate recognition for outstanding achievement. When you retire, you get the WHITE T-shirt, which is also worn by staff.

CHAPTER 1

HEAT

Billions of insects fizzed about in the sunset. James and Bruce had given up trying to swat them off. The boys had jogged ten kilometers along a twisted gravel path. It was uphill, heading towards a villa where two eight-year-olds were being held hostage.

"Better give us a minute," James huffed, leaning forward and resting his palms against his knees. "I'm wiped."

If James had wrung out his T-shirt, he could have filled a mug with sweat.

"I'm a year younger than you," Bruce said impatiently. "You should be the one pushing me. It's that gut you're carrying."

James looked down at himself. "Give over, I'm hardly fat."

"Not exactly thin either. You're gonna get crucified at your next medical. They'll put you on a diet and make you run all that off."

James straightened up and drank some water from his canteen.

"It's not my fault, Bruce. It's genetic. You should have seen the size of my mum before she died."

Bruce laughed. "There were three Toffee Crisp and one Snickers wrapper in our bin last night. That's not genetic, that's being a pig."

"We can't all have little stick-insect bodies like you," James said, bitterly. "Are you ready?"

"We might as well check the map now we've stopped," Bruce said. "See how far it is to the villa."

James got a map out of his pack. Bruce had a GPS clipped on his shorts. The tiny unit told you your exact position anywhere on the planet to within a couple of meters. Bruce transposed the coordinates on to the map and used his finger to trace the winding gravel path towards the villa.

"Time to go off road," Bruce said. "It's less than half a kilometer away."

"It's really steep," James said, "and the ground crumbles around here. It's gonna be a nightmare."

"Well," Bruce said, "unless your plan is to walk up to the front gate of the villa, ring the doorbell, and say, 'Excuse me love, can we have our hostages back?' I think we'd better cut into the bushes."

Bruce had a point. James gave up trying to fold the

map properly and stuffed it in his pack. Bruce led the way into the scrub, the tinder-dry plants crunching under his trainers. It hadn't rained on the island for two months. There'd been bush fires in the east. When the sky was clear, you could see the plumes of smoke.

James's damp skin soon had a coating of grit. He grabbed on to plants, using them to pull his way up the steep slope. You had to be careful: some plants had barbs, others erupted from the dry ground as soon as you pulled on them, leaving you holding a clump of roots, clutching desperately for something sturdier before you tumbled backwards.

When they reached the wire fence around the villa, they backed up a few meters and lay flat on the ground, collecting their thoughts. Bruce was moaning something about his hand.

"What are you whinging about?" James asked.

Bruce showed James his palm. Even in the half-light, James could see the blood trickling down Bruce's arm.

"How'd you do that?"

Bruce shrugged. "Somewhere coming up the hill. I didn't realize until we stopped."

"I'd better clean it up for you."

James tipped some water out of his canteen, washing away most of the blood. He got a first aid kit out of his pack; then lit a small torch and clamped it between his teeth, so he could see what he was doing while keeping both hands free. A thorn bulged under the webbing between Bruce's middle fingers.

"Nasty," James said. "Does it hurt?"

"What kind of stupid question is that?" Bruce snapped. "Of course it does."

"Am I supposed to pull it out?" James asked.

"Yes," Bruce said wearily. "Do you ever listen in class? Always remove splinters, unless there is severe and profuse bleeding, or you suspect you've punctured a vein or artery. Then apply disinfectant and a clean dressing or sticking plaster."

"You sound like you swallowed the textbook," James said.

"I was on the same first aid course as you, James. Only I didn't spend the entire three days trying to get off with Susan Kaplan."

"It's a pity she had a boyfriend."

"Susan doesn't have a boyfriend," Bruce said. "She was just trying to get rid of you."

"Oh," James said, crushed. "I thought she liked me."

Bruce didn't answer. He was biting down on the strap of his backpack. He didn't want anyone in the villa to hear if the pain made him scream out.

James lined up his tweezers. "Ready?"

Bruce nodded.

The thorn slid out easily enough. Bruce moaned as a fresh dribble of blood trickled down his hand. James mopped it up, rubbed on antiseptic cream, and wound a bandage tightly between Bruce's fingers.

"All done," James said. "Are you all right to carry on?"

"We can't turn back after going this far."

"You rest for a minute," James said. "I'll sneak up to the fence and check out the security."

"Watch out for video cameras," Bruce said. "They'll be expecting us."

When James switched off the torch, there was only

moonlight left. He shuffled to the fence on his belly. The villa looked impressive: two storys, four-car garage, and a kidney-shaped pool out front. The lawn sprinklers chugged gently, the spouts of water illuminated by the porch lights. There was no sign of any cameras or hi-tech security stuff; just the yellow siren box from a cheapo burglar alarm, which would be switched off while anyone was in the house. James turned back towards Bruce.

"Get up here. It doesn't look too serious."

James got out his wire cutters and snipped links in the fence until there was a slot big enough to squeeze through. He followed Bruce over the lawn, crawling swiftly towards the house. James felt something squish against his leg.

"Oh . . . man," James said, sounding totally revolted. "Jesus."

Bruce hushed him up. "Quiet, for God's sake. What's the matter?"

"I just dragged my knee through a colossal pile of dog crap."

Bruce couldn't help smiling. James looked set to puke.

"This is bad," Bruce said.

"Tell me about it. I've had it on my shoe before, but this is on my bare skin."

"You know what a massive pile of dog mess means?"

"Yeah," James said. "It means I'm extremely pissed off."

"It also means there's a massive dog around here."

The thought focused James's mind and got him crawling again. They stopped when they got to the wall of the villa, adjacent to a row of French doors. Bruce sat against the wall and checked out the room inside. The light was on. There were leather sofas and a snooker table inside. They tried sliding the French doors, but every one was locked. The keyholes were on the inside, so there was nothing to use their lock guns on.

WOOF.

The boys snapped their necks around. The mother of all rottweilers stood five meters away. The huge beast had muscles swelling through its shiny black coat and strings of drool hanging off its jaw.

"Nice doggy," Bruce said, trying to keep calm.

The growling dog moved closer, its black eyes staring them down.

"Who's a nice doggy-woggy?" Bruce asked.

"Bruce, I don't think it's gonna roll over and let you tickle its tummy."

"Well, what's *your* plan?"

"Don't show it any fear," James quaked. "We'll stare it down. It's probably as scared of us as we are of it."

"Yeah," Bruce said. "You can tell. The poor thing's cacking itself."

James began creeping backwards. The dog let out more volcanic barks. A metal hose reel clattered as James backed into it. He considered the reel for a second, before leaning over and unrolling a few meters of plastic hose. The dog was only a couple of steps away.

"Bruce, you run off and try to open a door," James gasped. "I'll try fending it off with this pipe."

James half hoped the dog would go after Bruce, but it

kept its eyes fixed, pacing closer to James until he could feel its damp breath on his legs.

"Nice doggy," James said.

The rottweiler reared up on its back legs, trying to knock James over. James spun away and the paws squealed down the glass door. James lashed out with the hosepipe. It cracked against the dog's rib cage. The beast made a high-pitched yelp and backed up slightly. James cracked the pipe against the patio tiles, hoping the noise would scare the dog away, but if anything the whipping seemed to have made it crazier.

James felt like his guts were going to drop out, imagining how easily the huge animal could rip into his flesh. James had nearly drowned once. He'd thought nothing could ever be scarier, but this had the edge.

A bolt clicked behind James's head and the French door glided open.

"Would Sir care to step inside?" Bruce asked.

James threw down the hose and leapt through the opening. Bruce rammed the door shut before the rottweiler made a move.

"What took you so long?" James said anxiously, trying to stop his hands from shaking. "Where is everyone?"

"No sign," Bruce said. "Which is definitely weird. They'd have to be deaf not to hear that psycho mutt barking at us."

James grabbed one of the curtains and used it to wipe the dog crap off his leg.

"That's so gross," Bruce said. "At least it's not on your clothes."

"Have you checked all the rooms out?"

Bruce shook his head. "I thought I'd make sure you weren't being eaten first, even if it meant we got caught."

"Fair play," James said.

They worked their way across the ground floor, creeping up to each door and checking out the rooms. The villa looked lived-in. There were cigarette butts in ashtrays and dirty mugs. There was a Mercedes in the garage. Bruce pocketed the keys.

"There's our getaway vehicle," he said.

There was no sign of life on the ground floor, which made the staircase likely to be some sort of trap. They stepped up gingerly, expecting someone to burst onto the landing pointing a gun at them.

There were three bedrooms and a bathroom on the second floor. The two hostages were in the master bedroom. The eight-year-olds, Jake and Laura, were tied to a bedpost, with gags over their mouths. They wore grubby T-shirts and shorts.

James and Bruce pulled the hunting knives off their belts and cut the kids loose. There was no time for greetings.

"Laura," James barked. "When did you last see the bad guys? Have you got any idea where they might be?"

Laura was red-faced and seemed listless.

"I dunno," she shrugged. "But I'm busting to pee."

Laura and Jake knew nothing about anything. Bruce and James had been expecting a battle to get at them. This was far too easy.

"We're taking you to the car," James said.

Laura started limping towards the bathroom. Her ankle was strapped up.

"We don't have time for toilet breaks," James gasped. "They've got guns and we haven't."

"I'm gonna wet my knickers in a minute," Laura said, bolting herself inside the en-suite bathroom.

James was furious. "Well, make it snappy."

"I need to go too," Jake said.

Bruce shook his head. "I don't want you disappearing. You can pee in the corner of the garage while I start the car."

He led Jake downstairs. James waited half a minute before thumping on the bathroom door.

"Laura, come on. What the hell is taking you so long?"

"I'm washing my hands," Laura said. "I couldn't find any soap."

James couldn't believe it.

"For the love of God," he shouted, hammering his fist on the bolted door. "We've *got* to get out of here."

Laura eventually hobbled out of the bathroom. James scooped her over his shoulder and sprinted downstairs to the garage. Bruce sat at the steering wheel inside the car. Laura slid onto the backseat next to Jake.

"It's kaput," Bruce shouted, getting out of the car and kicking the front wing. "The key goes in but it won't turn. It's showing a full tank of petrol. I don't know what's wrong with it."

"It's been sabotaged," James yelled back. "I bet you any money this is a trap."

Bruce looked awkward as the realization dawned.

"You're right. Let's get out of here."

James leaned inside the Mercedes.

"Sorry you two," he said, looking at Jake and Laura. "Looks like we've got to make a run for it."

But it was too late. James heard the noise, but only turned around in time to see the gun pointing at him. Bruce screamed out, as James felt two rounds smash into his chest. The pain knocked the air out of his lungs. He stumbled backwards, watching bright red streaks dribbling down his T-shirt.

CHAPTER 2

STINGING

Fired from close range, the next paintball knocked James backwards on to the concrete floor. Kerry Chang kept the gun on him as she closed in. James had his hands in the air.

"I surrender."

"Pardon?" Kerry said, blasting a fourth paintball into James's thigh.

It wasn't going to do permanent damage but, fired from close range, the paintballs had left him in a heap on the ground.

"Kerry, please, not again," James gasped. "That *really* hurts."

"Pardon?" Kerry said. "Can't hear what you're saying."

She stood astride James, pointing the muzzle of the paintball gun at him. On the other side of the car, Bruce screamed as Gabrielle shot him a couple more times.

Kerry fired into James stomach from less than a meter away, doubling him over.

"You mad *cow,*" James howled. "You could have my eye out doing that. You're supposed to stop shooting as soon as I surrender."

"Did you surrender?" Kerry grinned. "I misheard. I thought you said, 'Please shoot me again.'"

The girls rested their guns on the roof of the car.

"Did we whip your little pink butts?" Gabrielle whooped in her thick Jamaican accent. "Or did we whip your little pink butts?"

James struggled to sit up, clasping his hands over his stomach. The pain was bad, but losing to the girls on a stupid training exercise hurt a hundred times more.

The powered garage door started rolling upwards. A huge man stood silhouetted against the moonlight. It was Norman Large, CHERUB's head training instructor. He had the rottweiler on a leash at his side.

"Well done, ladies," Mr. Large shouted. "You've distinguished those pretty little heads on this one."

Kerry and Gabrielle smiled. Mr. Large stopped walking when his size fifteen boots were almost touching James's leg. James put his hand over his face, shielding his nose from the growling dog's rank breath.

"That thing's not gonna bite me, is it?" James asked.

Mr. Large laughed. "Luckily for you and Bruce, Thatcher has been trained to pin a man to the ground and never bite. Her brother, Saddam, now that's a different question. He's trained to sink his teeth in. We'd have been picking chunks of flesh off the lawn if you'd been up against Saddam. Unfortunately, the chairman banned me from using him. . . . Anyway, James, get on your feet. Gabrielle, help that other little idiot to stand up."

Bruce limped around the car, using the bonnet for support. The yellow paint from Gabrielle's gun trickled down his legs. Both boys stood with their backs against the car. Mr. Large hollered right in their faces.

"Tell me everything you did wrong."

"I'm . . . not sure, really," James shrugged.

Bruce looked down at the floor.

"Let's start at the beginning," Mr. Large bawled. "Why did it take you so long to reach the villa?"

"We jogged all the way," James said.

"Jogged?" Mr. Large shouted. "If I'm being held hostage at gunpoint, I at least expect my rescuers to have the decency to *run* to my rescue."

"It's boiling hot out there," James said.

"I could have run," Bruce said, "but James was knackered after ten minutes."

James gave Bruce a fierce look. Teams were supposed to stick together, not drop one another in it at the first opportunity.

"Can't manage a little ten-kilometer run, eh, James?" Mr. Large said, breaking into an evil grin. "Looks like you've let yourself get out of shape holidaying out here in the sunshine."

"I'm fit," James said. "It's just the heat."

"So, because you took so long to arrive, it was dark when you got to the villa, making it much more difficult to survey. Not that it matters, because you didn't do a proper survey anyway."

"I had a good look through the fence," James said, defensively.

Large banged his fist on the roof of the car.

"That's a survey, is it? What have you two been taught?"

"Before entering hostile premises, always do a thorough survey, investigating the building from all sides," Bruce said mechanically. "If possible, climb a tree or go to higher ground and get a look at the layout of the building from above."

"If you remember what it says in the training manual, Bruce, why did you decide that a glance through the fence was sufficient?"

Bruce and James both looked sheepish. Kerry and Gabrielle loved watching the boys squirm.

"If you'd done proper survey, maybe you would have seen the dog kennel. Maybe you could have planned a proper entry and exit strategy, instead of crawling up to the house and hoping for the best. Then, once you'd recovered the hostages, you decided to escape using the car. Didn't it occur to you that the car was the most obvious way to escape and was almost certainly booby-trapped? Or were you blinded by the prospect of lighting up the tires and taking it for a spin?"

"It did occur that it was obvious," James said.

"So why did you try to escape that way?" Large screamed.

"I mean . . . But . . . I only realized right before I got shot."

"This has got to be the worst performance on a training exercise I have *ever* seen," Mr. Large shouted. "You two have ignored every piece of training you've been given. If this was a real operation, you would have been killed ten times over. You're both getting grade F and James, I'm putting you on an emergency fitness plan. Ten kilometers running a day and, as you're so worried about the heat, I'll let you start when it's nice and cool. How does five in the morning sound?"

James knew better than to answer back, it only earned you push-ups. Mr. Large stepped back and took deep breaths. His head looked like a redcurrant after all the shouting.

"What grade did me and Gabrielle get?" Kerry asked, using her crawliest voice.

"B, I suppose," Mr. Large said. "You did a bang-up job, but I can't give you an A because you were up against such feeble opposition."

Gabrielle and Kerry smiled at each other. James wanted to knock their stupid smug heads together.

"Right, time to head back to the hostel," Large said. "Bruce, I need the car key."

Bruce chucked it over.

"That won't work," Gabrielle said. "That's for the front door of the villa. I put it on a Mercedes key ring so it looked like the car key. You want this one."

Mr. Large caught the real car key and loaded Thatcher the dog on to the front seat. Gabrielle and Kerry got in the back, squashed up with the two eight-year-olds.

"Oh no," Mr. Large grinned, as his massive body sank into the driver's seat. "Not enough room in the car. It looks like James and Bruce will have to find their own way home."

"But we drove in the van for ages before they dropped us off," James gasped. "I've got no idea how to get back to the hostel from here."

"How *awfully* sad," Mr. Large said, sarcastically. "I tell you what, if you manage to make it home before mid-night, I'll put your grade up to a D and you won't have to repeat the exercise."

Mr. Large turned the key in the ignition and the car started rolling forward. Thatcher poked her head out of the window and barked as the car crunched down the gravel driveway. James and Bruce looked despondently at each other.

"I don't think that it's that hard," Bruce said. "It's three hours until midnight and it's all downhill."

James looked totally miserable. "My legs feel like blocks of wood."

"Well," Bruce said, "I'm gonna start walking. You can go through this again if you want to, but I'm not going to."

"What I can't believe," James said, "is that everyone told me to get my act together and I never listened."

CHAPTER 9
SUN

Unless they're away on a mission, every kid at CHERUB spends five weeks in the summer on the Mediterranean island of C—. It's mostly a holiday: a chance to muck about on the beach, play sport, ride quad bikes over the sand dunes, and have a shot at being normal kids. But cherubs aren't normal kids: they could be sent on an undercover mission at any time. Even on holiday, they are expected to stay fit and do the odd training exercise.

Like loads of cherubs before him, James found it easy to slack off when there was a beach on the doorstep and tons of other kids to muck around with. For the last four weeks, he'd skipped fitness training. He'd spent his days messing about on the beach and his nights watching

DVD marathons while stuffing his face with popcorn and chocolate. When James got his training assignment, he ignored Kerry's advice to study it thoroughly and went out on a Jet Ski instead.

James considered his folly as he sauntered through the sticky night air toward the CHERUB hostel. The physical training instructors were going to make his life a misery. Once you gave them a reason, they didn't let you off until you were back in top shape. James couldn't make any excuses: Amy, Kyle, and loads of teachers had warned him to exercise and take the training seriously, but he'd lost all sense of responsibility the second he hit the beach.

Even after getting lost a couple of times, James and Bruce beat the midnight deadline for getting back. James had a grazed elbow where he'd tripped in a pothole in the dark and they were both gasping for a drink.

A bunch of older kids were having a moonlit barbecue in the gardens at the front of the hostel. Amy Collins came running over the lawn when she noticed James. She was beautiful, sixteen years old, with long blond hair. She wore denim shorts and a flowery top that stopped above the gold ring through her navel.

"Nice paint job, boys," she giggled. "Gabrielle and Kerry said they scrubbed the floor with the pair of you."

"You're drunk," James said.

Drinking alcohol wasn't allowed, but CHERUB staff turned a blind eye with the older kids, as long as they didn't go mad.

"Just a teensy drop," Amy said. "We went out on a boat and caught fish."

Amy spread her arms out to the size of a big fish, almost lost her balance and doubled over in drunken hysterics.

"You want barbecued fish?" she spluttered. "And there's fresh bread from the village."

"It's late," James said, shaking his head. "We'd better clean up."

"We emptied the whole ocean," Amy giggled. "Anyway, I'm busting to pee. I'll see you two scumbags in the morning."

As Amy staggered away, she thought of something and turned back.

"Oh, James."

"What?"

"I told you so."

James gave her the finger and wandered towards the main entrance of the hostel with Bruce in tow. The less contact they had with other kids, the less they would get flamed for mucking up the training exercise. They ducked down as they passed the recreation room, where about thirty kids were watching a horror movie on a projector screen. A couple of little red-shirt kids snickered at their paint-spattered clothes as the boys walked upstairs to the second-floor bedroom they shared with Gabrielle and Kerry.

The room was an L-shape, with the girls' beds at one end and the boys' around the corner at the other. It was basic compared to their individual rooms back at campus: ceiling fans, tile floor, wicker chairs and a tiny TV. It hardly mattered because the kids were always busy and only used the rooms to wash and crash out.

Kerry and Gabrielle had been back a couple of hours. The TV was showing an episode of *The Simpsons* in Spanish, which both girls could understand. They kept quiet, not even commenting on the stench of sweat.

"Well?" James said.

Kerry gave an innocent smile. "Well, what?"

"I know you're gonna start on us," James said, sitting on his bed and pulling off his trainers. "So go on, get it over with. Rub our noses in it."

"We'd never do that," Gabrielle said. "We're nice girls."

"My arse," Bruce said.

Kerry sat up on her bed. She was pink and shriveled, like she'd just finished a long bath. James dumped his filthy polo shirt on the floor.

"You better take that stuff down to the laundry when you've had your showers," Kerry said. "It'll stink the whole room out."

"If *you* don't like my stink," Bruce said, kicking off his trainers, "*you* take it down there."

He balled up his crusty sock and lobbed it on to Kerry's duvet. She flicked it away with the end of a biro.

"So, how come it took you so long to get back here?" Kerry asked, trying not to grin.

As soon as she said that, Gabrielle started cracking up.

"What are you laughing for?" James asked. "It's fourteen kilometers between here and the villa. I'd like to see you two do it any quicker."

"They're *so* thick," Gabrielle howled. "I can't believe it."

"What?" James asked. "What's thick?"

"Didn't you bother checking out the house?" Kerry grinned.

"We couldn't hang around," Bruce explained. "We had to be back here by midnight."

"There was money all over the kitchen cabinet," Kerry said.

"What good could that do us?" Bruce asked.

"And there was a working telephone," Kerry continued. "And a telephone directory."

James was getting impatient. "So what?"

"This isn't Outer Mongolia," Gabrielle said, making a telephone receiver out of her hand and putting it to her ear. "Why didn't you pick up the phone and call a taxi?"

"Eh?" James gasped, turning around and giving Bruce a blank stare.

"Taxi," Kerry snorted, hardly able to get the words out over her giggles. "T-A-X-I, they're a normal car, with a man to drive you and a little orange lamp on the roof."

"Oh . . ." James said bitterly, looking at Bruce. "Why didn't we get a cab?"

"Don't have a go at me," Bruce said. "You never thought of it either."

Gabrielle was rolled up in a ball, laughing so hard the frame of her bed was shaking.

"You two dickheads walked fourteen kilometers when you could have called a taxi and been home in an hour," Kerry said, pedaling her feet in the air with delight.

James's socks were bloody where they'd chafed on the long walk. His back and shoulders hurt from carrying the pack, his elbow was agony and his leg still stank of dog mess, even though he'd washed it. One day, he would be able to laugh about this, but right now he was ready to explode.

"This is *bull,*" James screamed, hurling his trainers against the wall.

He kicked out at his wardrobe, but he was tired and lost his balance. He ended up in a heap on the floor, making the girls laugh even harder. Bruce looked just as mad, but he concentrated his energy into ripping off his clothes and heading towards the shower.

"Give us two minutes before you go in there," Kerry said, wiping tears of joy from her eyes. "I want to go to bed in a minute. Can I quickly brush my teeth?"

Bruce tutted. "Go on then, but don't take all night."

Kerry padded barefoot into the bathroom and squeezed out a ball of toothpaste. Bruce and James waited by the open doorway in their boxers while she brushed. Kerry tried to control her laughing, but she couldn't resist having another dig.

"Fourteen kilometers," she shrieked, spluttering white toothpaste foam all over the bathroom mirror.

Bruce couldn't take any more abuse.

"Let's see how you like being laughed at," he shouted.

As Kerry bent over the tap to rinse her mouth, Bruce dunked her head. He only meant to nudge her so she got water over her face, but he did it too hard. Kerry's front tooth hit the tap and she sprung up furiously.

"You idiot," Kerry stormed, nervously feeling inside her mouth. "I think you've chipped my tooth."

Bruce realized he'd overdone it, but he wasn't about to go apologizing to someone who'd spent the last ten minutes taking the mickey out of him.

"Good," he snapped. "Serves you right."

Kerry grabbed a glass off the sink and threw it at Bruce's head. He ducked and the glass shattered against the wall.

"Cool it," James said. "This isn't worth fighting over."

"Do you think I'm gonna grow a new tooth?" Kerry screamed.

She stepped forward and gave Bruce an almighty shove. Bruce adopted a fighting stance.

"You want a piece of me?" he shouted.

Kerry looked ferocious as she wiped her lips on to the sleeve of her nightshirt.

"If you want to get your arse kicked by a girl for the second time today," she snarled, "that's fine by me."

James wedged himself between Kerry and Bruce. He was taller and stockier than the two kids he was trying to keep apart.

"Get out of the way, James," Bruce said.

"I'm going for Bruce whether you like it or not," Kerry said, drilling James with her eyes. "If you're in my way, you'll get damaged."

James could beat either Kerry or Bruce for strength, say in an arm-wrestle, but fighting was more about skill. Kerry and Bruce had done combat training at CHERUB for five years, whereas James had come to CHERUB less than a year earlier. He'd be out of his depth in a stand-up fight against either of them.

"You're not fighting," James said unconvincingly, hoping Kerry was bluffing. "I'm staying right here."

Kerry stepped forward, swept James's ankle away, and jammed two fingers into his ribs. It was an elementary technique for knocking someone over without seriously hurting them. James crawled towards his bed as violence exploded over his head.

Kerry was off balance after knocking James out of the way. Bruce used this to his advantage, putting Kerry out of action with one blow. Kerry staggered forward, gasping for breath as the end music for *The Simpsons* came on TV.

Bruce thought the fight was as good as won. He moved to put Kerry in a headlock, but she'd played Bruce for a sucker. She quickly regained her balance, spun out of the way, hooked a foot around Bruce's ankles, and swept his legs away.

James clambered on to his mattress; half horrified, half curious to see who would win. There was no way for him or Gabrielle to get help: the fight was blocking the doorway.

Within seconds of hitting the floor, years of self-defense training collapsed to the level of two drunks grappling on pavement. Bruce had a clump of Kerry's hair wound around his wrist and Kerry was dragging her nails down Bruce's cheek. They thrashed about, cursing one another and eventually rolling into the TV table. The first couple of knocks rocked the TV close to the edge. The third made the TV topple, face first, into the floor. The glass screen cracked and orange sparks spewed across the floor. Some of them hit Bruce's and Kerry's bare legs, then the lights went out and the ceiling fans went silent.

James looked out of the window. All the lights outside had gone too. The exploding TV had fused the electricity for the whole hostel. The fight kept going, but all James could discern were shadows and grunts.

Now Bruce and Kerry were over by the TV, James had an opportunity to get help. He sprang off his bed and grabbed the door handle. Gabrielle thought the same thing at the same moment and they nearly collided in the dark.

The corridor was tinged with green emergency escape lighting. Kids had their heads sticking out of their rooms, all asking each other why the electricity had gone off. James could hear Arif, a seventeen-year-old kid who was over six feet tall. He was exactly what was needed to break up the fight.

"Help us," James shouted. "Bruce and Kerry are killing each other."

That exact moment, someone reset the fuse and the lights came back on. Arif ran towards James's room, along with twenty other kids who wanted to get a look at the action. Arif was first into the room, followed by James and Gabrielle.

Bruce was nowhere. Kerry was in the middle of the floor. Her face was twisted with pain and she had her hands wrapped over her knee.

"Oh God," she sobbed. "Help me."

Kerry had shattered her kneecap in training a couple of years earlier. It had been repaired with titanium pins, but it was still weak. Arif scooped her off the floor and sprinted downstairs to the first aid room.

"Where the hell is Bruce?" Gabrielle asked angrily.

James shooed the onlookers out and slammed the door. He leaned into the bathroom.

"God knows. He's not in there."

Then he heard a sob under Bruce's duvet. Bruce was a skinny thing, so when he pulled the covers up over his head it was easy to assume he wasn't there at all.

"Bruce?" James asked.

"I didn't mean to hurt her knee," Bruce sobbed. "I'm sorry."

"If you start a fight, people get hurt," Gabrielle said severely. "That's how it works."

James had more sympathy. He sat on the edge of Bruce's bed.

"Leave me alone, James. I'm not coming out."

"Bruce, come downstairs with me," James said. "Everyone loses their temper sometimes. I'm sure the staff will understand—and speaking from personal experience—it's always best if you get your own side of the story in first."

"No," Bruce sobbed. "Go away."

Meryl Spencer, a retired Olympic sprinter who was James's handler, burst into the room. She'd been in bed and was wearing a nightshirt and unlaced trainers.

"What's happened here?" Meryl shouted.

"They got in a fight," James explained. "Bruce is under his duvet and won't come out."

Meryl smiled. "Won't he now?"

She leaned over the bed.

"Bruce," she shouted. "You're gonna have to face the music for hurting Kerry. Stop acting like a baby and get out of there."

"Go away," Bruce said, tightening the duvet around his head. "You can't make me come out."

"You've got three seconds," Meryl shouted. "Or I'm gonna seriously lose my temper."

Bruce didn't move a muscle.

"One," Meryl said. "Two . . . Three."

On three, Meryl grabbed the tubular frame of Bruce's bed and tipped it on to its side. Bruce thumped onto the floor and Meryl whipped the duvet off him.

"Stand up," she shouted. "You're eleven years of age, not five."

Bruce jumped to his feet. His face was a teary mess. Meryl grabbed his shoulder and shoved him up against the wall.

"I want all three of you in my office. You're in serious trouble. This kind of behavior is not acceptable."

"Me and Gabrielle didn't do anything," James pleaded. "We tried to break it up."

"We'll discuss it in my office," Meryl said. She took a deep breath and realized that James and Bruce still stank.

"You two have ten minutes to shower, put clean clothes on, and get downstairs. And if anyone starts up this hiding under the duvet nonsense again, I'll have them running laps until they puke, every day for the rest of their miserable lives."

CHAPTER 4

GRASS

"What did you do this time?" Lauren asked. "When did you get back to campus? How come they sent you home early?"

James was half asleep in bed and he wasn't in the mood for his nine-year-old sister. Lauren had knocked on his bedroom door three times. When James ignored her, she picked the lock. The most irritating things about living at CHERUB was that every kid knew how to pick locks. James was planning to buy a bolt next time he went into town. There's no way to pick a bolt.

"Come *on*," Lauren said, sitting herself on the swivel chair at James's desk. "Spill the beans. Everyone saw the ambulance take Kerry to the medical unit."

Lauren was James's only family since their mum had died the year before. James loved his sister, but he still spent a lot of his life wishing she'd go some place and stick her head in a bucket. She could be a total pain.

"Tell us," Lauren said sharply. "You know I'll just sit here bugging you until you do."

James threw back his duvet and sat up, picking at a gluey eye.

"Why are you up so early?" he asked. "It's pitch black outside."

"It's half past ten," Lauren said, turning slowly around on the chair. "But it's raining."

James swung out of bed and peered through the blind. Rain trickled down his window. The sky was gray and the outdoor tennis courts were under water.

"Great," James said. "There's nothing like British summer to cheer you up."

"You've got a good tan," Lauren said. "Mine's almost gone and I've only been back from the hostel three weeks."

"Best holiday I've ever had." James grinned. "We'll have to try and fix it so we go at the same time next year. Me, Kerry, and about six other kids had this massive race on the quad bikes."

"Racing's not allowed," Lauren said.

"Isn't it?" James smiled, guiltily. "Anyway, there was a humongous crash. Me and Shakeel. You should have seen the state the bikes were in. Front tires ripped off, petrol gushing everywhere. It was mad."

"Did you get hurt?"

"Shakeel twisted his ankle, that's all. I can't wait for next year."

Lauren smiled. "We dared Bethany's brother to drive one of the quad bikes through the dining room. It was so funny when he got busted. . . . Anyway, are you gonna tell us why they kicked your butts home early, or not?"

James slumped miserably back on his bed, realizing he was now about as far as you get from racing over sand dunes.

"I got totally stitched up," he said.

"Give over, James, you always say that."

"Yeah, but this time it's true. Bruce and Kerry had a punch-up. They trashed our room and Kerry busted her knee, but Meryl sent me and Gabrielle home early as well. We've got to go see the chairman this afternoon."

"You must have done *something*," Lauren said.

"Lauren, all me and Gabrielle did was try to break the fight up. It was a total miscarriage of justice. Meryl wouldn't let me get one word in."

"Makes up for all the things you haven't been caught for," Lauren grinned. "How's Kerry?"

"She's in loads of pain. They had to do a medivac: flew her home on a special plane because she can't bend her leg."

"Poor Kerry," Lauren said.

"I'll go and see how she is when I've got my uniform on. You coming?"

"I've got karate class in a minute," Lauren said, shaking her head. "I want to be in top form when my basic training starts."

"Oh yeah," James grinned. "Only a month to go now. I'm gonna have such a laugh hearing about all the ways the instructors make you suffer."

Lauren folded her arms and scowled at her brother. "You're not scaring me, you know."

The medical unit was a ten-minute walk from the main building. When James got to Kerry's room, Gabrielle was already there.

"Look what *your* friend did to her," Gabrielle said, as if it was somehow James's fault.

Kerry was propped up on pillows beneath a NIL BY MOUTH sign. MTV blared from the portable TV hanging over her bed. She was on painkillers, but still had wet eyes and looked like she hadn't slept.

James put Kerry's MP3 player on her bedside table.

"Thought some tunes might help take your mind off it," he said. "Hope you don't mind me going in your room."

"No problem," Kerry said. "Cheers."

"Has the doctor seen you?" James asked.

Kerry nodded, pointing to a light box on the wall.

"Show James the thing," she said.

There was already an X-ray mounted on the light box. Gabrielle walked up and switched on the lamp.

"That's Kerry's kneecap," Gabrielle explained, pointing to a round gray area on the X-ray. "See the four black bars?"

James nodded.

"Those are the metal pins put in when Kerry broke her kneecap two years ago. When Bruce twisted Kerry's leg, that pin there shifted. So now Kerry's got a piece of metal sticking out the back of her kneecap. Every time she moves, the metal cuts into the tendons underneath."

"Yuk," James said. "What can they do about that?"

"They're taking her to hospital," Gabrielle said. "They're operating this afternoon. Kerry can't eat or drink before the anaesthetic. They're going under her kneecap and cutting out the bent metal. The broken bone has grown back together, so the metal isn't doing anything now anyway."

James felt queasy imagining surgical instruments poking around inside his leg.

"OOOOOOOOHHH God!" Kerry screamed.

"What?" James asked, rushing over to the bed. "Are you OK?"

"It's nothing," Kerry said. "I just moved my foot. This is actually more painful than when I broke my knee."

She let out a low groan. James sat beside the bed and stroked her hand.

"Has Bruce been to see you?" he asked.

"No," Gabrielle huffed. "Like that little jerk would have enough class to come and apologize."

"James," Kerry said, "will you do us a favor?"

"Course," James said. "Name it."

"Go and see Bruce. Tell him I'm not making a big deal out of this."

"You call this no big deal?" James laughed. "You're joking."

"I'm not," Kerry said. "I don't want this turning into some massive feud. Remember I told you I broke Bruce's leg when we were red shirts?"

"Sure," James said.

"It was in karate practice. Bruce fell awkwardly. I came down on him full force and crunched his leg.

I never should have done something like that in practice. Bruce was cool about it. He shrugged it off like it was nothing. Everyone does stupid stuff sometimes. Remember that one, James?"

Kerry held out the palm of her right hand. It had a long scar where James had stomped it during training. "You can't hold grudges against people for every mistake they make," she said.

"Point taken," James said. "I'll speak to him."

James hated the row of plastic seats outside the chairman's office. If you had to see him for something good, Dr. McAfferty—usually known as Mac—let you straight in. When you were in trouble, he kept you hanging outside in suspense. James sat between Gabrielle and Bruce. He was combed and deodorized, in his neatest set of CHERUB uniform: polished boots, army-green trousers, and a navy T-shirt with the CHERUB logo embroidered on the front. The other two wore the same, except they were only entitled to wear gray T-shirts. Bruce had four red lines down his face where Kerry had clawed him.

Kerry might have forgiven Bruce, but Gabrielle wasn't talking to him. James felt like he was on a tightrope. Every time he said something to one of them, the other one huffed as if he was siding against them. James realized it was easiest if he kept quiet.

They waited a good half hour before Mac finally leaned out of his doorway. He was in his sixties, with a neat gray beard and a Scottish accent.

"Come on then," Mac said wearily. "Let's sort you three out."

James led the way towards Mac's mahogany desk.

"No, no, come and look at this," Mac said, heading towards an architectural model standing on a table by the window.

The kids stepped up to the model of a crescent-shaped building. It was a meter long, made entirely out of white plastic, with polystyrene trees and tiny white figures walking along paths outside.

"What is it?" James asked.

"It's our new mission preparation building," Mac said enthusiastically. "We're turning those shabby offices on the eighth floor into extra living space and building this beauty to replace them. Over five thousand square meters of office space. Every big mission will have its own office, with new computers and equipment. We'll have encrypted satellite links to our mission controllers all over the world, as well as to British Intelligence headquarters and the CIA and FBI in America. This model just arrived from the architect's office. Isn't it fantastic?"

The kids nodded. Even if they'd hated it, they wouldn't have wanted to get on Mac's bad side by saying so. Mac treated CHERUB campus like his own personal LEGO set. He was always having something built or knocked down.

"It's an eco-building," Mac enthused, lifting the plastic roof off so the kids could see the offices filled with miniature furniture inside. "Special glass retains the heat, so it stays warm in the winter. Solar panels on the roof power fans and heat the water."

"When's it being built?" Bruce asked.

"It's already being made in prefabricated sections in a

factory in Australia," Mac said. "That way we can minimize the number of construction workers we have to let loose on campus. Once the concrete base is poured, the whole lot is bolted together in a few weeks. Fitting out the interior should be completed early in the new year. You wouldn't believe the amount of arm twisting I've had to do to secure the funding."

"It's really cool," James said, hoping his enthusiasm would translate into a lighter punishment.

"Anyway, I suppose I have to sort you three hooligans out," Mac said. He clearly would have preferred to go on about his new building all afternoon. "Plant your bums at my desk."

The three kids sat in the leather chairs opposite Mac. Mac leaned over his desk, interlocked his fingers and stared at them.

"I've already spoken to Kerry," he said. "So what have you lot got to say for yourselves?"

"It's well unfair that me and Gabrielle got sent home," James said. "We were the ones who tried to break the fight up."

He noticed Lauren and her best friend, Bethany, with their noses squished against the outside of the window behind Mac's desk.

"As I understand Meryl Spencer," Mac said, "the four of you came back from a training exercise, went into your room, and began taunting one another and bickering. Is that true?"

The kids gave a mix of shrugs and nods. Outside, Lauren and Bethany were sticking their tongues out and mouthing rude words.

"As far as I'm concerned, that makes all four of you responsible for what happened," Mac said. "Gentle ribbing leads to teasing, which leads to nastiness and, as in this instance, it sometimes leads to violence and an eight-thousand-pound bill for an air ambulance. While each of you is serving your punishment, I want you to reflect that you'd all be enjoying another two weeks of holiday if you'd had the sense to behave decently towards one another instead of winding each other up. Is that understood?"

The three kids nodded. James hated how Mac's way of twisting the facts around made him feel partly responsible for Kerry getting hurt. What made him even more annoyed was Lauren sticking a sheet of paper up to the window that said JAMES SUCKS in giant black letters. Gabrielle couldn't stop herself smirking.

"By way of punishments, I want the three of you to report to the head gardener after you finish lessons every afternoon. We don't have enough staff to give the lawns the attention they deserve in the summer, but you guys putting in two hours' mowing a day for the next month will certainly help."

James groaned to himself. With extra fitness training in the mornings and mowing in the evenings, the next month was turning into a nightmare.

"Any questions?" Mac asked.

The kids shook their heads and stood up to leave.

"And James," Mac said.

James turned back. "What?"

Mac raised a picture frame off his desk and turned it towards James. It showed Mac standing with his wife, his six grown-up children, and an ocean of little grand-kids.

"James, would you kindly inform your sister that the glass in this picture frame gives me a very good reflection of everything that's going on outside my window. I want to see Lauren and Bethany in this office and you can tell them that they'll be joining you on gardening duty for the rest of the week."

CHAPTER 5

SLEEP

TWO WEEKS LATER

James got up at 5:30 a.m., despite his whole body begging him to stay under the duvet. He put on his running clothes and headed to the athletics track as the sun rose over campus. It took him an hour to run twenty-five laps: a distance of ten kilometers. He showered, then traded some homework with Shakeel over breakfast. Lessons went from 8:30 until 2:00, with half an hour for lunch. After lessons, there was karate practice topped off with forty-five minutes' circuit training. Boiling hot, James downed half a liter of orange juice and collected one of the ride-on mowers from the gardeners' storeroom. It wasn't hard driving the mower, but the sun was on him the whole time and the grass pollen made his eyes itch.

It was 6:15 p.m. by the time James got his first chance to relax. Dinner was a social event, with everyone mucking about and catching up on gossip. Most cherubs had done their homework before dinner and had the evening to themselves, but the mowing meant James hadn't even got started. Homework was supposed to be two hours a day. Some teachers were decent. Other piled on so much work it took heaps longer.

When James got back to his room it was gone 7:00. He sat at his desk, spread out his textbooks, and opened his homework diary. In the two weeks he'd been back on campus, James had acquired a backlog of homework that sucked up every second of his free time.

It was a warm evening, so James left his window open. A breeze clattered into the plastic slats of his blind. James's eyes were gluey and the words in his textbook drifted out of shape. His head slumped on the desk and he dozed off before he'd written a word.

Kyle lived across the hall. He was nearly fifteen, but he wasn't much bigger than James.

"Wakey, wakey," Kyle said, flicking James's ear.

James's head shot up from his desk. He opened his eyes, inhaled deeply, and looked at his watch. It was gone ten o'clock.

"OHHHHHH crap," James said, startled. "If I don't get this history report done by tomorrow, I'm dead meat. It's a two-thousand-word essay and I haven't even read the chapters in the textbook."

"Get a deferral," Kyle said.

"I've had a deferral, Kyle. And I've had a deferral of the deferral. I've got extra laps to run before school and mowing after. There aren't enough hours in the day. I spent all day Sunday doing homework and I still keep getting further behind."

"You should speak to your handler."

"I tried," James said. "You know what Meryl said?"

"What?"

"She said, if I was so snowed under with work, how come I had time to spend sitting in her office whinging?"

Kyle laughed.

"I swear, they're trying to kill me," James moaned.

"No," Kyle said. "They're trying to instil a sense of discipline in you. After a month of being worked like a dog, maybe you'll think twice about ignoring the rules next time. It's your own stupid fault. All you had to do on holiday was keep in half reasonable shape and study the briefing for the hostage training. Everybody warned you. Me, Kerry, Meryl, Amy. But you always reckon you know better."

James angrily swept his arm across his desk, shooting his books and pens on to the floor.

"Good idea," Kyle grinned. "That'll solve your problems."

"Spare me another lecture," James shouted. "I'm so knackered I can hardly keep my eyes open and I'm sick of everyone saying I told you so."

"What's that report you're doing?" Kyle asked.

"Two thousand words on the foundation of the British Intelligence Service and its role in the First World War."

"Interesting stuff," Kyle said.

"I'd rather eat a bowl of snot," James said.

"I might just be able to help you out, kiddo. I did that course two years ago. I've got my old notes and an essay in my room."

"Cheers, Kyle," James grinned. "You're a lifesaver."

"Ten quid," Kyle said.

"*What?*" James gasped. "Some friend you are, trying to make money out of me when I'm at my lowest ebb."

"This essay is a beauty, James. Grade A material. The girl I mucked it off is now studying history at Harvard University in the States."

"Fiver," James said. He reckoned the essay was easily worth a fiver. He'd have to swap bits around and rewrite in his own handwriting, but that would take about an hour, whereas doing the essay from scratch was a whole night's work.

"You're bleeding me dry," Kyle said, twisting his mouth as if he couldn't make up his mind. "But I'm a little low on funds. You can have it for a fiver, if you give us the money right now."

James went to his desk and got a fiver out of his cash box. Kyle stuffed it in his pocket.

"This better be a good essay," James said.

"Anyway," Kyle said, "I didn't come here to help with your homework. I'm the senior agent on a big mission that's coming up. We need three other kids. Me and Ewart Asker discussed it and you're on the team if you want the gig."

James wasn't that enthusiastic.

"I don't want to work with Ewart as my mission controller again. He's a psychopath."

"Ewart raves about you," Kyle said. "He thinks you did a great job on that antiterrorist mission. Plus, this is a big team. Ewart's wife will be there as well. She keeps him under her thumb."

"Who else is going?" James asked.

"Me, of course," Kyle said. "And Kerry. She's walking with a stick, but they reckon she'll be healed up before blast-off. There's a vacancy for another girl. It was going to be Gabrielle, but she's being held back for something in South Africa."

"Nicole Eddison," James said.

"Who?" Kyle asked.

"You know her," James said. "She was on my basic training and quit after one day. She got her gray shirt at the second attempt. I think she's done a couple of missions, but nothing major."

"I think I know who you mean," Kyle said. "Is it that girl with the huge chest you're always going on about?"

"She is *so* stacked," James grinned.

"James," Kyle said, indignantly, "you can't pick a girl for a mission because she has big breasts."

"Why not?"

"Well, for starters, it's unbelievably sexist."

"Come on, Kyle. Nicole's a really good laugh. She's in my Russian class and she's always getting chucked out for messing around. And as long as Kerry doesn't find out and kick my butt, who cares if it's sexist or not?"

"I'll ask Ewart to put her name on the list of candidates," Kyle said, reluctantly. "But he'll only pick her based on merit. The first mission briefing is tomorrow. There's tons of background studying to do."

"Oh, great," James said. "When am I gonna get time to do that?"

"Didn't I mention?" Kyle said innocently. "It's been arranged with Meryl. You still have to do morning laps, but we've cut out some of your lessons and Mac has agreed to knock the mowing on the head."

"Cool," James grinned. "Another two weeks of that workload was gonna send me under. What lessons have I been dropped from?"

"Art, Russian, religion, and history," Kyle said.

"Superb," James said, deliriously drumming his hands on his desktop. Then the penny dropped. "Did you say *history*?"

"Uh-huh," Kyle nodded.

"I just paid you five quid for a history essay."

"A good price for a good essay."

James leapt furiously out of his chair. "I don't care if it's written on gold parchment by that bloke who does the history shows on channel four," he spluttered. "I don't need the essay if I don't have to go back to history class."

"It goes to prove the old saying," Kyle giggled.

"What saying?"

"Cheaters never prosper."

"I tell you who'll never prosper," James stormed, grabbing one of the pens off his carpet. "You. And you know why? Because you're gonna have an extremely hard time prospering after I've rammed this biro up your nose. Give us my fiver back."

"What fiver?" Kyle asked. "I don't recall any fiver. Did you get a receipt?"

James gave Kyle a shove.

"You're a bandit, Kyle. Normal people don't go around conning their mates."

Kyle backed up, with a giant grin and his hands out in front of himself.

"I tell you what," he said, "I'm seriously short of cash. So, even though it goes against my sacred ethical code, I'll do you a deal."

"What deal?"

"If you let me keep the fiver, I'll get Nicole on to the mission."

"That's worth five quid," James smiled. "What's this mission about anyway?"

"Drugs," Kyle said.

CHAPTER 6

CLASSIFIED
MISSION BRIEFING:
FOR JAMES ADAMS, KYLE BLUEMAN,
KERRY CHANG, AND NICOLE EDDISON
DO NOT REMOVE FROM ROOM 812
DO NOT COPY OR MAKE NOTES

CHILDREN IN THE DRUG BUSINESS
Children are used by drug dealers throughout the world, to sell, smuggle, and deliver illegal drugs. There are a number of reasons why children are used:

(1) Kids selling or using drugs are usually viewed as victims rather than criminals. In most countries

children are punished lightly for drug offenses, whereas an adult caught with a large quantity of a drug like heroin or cocaine faces five to ten years in prison.

(2) Children have access to schools and young people. Drug dealers encourage children to give free samples of drugs to their friends. Someone who starts dealing drugs at twelve or thirteen can have hundreds of customers by the time they reach adulthood.

(3) Children have few sources of income and plenty of spare time. Many will do a drug dealer a favor, such as making a delivery for just a few pounds, or even for nothing, because they think it makes them look cool.

WHAT IS COCAINE?

Cocaine is an illegal drug extracted from the leaves of the coca plant (not to be confused with the cocoa plant, which is used to make chocolate). Coca grows at high altitude in the mountainous regions of South America. The leaves are refined into a crystalline white powder. Before reaching users, the powder is diluted with cheaper substances, such as lactose or borax, or it is mixed with other drugs such as methamphetamine (commonly called speed).

The powder is snorted up the

nose. It can also be injected, or mixed with other chemicals to form a smokable version of the drug called crack. Users of cocaine feel a sense of confidence and well-being that lasts fifteen to thirty minutes. Cocaine also causes numbness and was once used as an anaesthetic by surgeons and dentists. More effective anaesthetics are now available.

Unlike heroin or cigarettes, cocaine is not addictive. Despite this, many who try the drug enjoy its effects so much they use it to excess. Whereas a heroin or cigarette addict needs a regular fix, cocaine users often go days without using before going on a binge. Cocaine use risks serious side effects, including heart attacks, liver failure, brain seizures, strokes, and damage to the lining of the nose and mouth.

COCAINE IN BRITAIN

Cocaine was once the champagne of the drug world: a luxury only the rich could afford. A moderate user might get through a gram of powdered cocaine in an evening. In 1984, a gram of cocaine cost £200-£250. Twenty years later, the street price of cocaine has dropped to less than £50 a gram. In some areas of Britain, a gram of low quality cocaine can cost as little as £25.

The United States pays South American governments to hunt and destroy coca plants in the highlands where they grow. Despite this, the street price of cocaine has continued to drop, suggesting that supplies are still plentiful.

Most cocaine brought into Britain arrives via the Caribbean. There are thousands of smugglers in British prisons. Tough sentences have done little to stop the trade. Cocaine dealers continue to find people willing to act as drug couriers, often in return for less than a thousand pounds and an airline ticket.

It is impossible to catch every smuggler entering Britain. The police must aim higher and capture the people in control of the drug gangs. Close to one third of the cocaine entering Britain passed through an organization commonly referred to as KMG. The initials stand for Keith Moore's Gang.

KEITH MOORE AND KMG: BIOGRAPHY

1964 Keith Moore was born in the newly built Thornton housing area on the outskirts of Luton in Bedfordshire.

1977 After being caught selling cannabis in his school library, Keith was arrested by police and excluded from school. He became a chronic truant, suspected of many car thefts and burglaries.

1978 Keith began training as a boxer at the JT Martin Youth Center. JT Martin was a retired boxer and armed robber who controlled the underworld in Bedfordshire from the early 1960s until 1985. JT used his boxing club as a recruiting ground for young criminals.

1980 Keith was spotted in police surveillance photographs of JT Martin. In the pictures, Keith is a slightly built sixteen-year-old who looks out of place amongst JT's crew of boxers and nightclub bouncers.

1981 Keith became JT Martin's chauffeur when a previous driver was banned for speeding. Moving around with JT gave the seventeen-year-old an insight into all aspects of the drug business.

1983 After eleven amateur fights, with a record of one win, two draws, and eight defeats, Keith retired from boxing. Shortly afterwards, he married Julie Robertson, a girl he had known since infant school.

1985 Police captured JT Martin and a number of associates selling drugs. JT was sentenced to twelve years in prison. Keith Moore had been JT's driver for four years, but the rest of JT's crew regarded him as a wimpish hanger-on.

1986 With JT in prison, a power struggle erupted amongst

his former employees. Keith kept away from the violent struggles and developed an interest in JT's cocaine business. Cocaine was a tiny proportion of the criminal empire, which made most of its money selling heroin and cannabis. JT also owned nightclubs, pubs, and casinos, as well as dozens of small businesses such as laundrettes and hairdressing salons.

1987 The price of cocaine kept falling and supply was growing. Keith Moore was one of the first people in Britain to realize that the cocaine business was about to explode.

While his colleagues battled over heroin and nightclub profits, Keith traveled to South America and met with members of a powerful Peruvian drug cartel known as Lambayeke. He agreed to buy regular bulk shipments of cocaine at a discounted price. To sell this increased supply of cocaine, Keith launched a telephone delivery service, based on similar services that were thriving in the United States. It took advantage of two new technologies: mobile telephones and message pagers. Instead of having to go searching for a drug dealer, rich clients dialed a number and Keith had someone deliver drugs to their doorstep, usually within an hour.

1988 The cocaine business was earning Keith over £10,000 per week. This cash enabled him—at just 23 years of age—to take effective control of JT Martin's criminal empire. Keith avoided violence whenever possible. He manipulated jealous rivals, setting them against one another. When manipulation failed, he bought rivals off by handing them parts of the business that did not interest him.

Keith's next ambition was to build his profitable cocaine business into the biggest in the country. The only part of JT's empire Keith held on to was the youth center/boxing club in the neighborhood where he grew up.

1989 Keith's first son, Ringo, was born (now aged 15).

1990 Keith's business grew tenfold in three years.
Cocaine delivery expanded into Hertfordshire and London. He also began selling wholesale quantities of cocaine to other dealers all over Britain and mainland Europe.

1992 Julie Moore gave birth to twins, April and Keith Jr. (now aged 12).

1993 Keith's youngest child, Erin, was born (now aged 11).

1998 Drug dealing is often a short career. Anyone who is successful attracts attention from police and customs. They usually end up behind bars.

After investigations failed to gather enough evidence, police tried to get undercover officers into Keith's inner circle. Dozens of people working for KMG have been prosecuted. Even when they have agreed to cooperate, police have never been able to produce clear evidence linking Keith Moore with his drug business. At the core of KMG, an expensive legal team and fiercely loyal deputies have so far succeeded in keeping Keith Moore out of prison.

2000 As the cocaine business continued to thrive, Keith Moore's personal fortune was estimated at £25 million. After being arrested for non-payment of tax, he pleaded guilty to a minor charge and paid a £50,000 fine.

2001 Julie Moore left Keith after eighteen years of marriage. Keith kept custody of the children and the family home. Julie moved into a house across the street and remains on good terms with her ex-husband.

2003 Police launched Operation Snort, the largest taskforce of drugs officers ever assembled in Britain. The official aim was to stop the cocaine business. Unofficially, everyone knew Operation Snort was gunning for Keith Moore and KMG.

The operation descended into chaos when it uncovered corruption within police forces all over the country. Forty officers were found to have taken bribes from KMG. Eight of these were working on Operation Snort and included the chief superintendent who was in command of the whole operation.

Although Operation Snort is still running, its effectiveness has been blunted by infighting over the bribery allegations.

One national newspaper reporting on Operation Snort said, "If all the corruption allegations are true, it would appear that Keith Moore has more police officers protecting him than the queen and the prime minister combined."

2004 (Present Day) Despite a personal fortune now estimated at between £35 and £50 million, Keith Moore has shunned the trappings of the super rich. He lives with his children in a large detached house less than twenty minutes' drive from the housing area where he was born. His four children attend the local comprehensive school. He works from an office at home and socializes with family members and friends he has known since boyhood. His only extravagances are a collection of Porsche sports cars and a beachfront house in Miami, Florida.

MISSION REQUEST

In early 2004, frustrated by the lack of success in bringing down KMG and outraged by police corruption, the government asked the intelligence service to find a way of infiltrating KMG at the highest level. MI5, the adult branch of British Intelligence, could see no reason why it would have any more success at this than the police. CHERUB was suggested as a method of last resort.

Keith Moore is close to his four children. Appropriately placed CHERUB agents may be able to befriend them and gather vital information.

MISSION PLAN
Husband and wife mission controllers, Ewart and Zara Asker, will move into a house in the Thornton housing area with their baby son and four CHERUB agents. For the purposes of the mission, the agents will be adopted children of Zara and Ewart. The family surname will be Beckett. To minimize confusion, everyone will use their normal first names.

PRIMARY OBJECTIVE
Each agent has been selected to befriend one of Keith's children, as follows:

James Adams – Junior Moore (Keith Junior)
Kyle Blueman – Ringo Moore
Kerry Chang – Erin Moore
Nicole Eddison – April Moore

If the cherubs succeed in making friends, they must attempt to socialize out of school and try to get inside Keith's home, gathering information wherever possible. Each cherub will be placed in the same tutor group as the child they are supposed to befriend.

SECONDARY OBJECTIVE
Many children in the Thornton area run errands and deliver drugs for KMG associates. Each cherub should identify children who are working for KMG and try to get involved themselves. Children usually work for small-time dealers, delivering drugs to individual clients using mobile phones and pushbikes.

Evidence suggests that children who attend Keith Moore's boxing club and make reliable couriers are promoted rapidly and given responsibility for moving wholesale quantities of drugs. If these children can be identified, they may provide information that will enable police to prosecute senior figures inside KMG.

NOTE: ON THE 13TH DAY OF AUGUST 2004 THIS MISSION PLAN WAS PASSED BY THE CHERUB ETHICS COMMITTEE BY A 2:1 VOTE, ON CONDITION THAT ALL AGENTS UNDERSTAND THE FOLLOWING:

This mission has been classified HIGH RISK. All agents are reminded of their right to refuse to

```
undertake this mission and to
withdraw from it at any time.
Agents will be at risk of violence
and exposure to illegal drugs.
Agents are reminded that they
will be excluded from CHERUB
immediately if they willingly use
cocaine or any other class A drug.
```

It was breaking all sorts of rules, but Zara Asker let them take the mission briefings outside and read them in the sun. She'd made a picnic, spreading a tablecloth over the grass and covering it with sandwiches and snacks. It was a chance for baby Joshua to get used to Kyle, Kerry, Nicole, and James. The eight-month-old sat under a sunshade, wearing nothing but a nappy. Kerry and Nicole leaned over him with giant grins.

"Look at his tiny fingers, James," Kerry beamed. "He's so cute you could gobble him up."

James lay back in the grass with sunglasses on, thinking he looked cool and wondering how Kyle had managed to get Nicole on the mission.

"It's a baby, Kerry," he said, "I've seen one before, they all look exactly the same."

Kerry tickled Joshua's belly.

"That's James," she said. "Isn't he Mr. Grumpy today?"

"Ooogy woogy woo," Nicole added.

Ewart was striding across the grass towards them, carrying an icebox and some bottles of soft drinks. He was a big muscular guy, with bleached hair and half a dozen earrings. He wore a Carhartt T-shirt and old jeans with the legs ripped off.

Zara was older than her husband. She looked like a typical harassed mum, with scraggy hair and puked-up milk on her T-shirt. Like most CHERUB staff, she was a former pupil. She'd gone to university and worked for the United Nations before returning to CHERUB as a mission controller. Kyle had worked with Zara a couple of times before. He said she was one of the best mission controllers to get. Everyone agreed. Ewart was the toughest.

"Hey, Nicole," Kyle said, swatting a fly away from his paper plate. "You should have seen how happy James was when he found out you got on this mission."

James sat up, surprised by Kyle's outburst. Nicole turned away from the baby.

"Was he?" she said, breaking into a smile. "Is that right, James?"

James was flustered. Kerry would kill him if she found out he'd paid Kyle to get Nicole on the mission.

"That's right," James spluttered. "I've never got a chance to know you, but the few times I've spoken to you, you've always seemed . . . nice."

"Thank you, James," Nicole smiled. "I was worried I'd be the odd one out because you three are already close."

Kyle grinned. "And James fancies you."

"Piss off, Kyle," James said.

Kyle was one of James's best mates, but he was always trying to con you or wind you up. Sometimes it got annoying. Zara cuffed Kyle around the back of the head.

"I'm only telling the truth," Kyle said.

"Kyle, *behave,*" Zara said sharply. "And James, you watch your language in front of the baby."

James could feel his face burning with a mix of anger and embarrassment.

"I know James doesn't fancy me," Nicole said. "Everyone knows James and Kerry have a thing going."

"Says who?" Kerry gasped.

"Yeah," James said defensively. "Me and Kerry did basic training together and we're good mates. It doesn't mean we fancy each other."

Kyle laughed. "If you say so, lovebirds."

"At least I've *had* a girlfriend," James said, looking at Kyle. "You're nearly fifteen and I've never seen you anywhere near a girl."

Kyle looked offended. "I've had girlfriends."

James grinned, sensing he'd put Kyle on the back foot.

"Girls in dreams don't count, dickhead."

A second later, James found himself dangling in the air with Ewart eyeballing him.

"Fifty laps," Ewart barked.

"What?" James gasped.

"You shut that filthy mouth in front of my son."

"He's a baby," James said. "He can't understand a word."

"But he'll learn," Ewart snarled. "Get over to the running track, now."

Fifty laps of the track took two hours and left you for dead when you stiffened up the next morning. Zara intervened before James boiled over and told Ewart where to shove his laps.

"Ewart, darling," Zara said gently. "James needs to be here while we discuss the mission. I'm sure an apology will be sufficient."

James, still suspended in mid-air, didn't think anyone deserved an apology, but it was better than running laps.

"OK," James said. "I'm sorry."

"For what?" Zara asked.

"I shouldn't have sworn in front of the baby."

"Apology accepted, James," Zara said. "And Kyle, quit being smart. You're the senior agent on this mission. I expect you to help the less experienced agents, not keep stirring up trouble."

After Ewart had put him down, James straightened his clothes, sat on the grass, and started piling chicken drumsticks and sandwiches on to a paper plate. Nicole shuffled up beside him and pinched a couple of his crisps.

Zara began reading notes from a long list.

"OK, as you all know, we're leaving first thing the day after tomorrow. Pack light. There are seven of us and it's a small house. State school starts Tuesday, giving us nearly a week to settle in before term starts. I've prepared a hundred-and-sixty-page dossier on Keith Moore, his associates, and his family, I want all of you to read it and memorize as much as you can. . . ."

CHAPTER 7

MOVING

It was pandemonium. They had a big moving van and a people carrier. The van was already stuffed, mostly with baby stuff like pushchairs and walkers. Kerry had five bags of clothes and junk, which James had to hump downstairs because her knee was still weak. Kyle, who was always ridiculously neat, wanted to take his clothes rail, eight pairs of shoes, and his own ironing board. Ewart was going beserk, using language that would have earned James thousands of laps.

"I'm only making one trip," Ewart shouted. "So you lot better sort yourselves out."

James was the only one who'd followed instructions to pack light. He had a backpack, with toiletries, spare trainers, a jacket, and a few changes of clothes. His PlayStation and TV had gone ahead the day before with the furniture.

Lauren came tearing around the corner towards them. She was in uniform and she was crying. It was the last thing James expected.

"What's the matter?" he asked, bundling his sister into his arms.

Her T-shirt was sweaty and the sobs made her whole body shudder.

"Just . . ." Lauren sniffed.

James pulled her tighter and rubbed her back.

"Is someone bullying you, or something?"

"I'm ten in two weeks," she explained. "It's doing my head in thinking about basic training."

Lauren acted tough most of the time, but she couldn't always keep the nine-year-old girl inside herself under control. Whenever there was a chink in her armor, she came to James for comfort.

"Lauren, *I* passed training," James said, feeling a bit emotional himself. "I'd never done karate and I could barely swim. With all the fitness and combat exercises you've done, you're a million times better prepared than I was."

Lauren dragged her wrist over her eyes. Kerry got Lauren a tissue.

"Come on, kids," Zara shouted, as she climbed into the people carrier. "I want most of this drive out of the way before Joshua wakes up and starts screaming."

"I wish you weren't going away," Lauren said.

"Bethany's going into training with you," James

said. "She'll probably be your partner. You two will do great."

Lauren stepped back from James. Kerry gave her a quick squeeze.

"Just think, Lauren," Kerry said. "In four months, basic training will be a memory and you'll be able to go on missions. I'll bet you, any money you like."

Lauren smiled a bit. "Yeah. I hope so."

"If you want," James said, "I can probably arrange for you to visit us in Luton on your birthday. We can have a laugh."

Lauren looked surprised. "Will they let me?"

"They won't mind. It'll be good experience for you: getting a taste of what it's like being out on a mission and stuff."

"You better go then," Lauren sniffled, dabbing her eyes with the tissue. "I don't know what made me start crying. It just . . . Sorry . . . I feel really dumb now."

James pecked his sister on the cheek, before saying good-bye and climbing in the back of the people carrier.

Kyle leaned out of the side window. "You'll make it through training, Lauren," he shouted. "Don't go losing any sleep."

James pulled up the door and buckled his seatbelt.

"Sorry I shouted, James," Zara said, from the driver's seat. "I didn't realize Lauren was upset. Is she OK?"

"I think so," James nodded.

Lauren waved as they drove away. James's eyes were a bit damp, but he wasn't worried. Lauren had a good brain and she was fit. A serious injury was the only thing likely to stop her getting through basic training.

• • •

Ewart and Nicole traveled in the moving van with the luggage. Zara drove the people carrier, with Kyle next to her in the front. James and Kerry sandwiched Joshua's baby seat in the back. The baby woke up an hour before they arrived. Kerry had a go at feeding him, but he screamed his head off. She passed him over to James while she hunted round her feet for a bottle Joshua had batted on to the floor.

Joshua stopped screaming as soon as James took him. When Kerry tried to take Joshua back, he went nuts again. Kerry gave James the bottle and Joshua began drinking calmly.

"Looks like we've found James's job for this mission," Zara said, grinning. "He likes you for some reason."

Kyle laughed. "Kerry probably traumatized him with the funny faces she was pulling the other afternoon."

James wasn't used to babies. He was terrified he might do something wrong and either hurt Joshua or get puked over. It turned out OK, apart from a few dribbles of milk. After feeding, Joshua lay quietly in James's lap playing with the laces on his shorts. Once James got used to it, he thought having the warm little body wriggling on his lap was quite cool.

A third of the houses in the Thornton area were boarded up. The detached homes looked decent enough, but nobody wanted to live in them because of the airport a kilometer south. Every few minutes, a couple of hundred people thundered overhead, shaking the ground and filling the air with the sickly smell of jet fuel.

You only ended up living in Thornton if you didn't

have a choice. The residents were a mix of refugees, students, ex-convicts, and families who'd been chucked out of better places for not paying the rent.

A gang of lads had to stop their football match to let Zara drive through. Ewart and Nicole had arrived minutes earlier. Nicole had unpacked the mugs and started making tea.

The windows in the house were triple glazed to keep out the aircraft noise, but that didn't stop everything vibrating. Besides, it was too warm to leave every window closed.

There were three bedrooms between seven people. Kyle and James got a box room with bunk beds, a chest of drawers, and a tiny wardrobe.

"Just like old times," James said, remembering when he and Kyle shared a room in a council home before he joined CHERUB.

"There's nowhere to hang my clothes," Kyle said miserably. "They'll get creased."

"You can have the whole wardrobe," James said. "I'll just dump my stuff in the bag or under the bed."

"If there's anything that stinks in this room, I'm chucking it out," Kyle said. "I don't care if it's a sock or a seventy-quid pair of trainers—if it smells like you, it's going in the bin."

James laughed. "I'd forgotten what a complete tart you are."

Zara made dinner for everyone: fish fingers and oven chips, with frozen peas.

"Sorry," she said, handing plates to the line of kids in

front of the TV. "You better get used to my cooking. It's not exactly gourmet."

Something crashed outside the living room window. All the kids downed cutlery and bundled towards the window. There was rubbish all over the front lawn and a metal dustbin rolling towards the gutter. A couple of boys were sprinting off down the pavement. Ewart burst out of the front door, but they'd disappeared up an alleyway.

As James mopped his last chip through his ketchup, Ewart strode in and switched off the TV.

"I always watch *Neighbours,*" Kerry gasped.

"Not today you don't," Ewart said. "You kids have a job to do."

"Go outside and start making friends," Zara said. "There's bound to be some dodgy characters in an area like this, so stick together. I want you back here as soon as it gets dark."

"And James," Ewart said, "you better pick all that rubbish off the front lawn before you go."

"Why's it my job?" James said bitterly.

Ewart broke into a smile. "Because I said so."

James thought about starting a row, but you never win against someone like Ewart.

It was easy starting conversations. The summer holidays had dragged on for weeks and the local kids were bored. James and Kyle played street football until they got knackered. Kerry and Nicole stood by the curb, nattering with a bunch of girls. When it started getting late, the four of them got invited to a kiddies' playground.

There was nothing special about it: a burned-out park keeper's shed sprayed with graffiti, a busted roundabout, a climbing frame, and a slide. But once the sun started to go down, it came alive. Kids aged between ten and sixteen gathered in fours and fives; smoking, arguing, and being loud. There was a tense atmosphere. Flash kids dressed like Nike commercials ripped into refugees dressed out of the charity box. Boys were trying to get off with girls and there was a rumor going around about a gang from another neighborhood turning up and starting a fight.

Apparently, a kid had been stabbed in the playground a couple of months earlier. He'd ended up with between eight and two hundred stitches, depending on what version of the story you believed.

"This is boring," Kerry said, after half an hour of standing around without anything happening except a lot of talk. "We better go home."

"You go if you want," James said. "I'm staying to see if a fight breaks out. It might be good."

"It might also be dangerous," Kerry said. "I've seen a couple of kids with knives and Zara told us to be home before . . ."

James interrupted, mocking Kerry's voice. "Zara told us da-de-da-da. . . . Chill out, Kerry, what's the point of having a curfew unless you're going to break it?"

Kerry looked at Nicole for moral support. "Are you coming?"

"No way," Nicole said. "I want to see some action."

They all waited another twenty minutes. A guy aged about fifteen came over and started chatting up Nicole.

Then someone's mobile rang and a rumor shot around. There was a car coming.

"So what?" Kerry asked.

"Stolen car," one of the local kids explained. "Joy-riders. They usually put on a good show."

Fifty-odd kids piled out of the playground and hurried to a deserted car park a few hundred meters down the road. A cheer when up when everyone spotted the headlights. It was a Subaru Impreza turbo, metallic silver with a giant wing on the back. The driver did a couple of handbrake turns, spinning the car and stinking up the air with tire smoke. Then he overdid it and smacked into a bollard, leaving a massive graze down one side of the car. The audience whooped and cheered, even though he'd nearly splattered a couple of girls standing astride their bikes.

"These guys are nutters," James giggled. "I'd love to have a go at that."

Kerry gave him a filthy look. "It's so stupid. They could kill themselves, or an innocent bystander."

"Loosen up, Kerry," James said. "You sound like an old fart."

The Subaru squealed to a halt a few meters away. As the cloud of tire smoke cleared, the driver and his mate opened the doors and ran around the car to switch seats. They both looked about fifteen.

"Where are our babes?" the new driver shouted.

A couple of tarty-looking girls jogged to the car and clambered in the back. When they were inside, the driver lit up the rear tires and started driving circuits around the neighborhood. He skidded on every corner, nearly losing the back end a couple of times on sharp turns. When the car was out of sight, you could still hear the engine and squealing tires. The joyriders kept coming back to the car park for more adulation from their audience.

The excitement level went into overload when a police siren went off. James was hoping to see a chase, but the joyriders didn't fancy their chances. They slammed on the brakes, jumped out, and merged into the crowd of kids as three police cars turned into the car park.

Everyone started running. One of the guys they'd been playing football with tugged James by his T-shirt.

"Don't stand there gawping," he said urgently. "The pigs will bust you if they get hold of you."

Kerry, Kyle and Nicole were already gone. James sprinted off, but the whole of Thornton looked identical in the dark and he couldn't remember the way home. He ended up in the center of the neighborhood, in a large paved square with lanes of identical houses branching off in six different directions.

"You know which way?" a voice asked breathlessly.

James spun around. It was a massive relief to see Kyle. Kerry and Nicole were with him.

"We can ask one of the policemen," Kerry said.

"Are you totally brain dead?" James asked, tapping his head. "The police are looking for two boys and two girls. They'll nick us."

Kerry looked perplexed. "But we didn't steal the car."

"Kerry," Kyle said, laughing, "how naïve are you? In an area like this, cops and kids are like oil and water: They don't mix."

"Well," Kerry said indignantly, "none of this would

have happened if we'd gone home when I said."

"Oh, shut your smug hole," James said.

"So, which way?" Nicole asked.

They were all out of breath when they burst through the front door. It was pure luck finding the right street at the second attempt, without bumping into any cops. Zara leaned out of the kitchen into the hallway.

"Ahh . . . Here they are. My little monsters," Zara grinned. "Late as usual."

The kids were expecting a roasting, but they got off because there was an old couple sitting at the table in the kitchen, drinking tea with Zara and Ewart.

"This is the adopted family," Ewart explained. "Kids, meet Ron and Georgina. They live next door and they brought us homemade biscuits to welcome us to the neighborhood."

"You kids dip in," the old girl said. "My biscuits have won prizes."

They stuck their hands in the tin and grabbed one. They tasted like they'd been baked in 1937, but they could hardly start gobbing them out in front of the old lady.

"Delicious," James said, gagging for some water to get the stale taste out of his mouth.

"Would you like another one?" the old dear asked.

Zara clamped the lid on the biscuit tin.

"They're off to their rooms now," Zara said. "They're not really allowed sweet stuff this late. It's bad for their teeth."

They were all thankful that Zara had saved them from

another biscuit. James led the scramble upstairs to the bathroom.

"SHUSSSHH, you lot," Zara whispered after them. "Joshua's asleep."

The four of them queued at the bathroom tap to get a drink; then they slugged mouthwash to get the taste out of their mouths.

"It's like a single bite sucks every bit of saliva out of your mouth," Kerry said.

"I bet she knows how disgusting they are," Kyle said. "Probably gets a kick out of watching everyone suffer."

"Hope the old bag dies," Nicole said.

James started laughing. "I think that's a *tiny* bit extreme, Nicole."

"I can't stand old people," Nicole said. "Wait till they're sixty, then give all of 'em both barrels of a shotgun."

"My nan was great," James said. "I got a Kit Kat or Wagon Wheel every time I saw her . . . I was her favorite. She never liked Lauren much."

Kerry grunted. "No accounting for taste, I suppose. When did she die?"

"When I was ten."

"Is Lauren OK now?" Kyle asked.

"I haven't spoken to her since this morning," James said. "Suppose I'd better ring her before I go to bed."

After he undressed, James climbed into his bunk and gave Lauren a call on his mobile. She was embarrassed about crying earlier and didn't want to talk about it.

CHAPTER 8

CONTACT

It was the first day of a new school year. The lines of miserable kids had short haircuts and new uniforms to grow into. Kyle offered to run the iron over James's stuff to "make it nice and crisp," as he put it. James had forgotten how annoying it was to wear a tie and blazer all day. The only good thing was, Nicole looked fit in her white blouse, with her tie loose around the collar. She'd altered her skirt so it was half the length of Kerry's.

James had been to a few different schools since his mum died. Grey Park looked like it was the bottom of the pile. The smell was a mixture of toilets and floor polish. The curtains and walls in the entrance hall were stuck up with thousands of bits of chewing gum, half the kids weren't in uniform, and there was an aquarium full of dead fish with a chair floating in it.

James broke off from the others and found his classroom. He recognized Junior Moore straight away, sitting at the back with a mate. You could tell, by the state of their uniforms and the way they were sitting with their trainers on the desk, that they wanted everyone to think they were bad guys.

James had to work his way in with them gradually. If you went straight up and introduced yourself to kids like that, they'd treat you like a joke. James's plan was to act cool and win them over with bad behavior.

The teacher came in. He was a titchy little donut in a beige suit called Mr. Shawn. He seemed full of himself; the kind of teacher who gave you an urge to muck about, just so you got the pleasure of seeing him flip out.

"O-KAYYYYYY!" Mr. Shawn shouted, slamming a book on his desk to get everyone's attention. "Summer is over, welcome to Year Eight. . . . Find your seats and settle down."

James sat at an empty desk in the middle. This seriously weird kid sat next to him. He was tall, but stick thin. His uniform was too small and his walk was bizarre, like he was trying to move in twenty directions at once.

"You're new," the weirdo said. "I'm Charles."

James didn't want to be nasty, but a geeky pal was the last thing he needed if he was going to make friends with Junior.

"I can show you around if you want," Charles said.

"It's OK," James replied awkwardly. "I'll manage, but cheers for the offer."

Charles didn't carry a backpack like the other kids; he had a brown leather briefcase. Judging by the noise when he put it down, he kept a couple of bricks inside. Charles stooped over the desk and began frantically scratching at the back of his hand. A snowstorm of skin flakes drifted on to the table in front of him.

"I've got eczema," Charles explained noisily. "It gets worse in the summer when I sweat."

Mr. Shawn started handing out timetables and burbling on about the fabulous opportunities presented by the after-school chess and drama clubs. Ten minutes into school, James already wanted to burst out of the front gate and run for the hills. He'd always found school boring, but after being at CHERUB, where the classes were small and the teachers pushed you, normal school made him feel like his life was running in slow motion.

Charles was bored as well. He got an apple out of his briefcase and crunched into it. Mr. Shawn stopped talking and glowered at him.

"Charles, what on earth are you doing?"

"Eating an apple," Charles said, as if he'd been asked the world's stupidest question.

"We don't eat in class, do we?" Mr. Shawn said.

Everyone started laughing. If a cool kid had bitten the apple, they would have laughed at how funny it was. But they all had Charles down as class loser, so everyone was shaking their heads and there were a few murmurs of "spastic" and "retard."

"Put it in the bin, Charles."

Charles took a final bite of the apple, before hurling it at the metal bin behind Mr. Shawn's desk. He missed, so he lumbered over and picked it off the floor. The back of his trousers looked set to rip open when he bent down and you could see his bright green Y-fronts.

"Nice knickers, Charles," one of the girls shouted.

"Yeah," someone else shouted. "But they were white when he put them on."

The kids went into another round of laughs.

Charles missed the bin a second time, even though he was dropping the apple from less than a meter. He lost his temper and kicked out. The bin smashed against the wall and the metal got bent out of shape.

"Charles, calm *down*," Mr. Shawn shouted.

"I hate bins," Charles steamed, booting it again.

"Into your seat now, Charles, unless you want a detention tonight."

Charles stumbled back to his seat.

Their maths teacher was a fruitcake. She had the key for the wrong classroom. Everyone stood around in the corridor while she went looking for the caretaker. Junior and his pal wandered up to Charles. James was standing next to him.

"Did you miss us this summer?" Junior asked.

Charles kept quiet. Junior grabbed his wrist and bent back his thumb.

"Did you bring us any presents from your holidays?" Junior asked, tightening his grip until Charles's face twisted up in pain.

"No," Charles gasped.

"That's not nice. I think you deserve a slap."

Junior let Charles's thumb go and clocked him around

the face. It wasn't hard. It was mainly done for humiliation.

"And who's your new friend?" Junior asked.

"James," Charles stuttered.

Junior faced James off. He was a fair bit shorter than James, but he had beefy arms and shoulders, as well as a mate to back him up. He gave James a little shove.

James felt edgy. CHERUB training had taught him that your first encounter with someone sets the tone for everything that follows. If James appeared weak, Junior would never consider him an equal and they'd be unlikely to make friends. But if James lashed out, they might become enemies and that would be even worse. He had to get the right balance between the two.

"Try pushing me around if you want to," James said casually. "But I wouldn't recommend it."

Junior turned to his mate and smiled.

"What's this, Del?" he laughed. "Looks like the new boy thinks he's a hard man."

Junior tried to grab James's wrist. James dodged out the way and jabbed two fingers into Junior's belly, sending him into a spasm.

"Too slow," James said, shaking his head in contempt.

Junior lunged again. His fist hit James in the guts, knocking the wind out of him. The force behind it surprised James. In a flash of anger, he hooked his foot around Junior's ankle and shoved him over. All the other kids backed up, expecting a fight.

James stood over Junior with his fists bunched, defying him to get up. Junior didn't look too confident. After a couple of tense moments, James smiled and reached out his hand.

"If you want a row, there's plenty of easier targets than me," he said.

Junior looked pissed off, but grudgingly let James help him up.

"Where'd you learn to do that?" Junior asked, brushing off his uniform.

"From Zara, my stepmum," James said. "She's a karate instructor."

"Cool," Junior said. "What belt are you?"

"Black, of course," James said. "What about you? Who taught you to throw a punch?"

"Boxing club," Junior said. "I'm undefeated. Eight fights, eight victories."

By the time the teacher got the classroom door open, the lesson was half finished. There was a spare seat next to Junior.

"Mind if I sit here?" James asked.

"Free country," Junior shrugged. "This is Del and I'm Keith; but that's my dad's name, so everyone calls me Junior."

"I'm James. Thanks for rescuing me from sitting with freak-boy over there."

James was pleased with himself. It had only taken an hour to break the ice. He sealed the deal by blowing a massive raspberry when the teacher asked him to be quiet. Junior and Del cracked up laughing.

Junior slapped James on the back as they walked out to morning break.

"You've got bottle, James," he said. "What lesson's next?"

Del got a timetable out of his pocket.

"History," he said.

"Balls to that," Junior said. "What about this afternoon?"

"Maths and French."

"Don't fancy that," Junior said. "You coming, Del?"

Del looked anxious. "I dunno. I don't think we should bunk off first day. My dad's gonna kill me if we get suspended again."

"Well," Junior said, "it's sunny outside. There's no way I'm sitting cooped up in some classroom. You wanna tag along, James?"

"Where you going?"

"God knows. We can get burgers or something, hang around the shopping center."

"Whatever," James said. "Anything beats lessons."

One of the coolest things about missions was being able to break all the rules without getting into trouble.

The two boys crawled under the back gate and ran a couple of hundred meters away from the school. Junior did a strip. He had a Puma T-shirt and shorts under his uniform.

"If you're gonna bunk off," Junior explained, "it's best to get rid of the uniform. Otherwise you get some old bat spotting the badge on your blazer and ringing up your school to complain."

"Smart," James nodded. "But all I've got under here is bare skin, so unless you want me to walk around in my boxers, I'm stuck with it."

"You want to go to the Reeve Center?" Junior asked.

"What's that?"

"Big shopping place. You're seriously telling me you've never been there?"

"We only moved here a week ago," James explained.

"Why's that?"

"We were in London," James lied, repeating the cover story they'd all had to memorize. "My stepdad got a job at the airport, so we moved up here."

"If you've never been to the Reeve Center, we should definitely go. It's half an hour on the bus. There's sports shops, games shops, and a big food court."

"Sounds cool," James said. "But I've only got the three quid Zara gave me to buy lunch."

"I can lend you a fiver, James. But I'll send my geezers round to smash your legs if you don't pay me back."

James laughed. "Cheers."

CHAPTER 9

THEFT

They wandered round the Reeve Center for an hour, looking at trainers and computer games that they didn't have any money to buy. It wasn't as boring as school, but it wasn't exactly exciting either. When they got hungry, they got stuff off a Mexican stand in the food court.

"My dad's loaded," Junior said, taking a chunk out of his burrito. "But he's so tight. He says he doesn't want me turning into a spoiled brat. I'm telling you, half the poor scum living down in Thornton get more cool stuff than I do."

"That's where I live," James said.

"Sorry," Junior smiled. "No offense."

"None taken."

"Actually, it's quite a laugh hanging out in Thornton. I was down there in the holidays and some kids started chucking bricks at the police."

James laughed. "Excellent."

"It was brilliant. One cop car got the windscreen smashed and everything. I go to boxing club down there as well. Have you been round there?"

"No."

"My dad sponsors it, actually. You should come along, everyone who goes boxing is a nutter. It's a good crowd."

"Maybe I'll try it," James said. "Does boxing hurt?"

"Only when you get punched," Junior said, grinning. "So that's something you should definitely try to avoid."

"So how come your dad's loaded?" James asked. "What does he do?"

James knew what Keith Moore did, of course, but he wondered what Junior would say.

"Oh, he's a businessman. Import and export. He's a millionaire actually."

James acted impressed. "Seriously?"

"No kidding. That's why I get so pissed off he won't give me decent pocket money. There are six PlayStation games I want really bad. I'll get a couple of them for my birthday, but that's not till November."

"Steal 'em," James said.

Junior laughed. "Yeah, but knowing my luck I'd get busted."

"I know a few things about shoplifting," James said. "My mum was into it, before she died."

"Did she get nicked much?"

"Never," James said. "Shoplifting is a snip, as long as you use forward planning and kitchen foil."*

"How many times have you done it?" Junior asked.

"Hundreds," James lied.

In fact, the only time James had tried shoplifting was when he was in care shortly after his mum died. He'd ended up in a police cell.

"So what's the tinfoil for?" Junior asked.

"I'll show you, if you want to go for it."

"I'm in if you reckon it's safe."

James gurgled up the last of his Coke. "There's no guarantee, but I've never been caught before."

He reckoned shoplifting was a good way to cement his friendship with Junior. If they got away with it, he'd be a hero and he could invite himself round to Keith Moore's house to play the games. It would be trickier if they got caught, but the experience of getting in trouble together would probably bring them closer.

James wouldn't get in real trouble with the police, because they would arrest and charge James Beckett, a boy who didn't really exist. As soon as the mission ended, CHERUB would pull James Beckett's criminal file and have it destroyed, so no fingerprint or DNA evidence would ever be linked back to James's real identity.

---

* The author of this book would like to point out that the shoplifting technique described here only works with certain outdated security systems. I've got no intention of telling you which ones they are because I don't want angry dads turning up on my doorstep and kicking my head in because their little darling just got busted trying to nick something from a shop.

James bought a roll of tinfoil in one of those everything for a pound shops. They locked themselves in a disabled toilet. James gave Junior the stuff out of his backpack and lined it with a double layer of the shiny aluminum.

"What does it do?" Junior asked.

"You know those alarms that go off when you take something out of a shop?"

Junior nodded.

"They're metal detectors," James explained. "They put those sticky metal tag thingies on everything, and the alarm goes off when it detects them."

"So, won't the metal foil make it go off?"

"It only goes off when it detects the right-sized piece of metal. Otherwise, it would ring for every umbrella and belt buckle. So, as long as you wrap the security tags inside something made of metal, the alarm thinks it's something different and doesn't go off."

"Genius," Junior said, breaking into a grin.

"All we need is a shop where they keep the PlayStation disks in the boxes, not behind the counter."

"Gameworld does," Junior said.

"We'll have to go in separately. I'll go up and stick the games in my pack. Your job is to distract the security guard, or any staff that comes near me."

"How?"

"Anything to take their attention off me. Just walk up and ask where something is."

"You're sure this isn't going to go wrong?" Junior asked excitedly. "If we get caught, my dad will crucify me."

"Trust me," James said. "Besides, you're only a look-out. I'm the one taking the big risk."

James felt confident as Junior led him through the shopping center towards Gameworld.

The security guard stood in the entrance. James went straight up the back to the PlayStation games. His foil-lined backpack was already unzipped. He found four of the games Junior wanted, then realized he might as well grab a few for himself while he was taking the risk. It was dead easy: The security guard was picking his nose and the guy at the checkout was texting on his mobile.

James zipped the pack up and slung it over his back. Junior stood in the doorway, with the security guard pointing out the DVDs to him. James headed towards the exit as nonchalantly as he could, but his heart was thumping. As he passed through the detector, an alarm went berserk and a mechanical voice boomed out:

"We're sorry, an inventory tag has been left on your item. Please return to the store. We're sorry, an inventory . . ."

The guard took hold of James and tried to drag him into the shop. Junior could have kept his head down and nobody would have been able to prove he was involved, so James was impressed when he charged towards the security guard and punched him in the side of the head. James kneed the guard in the stomach and started running, with Junior a few paces behind.

The security guard in the store opposite had seen the whole show and came after them. When James glanced back over his shoulder, the guard was shouting into his walkie-talkie, requesting back-up.

"You tit," Junior shouted, as shoppers dived out of their way. "What a great plan."

James couldn't work out what he'd done wrong. Two security guards came out of a department store up ahead, blocking their path and forcing them to cut into a women's clothing store. A woman with a buggy went flying into a display of leggings as James crashed into her. The store was crammed with rails of clothing that brushed against James as he ran. Junior stumbled. One of the security guards got a hand on him, but he spun away and recovered his balance.

James burst out of the fire exit at the back of the shop, setting off another alarm. He'd hoped the door would lead out on to the street, but he'd emerged into the central concourse of the shopping centre. There was big fountain and a stand where they did temporary exhibitions. The yellow banner hanging over the exhibition stand sent James into shock:

BEDFORDSHIRE POLICE THEFT PREVENTION SQUAD.
FIND OUT HOW TO PROTECT YOUR
HOME AND CAR FROM CRIME.

There was a long fold-out table, with three policemen behind it handing out crime prevention leaflets.

"Holy shit," Junior gasped, stopping in his tracks.

With the police up ahead and security guards behind, their chances looked about nil. James considered surrendering, but Junior noticed a door with a toilet sign a few meters away and barged it open. He led James down a narrow corridor, with six pairs of men's shoes clattering after them. They passed the entrance to the ladies' toilet and crashed through a fire door, into the dim confines of a multistory car park.

They sped towards the lift, but there was no time to wait for it. Instead, they scrambled on to the staircase and ran down, leaping three steps at a time, fueled by adrenalin. James twisted his ankle, but he didn't have time to think about the pain, or the fact that if he tumbled he'd smash his head open on bare concrete.

The policemen were more cautious on the stairs and the boys had gained ground by the time they booted open a set of doors that led into a sunlit alley. There were massive steel bins and boxes of rubbish piled around them. They clambered over everything, reaching the front of the shopping center as the police emerged through the doors at the bottom of the stairs. The security guards had given up.

There was a pedestrian crossing, with two lanes of waiting traffic. James saw the green man flashing and they made a dash for it. They ran into the outdoor car park, crouching low and jogging between the bumpers of two lines of parked cars.

The police got stranded on the other side of the road, waiting for the lights to change. One cop tried to stop the traffic with a hand signal and nearly got splattered by a motorbike. By the time the cops had halted the traffic and made it across, James and Junior were crouching behind a car a hundred meters away.

The three cops stood on the pavement by the car park, staring hopelessly at row after row of parked cars. The boys kept low until they came to the far side of the car park. They pushed themselves through shrubs, emerging on to the narrow pavement beside a fast-moving dual carriageway. Junior started to run.

"WHOA," James said. "Keep cool."

Junior turned around. "What?"

"Walk," James said. "It looks less dodgy if we're spotted."

They walked nervously for twenty minutes, looking back over their shoulders and having miniature heart attacks every time they spotted a white car. When they noticed a bus coming, they sprinted to the stop and hopped on. They went upstairs and sat at the back, well away from the other passengers. James finally felt safe.

"Sorry about that," he said breathlessly. "You're not pissed off with me, are you?"

Junior burst out laughing. "That was *mental*. The look on those cops' faces when we lost 'em. Oh man . . ."

"I'm an idiot," James said. "You know what I did? When I put the games in, I must have pushed the foil down the bag so it wasn't covering them over."

"Who cares now?" Junior grinned. "Gimme, gimme, gimme."

James unzipped his pack and pulled out nine PlayStation games. Junior read out the price stickers.

"Forty, forty, twenty-five, thirty-five. How much is that?"

"A hundred and forty."

"Thirty-eight, twenty-four, and three at thirty- five."

"Three hundred and seven quid," James said.

"You add fast," Junior said. "Over three hundred quid's worth of games. That's so cool, we've got to do it again some time."

"I dunno," James said. "I'm not sure if my underwear can take the strain."

• • •

"You're late, James," Zara said. "Dinner's nearly ready."

Kerry and Kyle were sitting at the kitchen table while Zara did frozen lasagna in the oven.

"Sorry," James said.

"You could have rung us," Zara said. "We were all worried."

Kerry looked up. "Where were you? I didn't see you at lunchtime."

"I was around," James said, defensively.

"So, how was school?" Zara asked.

"Oh, you know," James shrugged. "Same old, same old. Boring as hell."

Zara wouldn't have minded that he'd bunked off with Junior, but James didn't want her to find out about the shoplifting and the chase. If cherubs steal something, or make money while they're on a mission, they're supposed either to return the goods or donate them to charity. James had no plans to give away five top PlayStation games after going through so much exertion stealing them.

"How did you get along with Junior?" Zara asked.

"Really good," James said. "He's my sort of person. I reckon we would have ended up mates even if I hadn't tried. Where's Nicole?"

"Doing homework with April Moore and a bunch of other girls," Kyle said.

"Wow," James smiled. "She's a fast worker. How did you two get on with your targets?"

"Erin Moore and her weird friends chucked paper at me and started calling me 'peg-leg' because of my limp," Kerry said miserably.

"Ringo's a swot," Kyle said. "Nice kid, taking his GCSEs very seriously. The thing is, I reckon he's too straight to be involved in his dad's drug business."

"James," Kerry said, "why's there tinfoil sticking out of your backpack?"

"What?" James gasped.

Kerry leaned towards the pack. James whipped it away before she got a chance to see inside.

"You've been up to something," Kerry grinned. "What's in there?"

"Nothing," James said, jumping up from the table. "I better go and um . . . I'll give Lauren a call before dinner's ready."

Kyle and Kerry exchanged looks as James thumped upstairs to his room.

"Tinfoil?" Kerry whispered, not wanting Zara to hear.

"Don't ask me," Kyle shrugged. "But he's been up to something, that's for sure."

CHAPTER 10

PUNCH

It was Friday, after school. James, Kyle, Kerry, and Nicole sat on the living room couches in their school uniforms, drinking cans of Coke. The TV was on but nobody was watching.

James looked at Kyle. "I'm going boxing tonight with Junior. You wanna come?"

"You in a boxing ring," Kerry giggled. "That's something I'd pay money to see."

James clucked. "It's training, stupid. They don't make you fight on the first night."

"I'll pass on getting punched in the head," Kyle said. "I got invited to a party."

"Oh," James said. "Thanks for inviting me."

"It's Ringo Moore and his mates," Kyle said. "Year Ten and Eleven kids. They won't want the likes of you biting their ankles."

"I'm meeting April at the youth club," Nicole said. "The boxing gym is upstairs."

"So, Kerry," James said, breaking into a grin. "I'm going out with Junior Moore tonight. Kyle's partying with Ringo Moore and Nicole's at the youth club with April Moore. What are you and Erin Moore doing?"

"Ha-ha, very funny," Kerry said miserably. "Erin is the biggest geek. There's this student Spanish teacher."

"Miss Perez," James said. "I've got her as well."

"That's her," Kerry said. "Erin and her little friends wound her up so much, they made her run out of the classroom in tears. I felt really sorry for her."

"Yeah," James giggled. "Perez is always crying. My class had her bawling three times on one lesson. It was *soooo* funny."

Kerry looked mad. "James, that's horrible. How must that poor woman feel?"

James shrugged. "Who cares? She's only a teacher."

"You know what, James?" Kerry snapped. "Teachers have feelings the same as anyone else."

"Whatever," James said. "I know you're only angry because you can't get on with Erin and you'll probably get your botty kicked off this mission."

"Oh, shut up, James," Kerry shouted, putting her palm in front of her face. "I spend all day stuck in a class with a bunch of stupid, noisy morons. I don't want to come home and deal with another."

"Touchy, touchy." James giggled.

Kyle gave James a nudge. "Leave it out, eh?"

James realized he'd overdone it. He was getting a filthy look off Nicole as well.

"Sorry, Kerry," James said. "But you were taking the mickey out of me going boxing just a second ago."

Kerry didn't answer. She just scowled into the bottom of her empty Coke can.

"You don't have to sit here all night watching telly, Kerry," Nicole said. "You can come to the youth center with me if you want."

"I don't want your pity, Nicole," Kerry said tersely. "Our mission briefing says if you can't get on with your target, you should try and get involved in KMG through another kid. So, for your information, I won't be sitting in front of the TV. I'll be at the youth center with someone tonight, the same as Nicole and Mohammed Ali over there."

Kerry got off the sofa and stomped up to her room. Kyle reached over and punched James's shoulder.

"What the hell was that for?" James asked, furiously.

"Being an insensitive pig," Kyle said. "You know what a big deal Kerry makes about being the best at everything."

"Jesus," James said, rubbing his arm. "I was only having a laugh. It's not my fault she's so touchy."

"Go up and apologize," Kyle said.

"I better not," James said. "She probably wants to be on her own."

James noticed the look he was getting off Nicole.

"OK then," James huffed, standing up. "I'll go and say sorry."

James went upstairs. Kerry and Nicole's room was at the end of the corridor. As James got closer, he started to bottle it. Kerry had a violent temper and he didn't want to get on the wrong end of it. For the first time ever, James was happy to hear Joshua crying. He leaned into Ewart and Zara's room, making sure they weren't in there, then walked over to the cot and picked the baby up. Joshua rested his head on James's shoulder and changed his bawling to a gentler sucking kind of noise.

"Come on," James said, rocking Joshua gently. "Let's find Mummy."

He went down to the kitchen. Ewart was at the table.

"Cheers for picking him up, James," Ewart said. "Zara's just gone down the shop for some bread."

"Get his bottle warmed up," James said. "I'll take him into the living room. He likes watching the telly."

Ewart smiled at James. "Joshua still won't let Kyle or the girls go near him. You know why I think he likes you?"

James shrugged. "Why?"

"You've got blond hair, the same as me and Zara."

"Maybe," James said.

He carried Joshua through and sat next to Nicole on the sofa.

"Look who's here," Nicole said, grinning and wiggling Joshua's big toe.

Since he'd been on the mission, James had learned something about girls: if you want them to like you, don't worry about buying them gifts, or saying the right thing, or where you take them. What you need to do is grab the nearest brat and stick it on your lap. Nicole, who'd been furious at James a few minutes earlier, shuffled up close to him on the couch.

"You know, James," Nicole beamed, "someday you're gonna make a really good dad."

The stairs leading up to the boxing club had signed photos and newspaper cuttings of boxers James had never heard of on the walls. The door at the top of the stairs creaked and James got a nose full of thirty-degree heat and old sweat. About twenty guys were working out. Dark patches on their clothes, lifting weights, punching bags. James felt awkward, imagining they were all sizing him up, estimating how many milliseconds it would take to punch him out.

A massive guy stopped a set of crunches and started mopping his bald head with a towel.

"New fish?" he asked, looking at James.

James nodded. "I um . . ."

The guy pointed his thumb. "You want the back room, with the other kids. Try not to tread on anyone."

James had to step over gym mats and barbells to get through. The back room was bigger, with twenty-odd boys aged between nine and fourteen working out. Two young coaches stood in a ring up the back, mucking about and taking punches off some little kids. James recognized Junior, Del, and a couple of guys he'd seen around Thornton and at school.

"You Junior's new pal?" a voice asked from behind.

James turned. The guy sat in a plastic chair. He wore tracksuit bottoms and a stained vest. His shoulders were a mat of wiry gray hair. Even though the guy was thirty years past his prime, he still didn't look like a man you wanted to mess with.

"I'm Ken," the guy growled. "If you're here for the night, it's fifty pence."

"Junior said it's cheaper if I get a monthly ticket," James said.

"Fifty pence for tonight," Ken said. "I don't want to rob you. This is too much like hard work for most kids. They don't come through that door more than once or twice. If you're one of the ones who sticks it, I'll take what you've already paid off the monthly pass."

James nodded and dug some coins out of his shorts.

"Go see your friend Junior and try to follow what he does," Ken said. "You're here to train. That means you don't stand around talking. You don't mess around and you don't make jokes. Any kid starts a fight without my say so and I'll give the nod to someone who'll make them sorry. You got that?"

James nodded. "Don't I get coaching or something?"

Ken laughed. "I sit here with my eyes open. Give it a week or so. Follow what the others do. When I think you're ready, I'll get one of the trainees to start you off with a little sparring."

James wandered over to Junior.

"Enjoy the lecture?" Junior asked, grinning.

Junior, Del, and a couple of other guys trained in a group. Everything was a competition: how many push-ups or crunches, how fast you could skip, how many times you could punch the hanging ball in thirty seconds. CHERUB training had made James fit. He could hold his own at everything except skipping, which he'd only ever tried in PE lessons years earlier. Everyone except James got a turn in the ring, either sparring with each other or getting coached by Kelvin and Marcus, the two brutal-looking seventeen-year-olds the club employed as apprentice coaches.

When they were all half-dead, the group piled into the locker room, showered off the sweat, and put on fresh clothes. On their way out, Ken blocked James's way with his leg.

"You coming back?" Ken asked.

"I'd like to," James nodded, still out of breath. "If that's OK."

"You've done some kind of martial arts training, haven't you?"

"Yeah, karate and judo. How could you tell?"

"You're in good shape and you can punch," Ken said, "but a boxer needs fast feet as well. You want to be able to skip a hundred and fifty times a minute. Take this home and practice half an hour a day."

James took the end of a frayed skipping rope. He stuck it in his carrier bag, on top of his damp clothes.

Junior slapped him on the back as they went down the staircase.

"He must think you've got talent, James. I kept coming here for three weeks before he said a word and my dad practically owns the joint."

James couldn't help smiling, though it was hardly surprising he showed promise after all the combat training he'd done at CHERUB.

"You coming down the youth club with me and Del?" Junior asked. "It's packed out with girls, Friday night."

The youth club was on the ground floor, under the gym. It was supposed to be a disco, but the music wasn't very loud and nobody was dancing. James sat with Junior and Del on some slashed-up seats in a dark corner. There were plenty of boys and plenty of girls, but everyone sat in single-sex groups.

"So," Junior said, "which babes are us three studs gonna snap up tonight?"

Del looked at his watch. "None. I'm off to work once I've drunk this."

Del always had money and James thought it probably came from delivering drugs. He straightened up in his seat, sensing an opportunity to get information, but trying not to make it obvious he was prying.

"Work?" he asked. "At this time of night?"

Junior burst out laughing. "Ah . . . The voice of innocence."

"I work for KMG," Del said.

"KM what?" James said.

"Keith Moore's Gang," Del explained. "I deliver coke for Junior's daddy."

"Who wants Coke at this time on a Friday?"

"Not Coca-Cola, you wazzock," Junior said. "Cocaine."

James acted like he was surprised. "Cocaine? Isn't that seriously illegal? You told me your dad was in import export."

"He is," Junior said. "Imports drugs, exports cash."

"Hell." James grinned. "No wonder he's so loaded."

Del went into his backpack. He pulled out a small polythene bag filled with white powder.

"Cocaine," he explained.

James grinned as he took the packet and inspected it.

"Don't let everyone see it, you moron," Del gasped, knocking James's hand out of the air.

"Sorry," James said. "So how much is this?"

"One gram in every bag. They give me ten grams at a time, then they ring me on my mobile and tell me where and when to deliver it."

"How much do you make?"

"Fifteen per cent," Del said. "This is sixty a gram, so I get nine quid. If I work Friday and Saturday evenings, I can easily make a hundred quid. Sometimes though, like at Christmas, you get people loading up for office parties and stuff. I had this one guy who lived two streets away from me. He was buying ten grams at a time. Ninety quid for a ten-minute bike ride. It was beautiful."

"Do you blow all the money?"

Del shook his head. "I used to, but you end up wasting it on junk. Now I only spend twenty pounds a week. I stick the rest in my savings account and when I'm eighteen, I'm gonna buy a ticket and go off backpacking."

James looked at Junior. "So how come you're always broke?"

Del burst out laughing. "This baby's not allowed to go anywhere near drugs."

Junior explained miserably. "My dad's paranoid that he'll get arrested. If I get caught with drugs, it gives the police an excuse to question Dad and search our house."

"That's a shame," James said.

"Tell me about it," Junior said bitterly. "My dad's

a millionaire and half my mates are making a packet selling coke. What have I got? Holes in my jeans and supermarket-brand football boots."

"Can't you do it on the sly?" James asked.

"Won't happen," Junior said. "The word is out. Anyone who gets me or Ringo involved in the drug business will be in serious trouble if my dad cops them."

"So you're stuffed," James laughed. "You reckon there's any chance I can get in on this delivery lark?"

Del shrugged. "I'll go upstairs and have a word with Kelvin if you like. I don't know if he needs anyone right now, but I can try and get him to set you up with a few bags of coke and your own phone."

"I've already got a mobile," James said.

Del shook his head. "You have to use the phone they give you, so the police can't trace it."

"But there's definitely a chance?"

"I haven't got a clue," Del said. "All I can do is put a word in."

"Thanks," James said.

Del stood up. "Anyway, I've got a nine o'clock delivery, so I better dive home and pick up my bike. I'll see you two hard-up losers at school on Monday."

James smiled. "Yeah, see you."

"I'll be thinking about you sweating away on your bike in a couple of hours," Junior said. "When I've got my hand up some girl's shirt."

"In your dreams, Junior," Del shouted as he walked towards the exit.

James shook his head, grinning in false disbelief. "I can't believe your dad is a drug dealer."

"Who cares?" Junior said. "Do you want to try and get off with someone?"

They both glanced around.

"Look at that bird sitting by the Coke machine," Junior gasped. "I've not seen her here before."

James turned around. He'd guessed it was Nicole before he even saw her.

"She's reserved for me," he said. "That's my stepsister."

"You can't get off with your sister, you pervert."

"*Step*sister," James said. "We're not blood relatives. Why don't you go for the one sitting next to her? She looks like a right dog."

"That's my twin, you cheeky git," Junior said. "And you better not call April a dog again, unless you want a slap."

April had her hair done differently from the surveillance photos. James hadn't recognized her.

"I tell you who else is good looking," Junior said. "Pity she's already with someone."

"Who?" James asked.

"At the table behind our sisters. That Chinese-looking girl, with long black hair. She's well tasty."

James peered over. All he could see was the back of the girl's head. Then she turned and he saw her in profile.

"That's my other stepsister," James gasped. "That's Kerry. Who's that she's with?"

"Dinesh Singh. He lives up my road. His dad runs a firm that makes those microwave meals for supermarkets. So, you want to go over?" Junior asked. "I'll go for Nicole and you can have a run at April. She's not too picky, to be honest with you, so even you might stand a chance."

"Jesus," James said, feeling like his head was going to burst with jealousy. "Dinesh just put his arm around her."

"What's the problem? Do you fancy all your sisters, or something?"

"It's just, Kerry's really young."

"How old is she?" Junior asked.

"Twelve."

Junior burst out laughing. "We're twelve."

"Yeah," James said. "But we're in Year Eight, she's only a Year Seven."

"If you ask me," Junior said, "it's none of your business what your stepsister is up to. But if it makes you feel better, Dinesh is a weed. Just go over there and slap him one."

"I've a good mind to," James said.

This was a total lie. Kerry would break him into fifty million pieces if he even thought about it.

"Anyway," Junior said, "I'm not sitting here all night. Are you gonna ask April out or not?"

"You go," James shrugged. "I'm not in the mood."

April Moore was OK-looking and being friendly with her would be good for the mission, but James couldn't get Kerry out of his head.

Junior pulled up a chair next to Nicole and started chatting her up. James sat by himself and kept glancing over to see what Kerry was up to with Dinesh. He realized he couldn't sit on his own all night being jealous of Dinesh and decided to go across to April, but company arrived before he got a chance.

It was Kelvin and Marcus, the two coaches he'd seen at boxing club. They were both over six feet tall and solid muscle. They sat either side of James, squashing him even though there was plenty of room.

"I'm Kelvin," the black one said. He pulled a mobile phone out of his pocket and stuck it on the table. "Del tells me you're interested in doing deliveries."

James nodded. "I could do with the cash."

"Del said you're a solid kid," Kelvin continued. "What you gonna say if the cops pick you up for holding drugs?"

"Nothing, of course."

Kelvin nodded. "That's right. You don't know us, you ain't never seen us. Tell 'em you found the drugs in a bush and stick to that story no matter how they try to mess with you. You know what happens if you grass us up?"

"I get beaten up?"

"Cut up, more likely," Kelvin said. "And that's just for starters. They'll send people round your house and start on your family. Smash the furniture, batter your mum and dad. Del said you have two sisters, they won't look so pretty after we finish with them. So you better understand, James, even if there's some massive cop threatening to lock you up and throw away the key, you better keep your trap shut."

"Don't worry," James said. "I'm no grass."

"You got a good bike?"

"It's pretty crap actually."

"Good," Kelvin said. "You don't want nothing fancy or you'll get mugged. How cool are your parents about you being out late?"

"It's OK until about half-ten."

"Marcus, set the kid up with three bags. I think we'll give him a trial run."

Marcus got three bags of cocaine out of his tracksuit.

"I want you on call school nights," Kelvin said. "Monday through Thursday. That means you keep your phone switched on and you're always ready to go. We don't want to hear that you're grounded, or you're busy doing something. Whenever they call, you jump to it."

"Can't I do weekends?" James asked. "Del reckons that's when you make the real money."

"Everyone starts at the bottom with weekday deliveries and no regular customers. The powers that be will see how you do. If you're reliable and you deliver fast, you get moved on to better paid work. Questions?"

"I've only got three bags of coke, how do I get more?" James asked.

"There's people at your school. We'll arrange for you to meet up with them when you need to."

"What if someone tries to rob me or something?" James asked.

"If you lose the stuff or get mugged, that's your problem and you owe us for what you lost. If the customer tries any funny business, don't sweat it. Give the customer what they want and some of our muscle will show them the error of their ways."

Kelvin and his silent pal got up from the table.

"One last thing," Kelvin said. "If you're out late, you'll get hassled sooner or later. Never carry more coke than you need to. A lot of kids carry knives, but if you ask me, you're safer throwing the stuff on the ground and legging it."

CHAPTER 11

KITCHEN

James ended up walking home from the youth club with Nicole. He didn't feel too good: a mix of nerves about his delivery job and seeing Kerry with Dinesh. They ended up in the kitchen, drinking glasses of milk. Zara and Ewart were already in bed.

"Did Kerry say anything to you about this Indian guy?" James asked.

Nicole grinned. "Jealous, are we, James?"

"No. It's just we're good friends and I like to look out for her."

"Can you smell something?" Nicole asked.

"No," James said, looking at the bottom of his trainers.

"I can," Nicole sniffed. "You know what it is?"

"What?"

"Bullshit."

"Very funny, Nicole."

"James, you *totally* fancy Kerry," Nicole said. "Why don't you just admit it and ask her out?"

"Give us a break, we're just friends. How did you get on with Junior?"

"He's not bad-looking," Nicole said. "But the kid could seriously use some mouthwash."

James laughed.

"So," Nicole said, "if you're not as keen on Kerry as everyone says, what do you think of me?"

James looked uneasy. "You're a nice person, Nicole."

"That wasn't what I asked."

"Well . . ." James squirmed. "Actually, yeah . . . You've got a nice body and that."

"You're not so bad yourself," Nicole said, leaning against the kitchen cabinet. "Come over here."

"Why?" James asked.

"Kiss us."

James laughed. He leaned in and pecked Nicole on the cheek.

"Is that all you've got?" Nicole asked.

The second time James moved in, Nicole wrapped her arms around his back and they started snogging.

The door clicked open and they burst apart. James crashed into the kitchen table as Kerry stepped into the room.

"Hello, hello," Kerry grinned. "Did I break something up?"

"No," James gasped. "It's nothing. We're just drinking some milk before we go up to bed. You want some?"

"Cheers," Kerry said.

James got a glass off the draining board and poured out some milk.

"Anyway," he said, stretching into a yawn. "It's gone eleven. I might as well go up to bed."

Kerry called him back.

"What?" he asked.

"You better wash the lipstick off your face," she said. "Unless you want it all over your pillowcase."

James walked up the stairs in a confused state. He fancied Nicole, but he didn't like Kerry knowing about it.

Kyle was in the top bunk when James got to their room.

"Some party animal you are," James said. "Home before eleven."

"Put the light on if you want," Kyle said, sitting up in bed. "I'm not tired. It was a decent party, but one of the neighbors complained and the cops came and broke it up. How was boxing?"

James explained about everything that had happened. He tried to make it sound matter of fact, but the Kerry and Dinesh thing was getting to him and he blurted out something he'd never admitted to anyone.

"Kerry kind of . . . Sometimes I lie awake at night thinking about her. She's really, I mean . . . She's not stunning . . . Not the sexiest girl in the world or anything, but there's something about her that goes through me like a big warm whoosh."

"You've *got* to ask her out," Kyle said.

"But I want her to carry on being my mate. What if we end up rowing and hating each other?"

"You've got to risk it," Kyle said.

"What if she doesn't even want to go out with me?"

"Look," Kyle said firmly. "You just got off with Nicole, so you should be excited about that; but all you're talking about is Kerry, Kerry, Kerry."

"What do I say to her?"

"Try the truth," Kyle said. "Tell Kerry how much you like her and then it's up to her."

"Maybe you're right," James said. "I'll say something to her first chance I get. I mean, you never know, it might even work out between us."

"That's right," Kyle said.

James clicked out the light and climbed under his duvet.

"Kyle, what I don't get is: How come I'm taking all this advice off you when I've never seen you with a girl?"

"I've never had a girlfriend," Kyle said.

James was surprised by the honesty. He'd expected Kyle to be defensive.

"Seriously?" James asked.

"Yep," Kyle said.

"But there's loads of girls at campus. I'm sure I could fix you up with one."

"I don't want a girlfriend," Kyle said.

"What?" James asked. "Did a girl hurt you really badly or something? Is it like one of those romantic films my mum used to watch?"

"No, James. I don't like girls."

"What, you mean you only like old birds? Like, in their twenties or something?"

Kyle laughed. "No. I like boys."

James shot up off his mattress. "Piss off you do."

"James, I'm gay."

"No bloody way," James said. "This is another Kyle wind-up."

"I'd appreciate it if you didn't go shouting it off to the whole world, but you were honest with me about Kerry, so there you go. It's the truth, whether you want to believe it or not."

"Wow," James said. "Do you swear that you're gay, on your life?"

"Yes," Kyle said.

"Wow," James said.

He felt like his head was going to explode. He already had too much going on in there, with Kerry and Nicole and the drug dealing.

"Who else knows?"

"I've told a few people," Kyle said.

"I can't believe it," James gasped. "You don't seem anything like a poof."

"Actually, I'd prefer it if you didn't call me that."

"Oh, right . . . Sorry."

James lay awake the whole night, listening to the airplanes rumbling over the house. He got up with the sun, had a shower, got a bowl of Shreddies and made himself tea. When the newspaper dropped through the letterbox, he read the sports page at the kitchen table, but it was like the words were going through his eyes and bouncing straight off his brain. All he could think about was Kerry with Dinesh and Kyle being gay.

Kerry and Nicole came downstairs. James didn't like that they were together; it made his paranoid side imagine that the two of them were working together and scheming against him.

"I'm making bacon sarnies," Nicole said. "You want one, James?"

"Mmm," James said. "Cheers."

Kerry sat on the opposite side of the table and poured orange juice. Kyle had asked him not to tell people he was gay, but James was practically bursting. He had to tell someone. It felt too big to keep locked up.

"I spoke to Kyle last night," James said.

Kerry looked up from the color supplement. "And?"

"He told me something. It's totally mind-blowing, but you can't spread it around."

"Whatever," Kerry said. "Spill the beans."

"Kyle told me he's gay."

Kerry smiled a bit. "Well duh. Of course Kyle's gay."

Nicole looked away from the spattering bacon. "It took you *this* long to work out Kyle's gay?" she said.

"He said he'd only ever told a couple of people."

Kerry smiled. "You must have at least suspected."

"No. Why would anyone suspect Kyle's gay?"

"Well, dingus," Kerry said. "He's always clean and neatly dressed. Unlike most of you guys, his room isn't covered in disgusting pictures of half-naked women and nobody has ever seen him within five kilometers of a girl. I mean, short of walking around with a plaque on his forehead saying 'Gay Boy,' how obvious do you want it to be?"

"But I share a room with him," James gasped. "He sees me naked."

"So what?" Kerry said. "I've seen you naked."

"Well, he's gay."

"You think he fancies you?" Kerry giggled. "I wouldn't flatter yourself."

Nicole turned away from the frying pan with a big smile on her face. "Come to think of it, I've seen him eyeing you up, James."

"Shut up," James said. "It's not funny. It's disgusting."

"You think being gay is disgusting?" Kerry tutted. "I thought Kyle was your friend."

"He is," James said. "But . . . I'm not comfortable with the whole gay thing."

"Do us some bread, Kerry," Nicole said. "Bacon doesn't take long."

Kerry got the loaf off the cabinet and started buttering.

"You know, James," she said, "it must have been hard for Kyle to admit something like that to you. Especially when you're always calling people faggots and queers."

Nicole moved the pan off the heat and helped Kerry make up the sandwiches.

"I heard that one person in ten is gay," Nicole said. "So it's not that unusual. If you think about it, every football team probably has one gay player on it."

Kerry giggled. "I wonder who the gay one at Arsenal is? Actually, the big clubs have loads of players and reserve teams. There's probably at least four or five."

James stood up from the table and boiled over. "That's not funny," he shouted. "There's no such thing as a gay Arsenal player."

Kerry slammed James's plate on the table in front of him. "Sit down and eat that," she said angrily. "Kyle's your friend, so you better be supportive. If you say anything that upsets him, I'll show you the meaning of uncomfortable."

CHAPTER 12

SUBURBAN

It was Wednesday evening, and James was on his third night making deliveries. His phone went off a couple of times a night; always the same calm female voice on the other end. James had no idea who or where she was, only that she seemed motherly, was happy to give directions, and always signed off with the same words: "You be careful out there, young man."

The deliveries were never more than a few kilometers' ride. The job would be nasty in the winter, but on sunny early autumn evenings it was no hardship. James had imagined his customers would be scraggy-haired women in night clothes holding screaming babies, or wild-eyed men with beards and motorbikes, but it was nothing like that.

• • •

James was breathless by the time he found the housing estate. The houses were brand new. There was a developer's signpost over the entrance: LAST FEW HOMES REMAINING—PRICES FROM £245,000. The houses were neat, with newly planted trees and recent-plate Fords and Toyotas parked on the driveways. There was no traffic and little kids played outside on skateboards and microscooters.

As James freewheeled down a gentle slope, he noticed the streets were named after musical instruments: Trumpet Close, Cornet Avenue, Bassoon Road.

He turned into Trombone Villas, the most exclusive street in the development. The gray tarmac became red and the cars on the driveways changed to Range Rovers and Mercedes. He was looking for Stonehaus, and like millions of delivery people before him, James had learned to hate house names. With numbers, you knew that 56 was after 48, and 21 was on the other side of the road. Stonehaus could be anywhere. He found it after a search, the signpost hidden behind a BMWX5 and a Grand Voyager. He wheeled up the driveway and pressed the bell, which sounded off in a tinny version of "When the Saints Go Marching In."

A boy ran down the hallway and opened the door. He was eight or nine, wearing the long gray socks and fancy uniform of a fee-paying school. At this time of day, the kid was in a state, with his bare chest showing under his unbuttoned gray shirt.

"Daddy!" the kid shouted.

A man holding a whiskey tumbler hurried down the stairs, while the kid ran back to the TV.

"HEYYYYY there," the man said, trying to sound cooler than the fat balding man he really was. "Four grams, wasn't it?"

James nodded. "Two hundred and forty quid." He went into his backpack and got the four bags of cocaine. The man peeled five fifties off a roll of notes.

"I don't have change," James said.

Del had taught James to pretend never to have change. If the customer kicked up a fuss, you miraculously remembered you had money from a previous delivery in your backpack; but you were hoping the average middle-class coke snorter didn't want to keep a drug dealer hanging about on his doorstep and simply said:

"No worries, son, keep the change for yourself."

James smiled and tucked the money in his pocket. "Thanks, mate," he said. "Enjoy yourself."

The man closed the door. James couldn't help smiling. He'd just earned thirty-six pounds commission, plus a ten-pound tip, for a half-hour bike ride.

It was gone nine when James got home. Everyone was waiting for him in the living room. Two weeks into the mission, Ewart and Zara wanted a conference to see what everyone was doing and to work out the best way forward.

"Sorry I kept you waiting," James said. "But I've got to deliver when I get a call."

Zara had rearranged the sofas in the living room and brought in kitchen chairs, so everyone could sit facing each other. James squeezed on to a sofa between Kyle and Nicole.

"OK," Ewart said. "I want each of you to say what you think you've achieved so far. Keep it short, you've all got to get up for school tomorrow."

"Nicole," Zara said, "why don't you start?"

Nicole cleared her throat. "You pretty much know. I've been getting on OK with April. She knows what her dad does for a living, but keeps out of it. I've been to Keith Moore's house a few times doing homework and stuff and I've met him; just exchanging hellos and that."

"That's a good start," Ewart nodded. "Do you think you can carry on getting regular access to the house?"

"Sure," Nicole said. "April likes having the girls round and showing off her giant bedroom. She likes to think of herself as the leader of our group. I'm going to a sleepover there this Saturday."

"Have you had much chance to nose around the house?" Zara asked.

"I thought I'd play it safe to start with," Nicole said. "You've got all the notes and stuff I copied from the cork board in the kitchen."

"Do you think you could place minicameras and listening devices around the house?"

"Easily," Nicole nodded. "The house is big, so if anyone asks what I'm doing, I can pretend I got lost and wandered into the wrong room."

"Excellent," Ewart said. "Could you get a nose inside Keith's office?"

"I doubt it, he's usually in there. The one time he was out, I tried and the door was locked. I suppose I could take my lock gun."

"No way," Ewart said. "If someone sees you with a lock gun, it will put you in serious danger and blow this whole operation."

"The next best target would be Keith's bedroom," Zara said. "He's the kind of guy who gets phone calls at all hours, so you can be sure he takes important calls in bed. Have a good snoop and put in a listening device."

"Why can't you tap the phones from out in the street?" James asked.

"They've been tapped for years and Keith knows it," Ewart said. "A serious villain like Keith Moore uses mobiles or face-to-face meetings. He'll pick up a pay-as-you-go mobile and use it for a day or two, then switch to another one before we know he's got it. He also speaks using code words, and uses something to disguise the sound of his voice, so you could never go into court and prove it was him saying what he said. Our only chance of getting useful information is to have a microphone in the actual room where Keith is talking."

"So, Nicole," Zara said. "That's your target. Get a microphone in Keith's bedroom and maybe a few others around the house. The risks are low, because nobody is going to suspect that a twelve-year-old girl is planting a microphone, but you should still be careful."

"OK," Ewart said. "Good work, Nicole, keep it up. Do you want to go next, James?"

James nodded. "Me and Junior are top mates, bunking off and going to boxing and stuff."

"How much do you think Junior knows about his dad's business?"

"He comes out with stuff," James said. "He's curious

about what his dad does. If any one of Keith's kids knows anything worth knowing, I'd bet on Junior."

"And the deliveries," Zara said. "How are they going?"

"Good," James said. "It's mostly nice houses and offices I'm going to. I was worried at first, but it's like having a newspaper round, only with decent wages."

Ewart spoke. "The mission briefing mentioned that kids around here aren't just delivering small amounts of drugs to individuals, but are getting deeper into the organization and delivering in bulk to dealers from other parts of the country. Have you seen any sign of that?"

James shrugged. "Some kids are making serious money, so it wouldn't surprise me."

"Your number one job is to find out how they're making that money," Zara said. "Make friends, ask questions, and keep pestering until you get an answer. Remember to keep safe when you're out on deliveries. If you think a situation is dangerous, pull out and we'll clean up the mess afterwards. We'd rather abandon the whole mission than risk one of you guys getting hurt."

"Kyle," Ewart said. "Your turn."

"Ring's a bust if you ask me," Kyle said. "He's a straight-up guy, though he smokes a fair bit of cannabis. I'm getting in with his crowd. There are drug dealers at their parties and plenty of kids using all kinds of drugs. I might get some information from one of them, but I'm not hopeful."

Ewart and Zara looked at each other.

"Just keep trying, Kyle," Zara said. "That's all you can do until we think of something else."

"So," Ewart said. "Last but not least, Kerry."

"Me and Erin can't stand each other," Kerry said. "She's weird and immature and her friends sit in a group and don't talk to anyone else."

"What did you do to try and get in with them?" Ewart asked.

"We're just so different," Kerry explained. "I don't think we'll ever get on."

"The thing is, Kerry," Ewart said, "you've been trained to work out what type of person your target is and then act in a way that makes them your friend. If Erin mucks about and upsets teachers, then that's what you should do, even if you think it's silly and immature. If Erin swears and bunks off, you should do that too. I know you can't guarantee forming a friendship with a target, but I don't ever expect to hear a cherub say they're too different from someone to get along."

Kerry looked angry. "You'd need a world-class psychiatrist to work out Erin. She's part of a weird little clique and they shut everyone else out."

Zara spoke. "If you haven't hit it off with Erin by now, I doubt it's ever going to happen. I can't see much reason for you to stay on this mission. We can send you back to campus and say you've moved back to live with your real parents, or something."

Kerry looked close to crying. "I don't want to be sent back. I'm trying to get involved with someone else, like it says in the briefing."

"I can't see much point," Ewart said. "If you were a boy, you might be recruited as a courier, but that's all done through the boxing club, which is boys only."

Zara nodded, agreeing with her husband. "I'm sorry this mission didn't work out, Kerry, but don't be disappointed. Think of it as a learning experience."

"Let me stay," Kerry begged. "There's a boy in my class called Dinesh. I'm getting friendly with him and I think he knows something."

James put his wrist up to his lips and made a loud smooching noise.

"Grow up, James," Zara said wearily. "Kerry, what is it you think Dinesh might know?"

"His dad runs a company that makes microwave meals for supermarkets. When I was talking to him about Erin, he mentioned that his father has dealings with Keith Moore."

Zara didn't look too impressed. "Keith is a wealthy man, Kerry. He has business dealings with lots of people."

"But it's the way Dinesh said it," Kerry explained. "It's like Dinesh had a bad taste in his mouth. It might be nothing, but I'd like a chance to dig deeper."

Ewart and Zara looked at each other.

"*Please* don't send me back to campus," Kerry groveled. "Just give me a few more days."

"You're fond of this boy Dinesh, aren't you?" Zara said. "Is that the real reason you're so keen to stay?"

"I'm a professional," Kerry stormed. "It's not because I've fallen for some boy. I've got a hunch and I'm asking you guys to show faith in me."

"OK, Kerry," Zara said gently. "There's no need to get upset. Ewart and I will postpone our decision on sending you back to campus until next week. How does that sound?"

Kerry nodded. "Thank you."

"Anything else, before we all go off to bed?" Ewart asked.

"Yeah," James said. "It's Lauren's birthday this weekend, is it still OK if she visits?"

"No problem," Zara said. "If she meets up with any of the local kids, you'll have to tell them she's your cousin. It'll seem weird if you suddenly have a sister popping out of nowhere."

"If that's everything," Ewart said, "let's all get some shut-eye."

With only one bathroom, there was a scrum over the toothbrushes. Kerry stayed on the couch sulking and James thought he'd give the others a few minutes to fight it out.

"You're really good at this," Kerry said, looking at James.

"What?" he asked.

"Missions. You go into a room and everyone likes you. Good old James, even the baby likes you. I study hard and I get some of the best marks on campus, but I'm rubbish out on missions where it really counts."

"Come on, Kerry," James said. "You're being way too hard on yourself. This is your first important mission. Nobody expects you to be brilliant."

"And it'll be my last big mission, after this disaster," Kerry said. "I'll probably spend the rest of my CHERUB career doing mundane security tests and recruitment work."

James moved across to the other couch, next to Kerry. "I've been meaning to talk to you," he said.

"Talk about what?"

"We haven't been getting on that well since this mission started," James said. "But you still like me, don't you?"

"Of course I like you," Kerry said, breaking into a smile. "You're one of my best friends."

James decided to be bold and put his arm around Kerry's back. She smiled and rested her head against his shoulder.

"You've done all you can on this mission," he said. "And there's no way they're not gonna give you another shot at a big mission. With your fighting skills and the five billion languages you speak, who'll be able to turn you down?"

Kerry smiled. "For someone who acts like a moron half the time, you can be a really nice guy sometimes."

"Thanks," James grinned.

He thought about starting the speech he had prepared in his head, telling Kerry how kissing Nicole was a one-off and how he liked her a hundred times more than any other girl and wanted to be her boyfriend. But Kerry still looked upset. It wasn't the right moment.

CHAPTER 19

VISIT

One of the CHERUB staff dropped Lauren off on Saturday morning. James was barely out of bed when he heard the doorbell.

"Happy birthday," he said, giving his sister a hug. "You made double figures, the big one zero."

Lauren smiled. "I missed you, James . . . for some strange reason."

They walked inside. Everyone was wandering between the kitchen and living room, munching on triangles of toast. Joshua was shuffling down the hallway on his bum. Lauren had never seen him before.

"OOOH," she said. "Aren't you cute? What's your name?"

Joshua gave Lauren an odd look, as if to say, "Oh God, not another kid," and started bawling for Zara.

"Hey, Ewart," James shouted, "there goes your theory that Joshua likes anyone with blond hair."

Lauren wandered into the living room, threw off her bomber jacket, and sat on the couch. Kerry and Kyle wished her happy birthday.

"So," Lauren asked, "where's all my prezzies?"

"Actually," James said, "I haven't got you one yet."

"Typical," Lauren huffed.

"Now I'm a bona fide drug delivery boy, I thought you might like to spend my ill-gotten gains." James burrowed down his jeans, pulled out a fistful of scrunched-up bank notes and dumped them in Lauren's lap.

Lauren grinned. "How much is this?" She straightened out the notes and started counting. "Twenty, forty, sixty, eighty, a hundred, and ten, fifteen. Wow . . . How long did it take you to make a hundred and fifteen pounds?"

"Four nights," James said. "The only thing is, if you want me to take you shopping you'll have to pay my bus fare. I've only got sixty pence left."

"Is there a Gap near here?" Lauren asked eagerly. "I want some new jeans. And a Claire's Accessories? If there is, I can get those cool black hair scrunchies like Bethany's got."

"Can't you just use an elastic band?" James asked.

Lauren ignored her brother and glanced at her watch. "What time do the shops open?"

"Calm down, you idiot," James said. "The money's still gonna be there in a couple of hours. Why don't you go in the kitchen, get some toast and say hello to Zara and the others."

"Whatever," Lauren said. "But let's go early. The shops get really busy on Saturday."

Zara dropped the kids at the Reeve Center. James hoped none of the security guards remembered him.

"Why are you wearing those sunglasses?" Lauren asked.

James shrugged. "Am I? I forgot to take them off."

"You look a right twit," Kerry said.

"It doesn't have anything to do with the five PlayStation games you've got stuffed under your bed, does it?" Kyle asked.

"What were you doing spying under my bed?" James asked indignantly.

"Remember Monday, before school?" Kyle asked.

"No."

Kyle mocked James's voice: "I can't find my PE shirt, Kyle. Will you help us look for it?"

"Oh yeah," James said, "that."

"So let me guess," Kyle said. "You don't want to go anywhere too near Gameworld either."

"But if he stole them as part of a mission, he's allowed, isn't he?" Lauren asked.

"He's supposed to give the proceeds of any crime to charity," Kerry explained.

"Well he should give them to charity then," Lauren said. "You're not on this mission to make a profit, James."

"Does that include the birthday money in your pocket?" James asked.

"Oh," Lauren gasped.

"Yeah," James giggled. "That shut you up, didn't it?"

Normally, going around the girly shops would have driven James mad, but being the big brother treating his sister felt good. Lauren, who wouldn't be seen dead in a skirt, got two hooded sweatshirts in the Gap, a pair of faded jeans, and some silver stud earrings. She treated everyone to lunch in the food court and even got James a pair of novelty socks as a thank-you. He was never going to wear the ghastly things, but it was a nice moment when she gave them to him.

After lunch, Kerry went off to meet Dinesh. She told James to give Zara a message that she wouldn't be back until after dinner. Kerry being with Dinesh pissed James off, but he didn't want to spoil Lauren's birthday, so he tried not to think about it.

When they got home, Zara had ordered a fancy cake. The icing was camouflage green and there was a miniature assault course built out of marzipan, with a climbing tower, a water jump, and toy soldiers running around. The iced message around the edge said HAPPY BIRTHDAY LAUREN & GOOD LUCK IN TRAINING.

Joshua thought the cake was a toy and kept lunging out of Ewart's lap towards it. After Lauren had blown out her candles, everyone sat around the table, cracking up at the huge mess Joshua made with his tiny piece of cake.

Lauren was tired out by half-nine and James decided to go up to bed with her. She started off with a sleeping bag on the floor, but she decided it was uncomfortable and climbed in with James. She'd always gotten into his bed when they were little, but they'd grown since those days.

"This is ridiculous," James said, wriggling up to the wall so she had more room.

"I'm still scared about training," Lauren said quietly. "I don't even see the point of it."

"You'll understand after you've done it," James said. "Training's horrible, so when something tough happens on a mission, instead of being scared, you remember that you've been through worse and you can handle it."

"Sometimes," Lauren said, "just thinking about it make me feel like puking."

"The fear is worse before training starts," James said. "Once you're there, you're too worn out to think."

There was a knock on the door.

"Yeah," James shouted. "We're awake."

Zara pushed the door open and stuck her head in.

"James, when Kerry left you earlier, did she say if she was going anywhere after she left Dinesh's?"

"No," James said.

"I rang their house," Zara said. "Dinesh said Kerry left before eight. She ought to be home by now."

"Did you try her mobile?" James asked.

"That's the first thing I did. I even sent a text."

"Maybe we should go out looking," Lauren said.

"I wouldn't panic yet," Zara said. "She'll probably turn up. You two get some sleep and try not to worry."

A mobile woke James up. He'd forgotten Lauren was asleep next to him and bumped into her as he sat up.

"That's your tasteless ring tone," he said, giving her a kick. "I bet it's that idiot Bethany."

Lauren got out of bed, flicked on the light and found her phone inside her jacket. James looked at his clock. It was gone midnight.

"Hello?" Lauren answered. "Kerry, *wow*. Everyone's looking for you. . . . Hang on, yeah, James is here."

James snatched the Nokia off Lauren.

"Kerry?"

"Oh, thank God," Kerry said. "Why did you switch your phone off?"

"It's probably gone flat," James said.

"I couldn't get an answer from Kyle, or Nicole either. I tried Lauren as a last resort."

"Where the hell are you?" James asked. "Zara's going frantic. She's sitting downstairs waiting for you to get in."

"I'm outside Thunderfoods. I need a huge favor."

"What's Thunderfoods?" James asked.

"Dinesh's dad's company," Kerry explained. "I think I'm on to something, but I need you and one of the others to ride out here and give me a hand breaking in."

"Why don't you explain everything to Ewart or Zara?" James said. "They'll know what to do."

"Because if I'm wrong, I'll look like an idiot and they'll boot me back to campus."

James couldn't refuse. After all, he spent half his life telling Kerry to be more relaxed about rules.

"OK," he said. "What is it you want?"

"I'd like Nicole or Kyle to come as well," Kerry said.

"Nicole's at her sleepover. Kyle's out partying."

"But I'm here," Lauren said, sounding excited.

James looked at his sister. "No way, you're not trained."

"It's better if there's three of us to search," Kerry said. "But two is OK. I need you to bring some stuff: torches, your lock gun, your digital camera, and some beer."

"Where the hell can I get beer at this time of night? Even if there *was* some somewhere, I'm too young to buy it."

"There's a few cans in the bottom of our fridge," Kerry said. "Sneak one out."

"What do you need beer for, anyway?" James asked.

"James," Kerry snapped, "I don't have time for two hundred questions. Get the stuff, get on a bike and ride your butt out here."

James took down directions and ended the call.

"What's happening?" Lauren asked.

"God knows why," James said, "but Kerry wants to break into some food factory. She doesn't want Ewart or Zara to know what she's doing in case she's wrong about whatever it is she thinks is going on."

He stepped into some tracksuit bottoms and trainers.

"I'll go get the beer for you," Lauren said.

"Thanks."

Lauren crept down to the kitchen, while James churned through the mess under his bed and got his lock gun and camera. He grabbed Kyle's camera in case they needed two and took Lauren's phone because his was flat.

Lauren came back with the cold beer.

"Thanks," James said. "It's gonna be well hard, sneaking my bike out of the garage without Ewart or Zara noticing."

Lauren started putting on clothes.

"What do you think you're doing?" James asked. "You're not coming. No way."

"Kerry asked for a third person."

"You're not trained."

"I'll ride along," Lauren said. "If Kerry doesn't want me, I'll look after the bikes."

James knew how stubborn Lauren could be. He didn't have the time or energy to argue.

"Fine," he said. "But don't think I'm taking the rap for you if we get in trouble."

"I'm ten years old," Lauren said proudly. "I can make my own decisions."

CHAPTER 14

CURRY

There wasn't much traffic, but what there was drove dangerously fast. It took twenty minutes to ride across to the industrial park. Thunderfoods had a full car park and lights on everywhere. The factory worked 24/7, sending out truckloads of chilled pastas and curries to supermarkets.

Kerry led them to an alleyway between two warehouses.

"Are you sure you want to do this, Lauren?" she asked. "We could get in serious trouble if we're caught."

"If you want me to help, I'm up for it," Lauren said.

"So what's this about?" James asked.

"I got more information from Dinesh," Kerry explained.

"It's amazing what you can wheedle out of a boy if he think you're up for a snog."

"Did you snog him?" Lauren asked.

Kerry laughed. "No chance."

James was relieved. It was worth being dragged out of bed at midnight just to hear that.

"Anyway," Kerry said, "Dinesh doesn't get on with his dad. He reckons Mr. Singh is a hypocrite when he tells him to behave and do his homework, when he's a crook himself. So I go: 'How is your dad a crook?' And Dinesh started explaining how his dad nearly went bankrupt and KMG bailed him out. I said I didn't believe him. Dinesh tells me there's a storage building at the back of Thunderfoods' production plant. He says he's been inside and seen bags of cocaine. Security seems pretty lax: I've already sneaked right up to the warehouse door, but I can't get inside without my lock gun."

"What if there's a security system?" James asked.

"There is," Kerry said smugly. "You need a swipe card."

She pulled a plastic card out of her shorts. "I nicked this one off Mr. Singh."

"And what about the beer?" Lauren asked.

"We need a cover story," Kerry explained. "If we get caught, we act like kids who got drunk and decided to cause some mischief."

Kerry took the beer off Lauren. She pulled the tab and swallowed a few mouthfuls, then dribbled some down her T-shirt.

"It's more believable if we've got the smell of drink on our clothes and breath."

James took the can off Kerry and did the same. Lauren hated the taste and spat hers in the gravel. "I don't want to get beer on my new top," she said.

"Give us," James said.

He snatched the can off Lauren, poured most of it on the floor and splashed the dregs over her hair.

"OK," Kerry said. "Don't forget to act drunk."

They staggered through the Thunderfoods car park, keeping behind the cars. Then it was over a stretch of lawn to the side door of the warehouse. James handed Kerry his lock gun.

"You're quicker than me," he said.

Kerry fiddled with the lock, while James and Lauren sat in the grass yawning. It was an eight-lever deadbolt, one of the trickiest kinds to pick.

"You want me to try?" James asked.

Kerry sounded edge. "You won't do it. It needs a different attachment."

She unscrewed the back of James's lock gun. There were nine different-shaped picks inside and it was tough to tell them apart in the dark.

"This one or bust," Kerry said, clicking a different pick on to the gun.

She rattled about for another half minute.

"Finally," she sighed, pushing the door open.

The alarm pipped until she swiped the security card. They couldn't turn the light on in case someone saw it through the windows. It felt spooky, shining their torch beams around the cavernous black space. The racks of metal shelving were filled with sacks and tins of ingredients for the factory next door.

"Maybe that's how they get the cocaine into the country," James whispered. "Disguised as curry powder or something."

"No," Kerry said. "Dinesh described clear bags filled with white powder. And he said KMG people came and did something with it upstairs."

"Kerry," James said, "I hate to say this, but maybe your little boyfriend is just trying to impress you. This building doesn't even have an upstairs."

"We should split up," Kerry said, deliberately ignoring James. "There's a lot of shelving to cover."

They each took a row of shelves and started working along, searching for the white powder. The shelves went up ten meters. You'd need a forklift to access the higher bays.

Lauren whispered to Kerry between the rows of shelves. "Come look at this."

Kerry dashed over. Lauren's torch shone on a few clear polythene sacks filled with white powder.

"Borax," Lauren said. "It's what you mix with pure cocaine to make the weaker stuff they sell on the street."

"How do *you* know that, Miss Smarty-Pants?" James asked.

"I read your mission briefing," Lauren said casually.

James tutted. "Lauren, do you know how much trouble you could have got in if you'd been caught reading someone else's mission briefing?"

Lauren laughed. "Less than the amount you'd have been in for leaving a secret briefing lying on your bathroom floor."

"James," Kerry gasped, "you're not even supposed

to take briefings out of the mission preparation rooms."

"I know," James said, shrugging. "But I usually smuggle a few bits to read while I'm on the toilet."

Kerry took photos of the borax.

"So, Keith Moore stores his borax here," James said. "There's nothing illegal about borax. Mr. Singh will just say they use it as disinfectant."

"There must be more to it," Kerry said. "Keith wouldn't bail out a company this size in return for shelf space. Dinesh said about upstairs."

"I hate to keep saying it," James said, "but there *is* no upstairs."

"Yes, there is," Lauren said. "This building has a pointed roof, but the ceiling in here is flat."

"Good thinking, Lauren," Kerry said. "You obviously got all the brains in your family. There must a loft up there."

The three of them pointed their torches at the ceiling. The beams got dim over such a distance, but they eventually spotted a hatch that had to lead into the loft.

"How can we get up there?" Kerry asked.

"Easy," James said. "It's like a computer game. If you look, the shelves in some bays are closer together. You can use them like a ladder."

"And we thought all those hours on the PlayStation were wasted," Kerry said, smiling. "Lauren, you stay down here and keep lookout. Me and James will climb up."

Lauren nodded. James doubted she'd have been so agreeable if he'd been giving the orders. They clambered up the closely spaced shelves, feeling their way with their hands. They walked along the shelves, stepping over sacks and tins until they came to the next easy-to-climb section. Lauren shone her torch on them, lighting their path as best she could.

The top level was fifteen meters above ground, but the shelves were three meters deep, so if felt safe. There was a wooden pole with a hook on the end for undoing the loft hatch. Kerry pulled it open. James shone his torch into the hole while she pulled out the ladder. It clattered down, banging against the metal sheet on which they stood. The hundreds of fluorescent tubes in the ceiling a few centimeters from their heads started plinking to life. James and Kerry stared down and shielded their faces while their eyes adjusted to the light.

"What the hell did that?" James whispered.

"Someone must have come in," Kerry said. "They'll never see us up here, but where's Lauren?"

They crawled to the edge of the shelves on their bellies. James leaned over one side, Kerry over the other.

"I can't see her," Kerry said. "It looks like she's had the sense to get out of sight."

There were two sets of footsteps, accompanied by women's voices. James caught a glance of them. They were both fat, wearing hairnets and dark blue overalls.

"Bay forty-six," one woman said.

They walked slowly, reading the numbers printed on the shelves.

"Potassium carbonate," the woman said, leaning into the bay. "This is it, in the blue drums."

Something whumped against the floor, echoing around the warehouse. James peeked over the side. A sack of orange powder had exploded on the ground, almost directly below them. Lauren must have knocked it off a shelf.

The two women started walking towards the spill.

"I better see if Lauren's OK," James said.

Kerry nodded. "Be careful. Keep out of sight."

But when he turned around, Lauren was crawling along the metal towards them.

"Why didn't you hide behind something?" James whispered angrily.

"Sorry," Lauren said, looking ashamed of herself. "I wanted to be with you guys."

Even though it was tense, James couldn't help smiling. "Now you know why you need training: so you don't get scared so easily."

"I wasn't scared," Lauren said defensively. "Just . . ."

Kerry anxiously shushed the pair of them. "You're making too much noise."

Down at ground level, the two women were standing by the burst sack, hands on hips, staring up at the ceiling.

"We must have a ghost," one woman grinned.

The other one laughed. "I'm not sticking around to see if he chucks another one at us and it's not gonna be muggins here who cleans that mess up, either."

The women picked up their boxes and switched out the lights as they left. The three kids kept still, making sure the women were gone and letting their eyes readjust to blackness. Kerry lit her torch and shone it up the metal ladder.

"Bet you a pound there's nothing up there," James said.

Kerry didn't find him funny. "There better be after all this messing about."

She went up the ladder first. There were no windows in the loft, so it was safe to switch on the lights. Even before James got up the ladder, he could tell they'd found something good from the grin on Kerry's face.

Kyle woke up at 3:30 a.m., in a smoky room snarled up with sleeping bodies. He didn't know if he'd passed out or fallen asleep, or what the stain on his trousers was, but he remembered it was the wildest party of his young life. The host would be grounded for years when her parents got back from the Lake District.

Kyle had hammered himself with alcohol and thumping music. Now he was suffering. Anyone else would have crashed back to sleep, but Kyle wanted to get home, have a shower, and put his clothes to soak. He'd always been neat. One of his earliest memories was of chucking a tantrum over going on to a beach with a load of other kids because he didn't like getting sand in his clothes.

It took Kyle a while to find the room where he'd dumped his sweatshirt. He got abused when he trod on some naked guy's ankle in the dark. He stepped over more kids crashed out on the front lawn as he went out of the front gate towards the bus stop. He waited forty minutes for the night bus, which dropped him on the wrong side of Thornton at half-four in the morning. Everything looked wrong as he stumbled towards the house: All the lights were on and there was a gray Toyota he didn't recognize parked on the drive.

Nicole wasn't home, but everyone else was in the living room. Lauren had dropped to sleep on the couch.

Ewart had his laptop computer on the coffee table. A balding man in a suit and tie sat next to him.

"What's going on?" Kyle asked. "Did I miss something good?"

"Yeah," James grinned. "It turns out bringing Kerry on this mission wasn't a dumb waste of time after all."

Kerry gave James a look, but she was too full of herself to get offended.

Zara introduced Kyle to the stranger. "This is John Jones. He's in charge of the MI5 taskforce that's targeting KMG, so we called him over to look at the pictures."

John Jones reached over and shook Kyle's hand before speaking. "You kids are amazing," he grinned. "When Dr. McAfferty offered me a CHERUB unit, I thought it was some kind of joke."

James looked surprised. "You must have heard about missions where cherubs have done a good job."

John shook his head. "I'd been an MI5 agent for eighteen years without ever hearing of CHERUB."

Zara explained. "Thousands of people work for MI5, but only the most senior ones know about CHERUB. People like John only find out if they have to work with us."

"Even then," John said, "there are forty-three MI5 agents working on Operation Snort and I'm the only one who knows about you kids."

"So what's happened?" Kyle croaked, his throat raw from the smoke at the party.

"Come and look at the pictures James and Kerry took," Zara said.

Kyle leaned over the laptop screen while John Jones explained what had been photographed.

"KMG smuggles in cocaine at a very high purity, ninety percent or more. The stuff that gets sold on the street is between thirty and fifty percent pure. What you see in these pictures is a production plant. The pure cocaine gets mixed with borax and some other stuff in those aluminum vats. Then . . ."

John Jones clicked on the mouse, changing to a different picture.

"The machine in this picture is a real beauty. It must have cost over fifty thousand pounds. It's designed to package seasonings, like soy sauce or pepper. You turn it on, load up a roll of polyurethane bags, and tip your powder or liquid in the top. This one has been set up to package one-gram bags of cocaine."

"So did you find much coke?" Kyle asked.

"None at all," Kerry said.

"There could be drugs hidden in the warehouse," John said. "Or somewhere else on the Thunderfoods site, but I doubt it. Most probably, a couple of guys turn up with a few kilos of cocaine, spend a few hours mixing and bagging it, and then take it away with them when they leave."

"So," Kyle asked, "are you gonna bust this place up?"

"No," John said. "We're going to put it under surveillance. We'll get an undercover team to rig the loft up with video cameras and microphones. We'll watch who comes and goes and where they're coming from and going to. Hopefully, we can track the drugs that are processed at Thunderfoods back to wherever they're being smuggled in."

"So it's really only the beginning," James said.

"You kids have got our foot in the door," John said.

"That's not the same as bringing down KMG, but it's going to be a lot easier now we know where their cocaine is being processed."

John shook everyone's hand before he left. The sun was on its way up and Lauren was the only one who'd managed any sleep.

It was three in the afternoon when James surfaced from under his duvet. He was busting for a pee, but Kerry was in the shower, merrily singing her head off. Lauren had left a note on the kitchen table.

> *James*
> *U looked peaceful! Didn't want 2 wake U up. CU soon.*
> *Lauren*
> *XXX*

James was miffed. He'd wanted to say a proper good-bye and wish Lauren luck in training. He sprinted back upstairs as soon as he heard Kerry unlock the bathroom.

"What took you so long?" James gasped, lifting the toilet seat and starting to pee without bothering to close the door behind him.

"Sorry," Kerry said, toweling her hair. "Have you seen Ewart or Zara?"

"Not yet. They're at the supermarket."

"They want a word with us later on," Kerry said.

"You think we're in trouble for not asking before we broke in?" James asked.

"Lauren got a blasting from Ewart before she left."

"Was she upset or anything?"

Kerry shook her head. "She seemed to handle it OK."

"So, what do you reckon they'll do to us?"

"Kyle overheard Ewart and Zara talking," Kerry said. "Apparently we've landed ourselves washing-up duty for the rest of the mission."

James shrugged. "We could have got worse, I suppose."

CHAPTER 15

CONTENDER

Not much happened in the three weeks after they broke into Thunderfoods. That's how undercover mission usually work: You find a few things out quickly, then it starts getting tougher. You have to be patient, slowly winning the confidence of your targets and working your way deeper in to the organization.

Meryl Spencer sent James an e-mail to say Lauren had completed her first week of training and was coping well.

Nicole had put listening devices and miniature cameras around Keith Moore's house. James still liked Nicole, but he hadn't kissed her after the first time because he was more interested in Kerry.

Kerry had wired Mr. Singh's house with microphones and was spending a lot of time with Dinesh, trying to squeeze out more information. James still hadn't found the right moment to tell Kerry how he felt about her. At least, that's what he told Kyle. There had been loads of opportunities, but James always chickened out.

Kyle had given up targeting Ringo Moore and was helping a couple of Year Ten kids make deliveries for KMG on weekends. James still couldn't get his head around Kyle being gay, but it hadn't changed anything in their day-to-day lives.

Some days, James almost forgot he was on a mission. It was like being a normal kid: getting up and playing with Joshua, going to school, sitting through boring lessons or bunking off, coming home, and eating whatever frozen delight Zara had warmed in the oven, then going out making deliveries.

It wasn't a bad life. There was a hundred a week in drug money to spend. James had got new jeans and tracksuit tops, video games, and the dearest Nike trainers he could find. School was a doss and Junior and James always messed around and had a laugh. The two boys had loads on common: They both supported Arsenal, hated school, liked PlayStation, and had similar tastes in music and girls.

James hadn't been in a proper three-round fight yet, but he'd done some sparring and loved the buzz you got in the boxing ring. As soon as you get punched, the chemicals in your body rise up and make you mad, like somebody plugged you into the electricity. Your bad side takes over and you're not scared of anything.

James couldn't manage Ken's target of a hundred and fifty skips a minute, but he'd got well past the stage where the other boys pissed themselves laughing every time he picked up a rope. He stopped skipping and mopped the sweat off his face when Kelvin called him to ringside.

"One round sparring with Del," Kelvin said.

Del had a longer reach and seven fights under his belt, but James wasn't worried as he stepped through the ropes wearing gloves and a head guard. James was built for boxing: solid arms, big shoulders, and strong enough to take a punch.

"Touch gloves," Kelvin said, stepping back from the two fighters.

James charged forward on the bell. Del landed the first hit, a glancing blow on the side of James's head guard. James hit Del's head harder, sunk another punch in Del's guts, and then covered his face, blocking Del's jabs while spying for an opening through the crack between his gloves. When it came, James pounced forward and landed his glove in Del's face. The next punch caught Del off balance, sprawling him out over the canvas.

James wanted Del to get up so he could thump him again, but Del waved his gloves in front of his face and crawled to the ropes. James was disgusted. He spat out his mouth guard before tugging off his glove and hurling it at Del's back.

"Call that a fight?" he shouted. "Come back for some more, you little wimp."

Kelvin grabbed James by his shoulders and pulled him backwards. "Cool it, tiger," he grinned. "Try and remember this is amateur boxing. You win on the number of clean punches you land, not on how hard you punch or even how many times you knock the other guy down."

"I wanna fight somebody really good next time."

Kelvin laughed. "You're a strong lad, James, but you need to work on your speed, so don't start getting cocky."

James unbuckled his head guard and jumped out of the ring. Junior was walking towards him.

"You almost look good enough to fight me," Junior said, smiling.

"I'd fight you now if they'd let me."

Del had staggered around from the other side of the ring. His hair was soaked in sweat where it had been trapped under his head guard.

"You're too strong for me," Del gasped.

"Sorry I called you a wimp," James said. "I got carried away."

Del and James gave each other a sweaty hug. It was always the same: in the ring you wanted to kill someone, but once you got out you were mates again. As James walked over to his training pals, Kelvin called him back.

"I hear you've been a reliable delivery boy since you started," Kelvin said. "Don't think it's gone unnoticed."

"Cheers," James said, his mind still fixed inside the ring.

"You fancy a little train ride tomorrow evening?"

"How far?" James asked.

"We need a package delivered down St. Albans way. You up for it?"

"Sure."

"There's twelve kilos of coke split into four bricks. Get someone you can rely on to help you carry it. You'll earn forty pounds each."

"Sounds fair," James said. "Where do I pick the stuff up?"

"You know Costas?"

James nodded. "I've seen him around."

"He'll meet you in the Thornton playground at about six o'clock. Bring your mate so we can check him out."

Kyle was on another delivery, so James offered the job to Kerry.

"It's fifteen minutes' ride on the train," James said, "and we'll be earning twenty pounds each."

Kerry shrugged. "I was gonna do homework with Dinesh after school, but I'm not getting anything new out of him."

It was a drizzly night, so nobody else was in the playground. Costas was a burly sixteen-year-old who'd dropped out of school the year before. His face was a mass of zits and he didn't like the look of Kerry.

"Are you kidding me?" he asked. "You weren't supposed to bring your girlfriend. You need someone with a bit of presence in case there's trouble."

"This was arranged at short notice," James said. "Kerry's all I could get and she's well up to the job."

Costas looked at Kerry. "No offense, babe, but we don't use little girls."

Unless you were a very large person, preferably armed with a baseball bat, calling Kerry "babe" was a seriously bad idea.

"I'm not your babe," Kerry sniffed. "And I'm quite capable of defending myself."

"I'm sure you are, sweetie," Costas sniggered. "Sorry, James, but this is not gonna happen. Bringing a chick on a delivery, man . . . What are you thinking?"

"Give us those drugs," Kerry said furiously. "Or you're in deep trouble."

James smiled at her. "Kerry, calm down. I'll make a couple of phone calls and smooth this out."

"No," Kerry said. "I'm not letting this bag of pus talk to me like that."

Costas snorted noisily.

"What you gonna do, baby cakes, pull my hair?"

Kerry lunged forward, slamming a karate chop into the front of Costas's neck and sweeping his legs away as he stumbled backwards. Costas was on the ground with Kerry's knee crushing his windpipe before he even realized the fight had started.

"Baby cakes?" Kerry shouted, pressing her knee in harder as Costas gasped for breath. "Nobody calls me baby cakes."

"OK," Costas gurgled. "I'm sorry. You can go with James."

Kerry stood up and let Costas sit while his face returned to its normal color.

"You surprised me," Costas said angrily, as he got to his feet. "But you better not try anything like that again or I'll seriously hurt you."

Kerry couldn't help grinning. "I'll try to keep that in mind."

Costas made sure nobody was around before unzipping his backpack. Kerry and James each grabbed two plastic-wrapped bricks of white powder and tucked them in their backpacks. James started walking away.

"Hang on," Costas said. "Unless you want me to keep the eighty quid."

Kerry snatched the money out of Costas's hand.

"Pleasure doing business," she said.

She started jogging after James.

"Eighty quid, James?" Kerry said angrily. "I can't believe you tried to rip me off when you've got a roll of twenties in your pocket and I'm only getting pocket money."

"It was a mistake," James lied. "You can have half, of course."

"I'm keeping the lot," Kerry said, tucking the money into her jeans. "Unless you want to fight me for it."

CHAPTER 16

LOST

James and Kerry stepped off the train on to the platform at St. Albans.

"It's a shame we couldn't have got here earlier in the day," Kerry said. "St. Albans is really historic. There's Roman ruins and mosaics and stuff."

"Tragic," James said sarcastically. "Nothing gets my pulse racing like a good mosaic. We're not going into town anyway. We've got to get out to some housing area."

Taxis were lined up outside the station. The driver wanted to see James's money before he'd take them anywhere. The ride took them past farms and some seriously expensive houses, then from nowhere they found themselves surrounded by graffiti and concrete. It was like an alien spaceship had sucked a neighborhood out of the middle of London, then decided it didn't like the look of it and dumped it in the middle of nowhere.

The cab pulled up outside a shopping arcade. Everything was boarded up, except a pub that had been converted into a snooker club. It had a reinforced metal door and bars over the slits of glass that passed for windows.

Kerry looked around nervously as the cab pulled away. It was already turning dark.

"It must be the pits living in a place like this," James said. "Thornton may be a dump, but at least it's near to town. Out here you've got nothing."

It turned out the shops were the high point of the area. Beyond them were eight low-rise housing blocks. Three were boarded up, with CONDEMNED BUILDING notices and signs warning people not to go inside without masks to protect them from the asbestos dust. There was a pack of dogs roaming around, druggies in dark corners, and the only normal-looking people you saw walked fast, like they were afraid of being mugged.

James got the directions out of his pocket.

"Twenty-two, third floor, Mullion House."

They found Mullion House, then walked up a foul-smelling staircase and along the third-floor balcony. The door numbers ended at twenty. James rang the bell and an Eastern European–sounding woman shouted out of the letterbox in bad English.

"What is you like?"

"Do you know where number twenty-two is?" James asked.

"What?" she shoutd.

"Number twenty-two."

"Wait. I fetch my son."

The kid who came to the letterbox was about ten. His English was perfect.

"There's no number twenty-two," he explained. "I think all the floors are the same. It only goes up to twenty."

"Cheers," James said miserably, turning away from the letterbox. "Sorry to bother you."

"What do we do now?" Kerry asked.

"There's obviously a mistake with the address," James said. "I'll call the lady who rings my deliveries through. She'll sort it out."

James pulled the mobile out of his tracksuit and dialed. The phone made a bleep and a message flashed on the display: NO SIGNAL. Kerry tried hers and got the same.

"Crap," James said. "You really know you're in the middle of nowhere when you can't get a mobile signal."

Kerry looked down off the balcony towards the shops.

"There's a phone box by the bus stop," she said.

James looked down. "I'd put the odds of it working at something like a million to one."

They didn't have any other choice, so they went to take a look. The phone wasn't so much vandalized as annihilated. There was no glass, no handset, and no buttons; just a burned-up mess.

"This place is giving me the creeps," Kerry said. "Do you think they'd let us phone from inside the snooker club?"

"I wouldn't chance it," James said. "It looks like the kind of place where you'd get your throat cut."

"So what then?" Kerry asked.

"Let's get the hell out of here. There's no way to call another cab, so we'll wait for the bus. Our phones will work once we get to town. I'll make some calls and sort this shambles out."

They wandered across to the bus stop. Kerry glanced at the timetable.

"There's only one bus an hour," she said. "I think we just missed one."

There was hardly any traffic about. They sat on the pavement near the bus stop with their feet in the gutter. Kerry picked a dandelion from a crack in the tarmac and twirled it between her fingers.

"Do you think you'll get in trouble with KMG for this?" she asked.

"I've got the bit of paper with the address written in Kelvin's writing, so they can hardly blame me."

"It's pretty incredible," Kerry said.

James nodded. "Especially when you think what these drugs are worth."

"How much?" Kerry asked.

"There's twelve kilos. I sell coke for sixty a gram and there's a thousand grams in a kilo. So each kilo is worth sixty thousand pounds. That's . . . seven hundred and twenty thousand altogether."

"*Wow,*" Kerry gasped. "That makes our eight-pound delivery fee look a lot less generous."

"Course, that's the street price and this is being sold wholesale, but I'd still bet KMG isn't shifting this lot for any less than three hundred grand."

"You could buy a nice house with that sort of money."

James giggled. "Maybe we could do a runner."

"You know, it's cool the way you can do those sums in your head."

"I've been able to do it since nursery," James said. "Before my mum died, she ran this huge shoplifting gang and she got me to work out her sums; like, who owed how much and who was due what wages."

"Did she ever get busted?" Kerry asked.

James shook his head. "Nope. But when I was little, I used to have nightmares where the police came and took Mum and Lauren away. Junior made some comment the other day about his dad ending up in prison. He acted like it was a joke, but I could tell it worries him. I remembered how I used to be, and it made me feel really shitty about us using him to help put his dad in jail."

"I suppose every bad guy has someone who loves them," Kerry said.

They watched the sunset as the minutes dragged by. When the streetlights flicked on, James looked at his watch.

"The bus shouldn't be long now," Kerry said.

Three lads came out of the snooker club and started walking towards them. One was a big guy in his twenties, with a beard and curly brown hair down his back. The other two were skinheads in their late teens. Probably brothers, with ghostly complexions and spindly limbs. They weren't the first people who'd passed by, but something about them put Kerry and James on edge.

The taller skinhead stopped by Kerry.

"Waiting for a bus?" he asked.

"Yes," Kerry said, standing up. "That's what people usually do at bus stops."

"I thought you might be waiting for a hunk like me to come by and sweep you off your feet."

The shorter one gave James a shove. "You her boyfriend, blondie?"

"Piss off," James said, shoving him back.

"Got any money?" Shorty said, eyeballing James. "Not for very long you won't have."

Both skinheads pulled knives out of their pockets. CHERUB training teaches you to make an instant decision when you see a knife: either grab the assailant's wrist before the blade is in a threatening position, or back away if you don't have time. James and Kerry went for the first option, grabbing the two skinny wrists and yanking their arms behind their backs. Kerry twisted the tall one's thumb until his knife dropped on to the pavement, then smacked his head against the concrete bus stop. After freeing the other knife, James punched Shorty in the back of the head, before ducking down and picking both blades off the floor. He handed one to Kerry.

"We don't want trouble," Kerry said, waving the knife. "We're just waiting for the bus."

The two skinheads didn't back off, but they didn't look confident either. The guy with the long hair had waited in the background the whole time. He moved up between the skinheads and smiled.

"You two seem to know some pretty fancy moves," he said, breaking into a grin. "You got any that will stop one of these?"

He slid a sawn-off shotgun out of his jacket and pointed it at them. James looked at Kerry, hoping she had some smart move up her sleeve, but she looked as scared as he felt.

"This is a twelve gauge," the guy with the big hair explained. "One shot will blow the pair of you to smithereens. So, if you want to live beyond the next few minutes, you're going to do exactly what I say. OK?"

James and Kerry both nodded.

"First of all, pass the knives back to their owners, handles first."

The skinheads took the knives.

"Now put your hands on your heads."

Once their hands were on their heads, the skinheads rummaged through James's and Kerry's pockets, taking their money, keys, train tickets, and phones. Then they stripped off their watches.

"Now, lose the backpacks."

"You know you'll be in serious trouble if you take those packs?" James said. "You've no idea what's in them."

"I know exactly what's in them," the hairball laughed. "And you can tell Keith Moore that if he sends any more grubby little brats down here, we'll give them a lot worse than the beating we're about to give you."

Shorty looked at the gunman. "Can I have his trainers before we batter them?"

"Eh?"

Shorty pointed at James's trainers. "You said we could keep whatever we knicked off them. Those trainers are a hundred and nineteen ninety-nine. My little brother would love 'em."

The gunman shook his head in disbelief. "Go on, then."

James looked mortified as he surrendered his almost-new Air Max.

"Now," the gunman said, smiling sweetly, "after we go, you're gonna walk or crawl the hell out of here. If I ever see you again, I'll be the last thing you ever see. And I wouldn't bother waiting for the bus. Kids kept chucking bricks through the windscreen, so they stopped running them after dark."

The gunman made James and Kerry lie flat on the ground with their hands behind their heads, then he told the skinheads to give them a good going-over.

CHAPTER 17

CRAZY

Kerry and James crawled out of the road and lay in the grass verge behind the bus stop, catching their breath. As kickings go, it hadn't been bad, but they'd have plenty of bruises in the morning.

"I guess they wanted us fit enough to walk home and give Keith his message," Kerry said.

"How's your knee?" James asked.

"I'm OK. Your lip's bleeding."

"You feel up to walking, or do you want to rest for a minute?"

"I can walk," Kerry said. "What are we gonna do?"

"Exactly what the man with the gun told us to do," James said. "It'll take at least an hour to get into town.

Or if we pass a phone box that works, we can call home and reverse the charges."

"This will ruin the mission," Kerry said.

"Nah. I'll just explain what happened to Kelvin. It's obvious we've been set up."

"What if they think you were in on it?" Kerry asked. "There's plenty of delivery boys. If there's any doubt, KMG will just dump you and use someone else."

James realized she was right. "They're not exactly gonna be happy about me losing three hundred grand's worth of coke, are they?"

"They'll check all of us out," Kerry said. "Not just you and me. Kyle, Nicole, Ewart, and Zara will be under the spotlight as well. The whole mission will be down the toilet."

"I don't see how we can get the drugs back," James said. "That guy had a gun. I don't even have trainers."

"He was small-time," Kerry said.

"What makes you say that?"

"You heard what the skinhead said when he took your trainers. That hairball was paying them by letting them keep our stuff. That's hardly the modus of a big shot."

"OK," James said. "He's small-time, but he's still got a gun."

"He won't kill us in a million years," Kerry said. "He's been paid a few hundred quid to scare us, grab the drugs, and send a message to Keith Moore. There's a huge difference between that and murdering two kids."

"Supposing you're right," James said. "How do we find this guy?"

"I think there's only one road in and out of this chunk of paradise, and we haven't seen him leave. We're looking for a tall, fat drug dealer with tons of curly hair and a beard. I bet one of the scumbags hanging around here will be able to put a name to a description like that."

"And we just walk up and they'll tell us?"

Kerry shrugged. "We'll make some excuse why we need to find him."

"The thing is," James said, "if you've just ripped off KMG for three hundred grand, you won't be hanging around here for long."

"I know," Kerry said. "But he doesn't think KMG will know what's happened until we get into town. He'll be off his guard the next hour or so."

"You're serious, aren't you?" James smiled. "I'm really gonna go chasing after some gun-toting drug dealer in my socks?"

"I think it's worth the risk, but I'm not forcing you. If you're not up for it, we'll head home."

James thought for a second as he dabbed his bloody lip on the bottom of his T-shirt. He didn't fancy their chances. If it had been anyone but Kerry, he would have said no.

"Let's go and get shot," he said, climbing to his feet and taking his first painful steps since the beating.

They cut around the back of the shops, dodging the snooker club in case anyone inside spotted them. They found a couple of skinny women at the bottom of a staircase and got blank stares when they described the hairball. They got lucky on their second attempt, when Kerry described him to a group of teenagers.

"Was it some kind of heavy metal T-shirt?"

"Yeah," Kerry said. "Do you know where we could find him? He dropped his keys outside the snooker club and we picked them up."

"Sounds like Crazy Joe," one kid said. "He lives in Alhambra House. You want to be careful, he's a serious lunatic and he's drugged-up half the time."

"You know where exactly?" James asked.

"What do I look like?" the kid laughed. "Directory enquiries? Try the second or third floor."

"Cheers," James said.

"Nice socks," the kid replied.

Alhambra House was the furthermost block. There were twenty flats on each floor, but finding the right one was easier than they expected. Loads were boarded up and most of the others didn't look the part: old-person-style wallpaper in the hallways, or ethnic names written under the doorbells. Joe's flat turned out to be a give-away: the front door was painted black with a devil's-head knocker and underneath the word "Joe's" was written in Tippex. They peered through the glass. There was an Aerosmith poster pinned to the kitchen wall and all the lights were on.

James and Kerry didn't have their lock guns or anything with them. They couldn't get in, so they had to lure Crazy Joe out.

"Check he's at home first," Kerry said. "Ring the bell and run."

James pressed the buzzer and they sprinted to the end of the balcony and hid in the stairwell. Crazy Joe waddled on to his doorstep in his T-shirt and boxers and looked down the balcony. He swore about "bloody kids" and went back inside.

"So now what?" James said. "If he's half undressed, he's probably home alone."

"There might be a girlfriend in there as well."

"I don't reckon any woman lives in that house," James said.

"Based on what?" Kerry asked.

"Did you see the filthy sink and cutlery piled up on the draining board?" James asked. "That's a single man's kitchen if ever I saw one."

"There's something messed-up about this," Kerry said. "You'd think he'd be running or driving some place in a hurry, not sitting around in his underwear."

"None of this makes any sense," James said. "We need to take him down quickly and without making any noise."

Five minutes later, Crazy Joe emerged from his flat a second time to find James grinning at him.

"I warned you," Joe sneered.

As Joe lunged for James, Kerry landed her hardest punch into the side of his head. It hit the sweet spot above the eye socket where the skull is thinnest, giving Joe's brain a good rattling. All his muscles went limp and James had to dodge out of the way as he slumped across the balcony.

"Get moving," Kerry said anxiously, looking at James. "He'll start coming around in no time and I don't want to have to knock him out twice."

James stepped over Joe and ran into the flat, checking inside every room to make sure nobody else was home.

There were pizza boxes and rubbish everywhere. The smell of stale cigarette smoke made his eyes water. Once he knew the flat was empty, he helped Kerry drag the semiconscious Joe through to the living room.

"Find something to tie him up with," Kerry shouted.

James ripped the electric cables out of the back of the video and satellite box. Joe struggled a bit, but they managed to knot the flex tightly around his wrists and ankles.

"Where's our drugs, Joe?" Kerry asked, bunching her fist in the air above him.

"How old are you guys?" Joe grinned. "Thirteen, fourteen?"

"Nearly thirteen," James said.

"I've seen it all now," Joe said. "You guys were supposed to get scared and run home to Mummy."

"Shut it," Kerry said in a firm voice. "From now on, you talk when I say so and you better make sure I like the answer. So, for the second time, Joe, where are our drugs?"

"Found 'em," James said, spotting the two backpacks beside the couch.

He unzipped them, making sure the stuff was still inside.

"Look for the gun, and anything else you don't want him coming after us with," Kerry said. She kept Joe under control while James searched the flat. The shotgun was inside Joe's leather jacket, hanging up by the front door. James found a pistol and more drugs under the bed. It was cocaine in one-gram bags, identical to what James delivered most nights.

He'd been trained where to look for hidden stuff and an uneven piece of skirting board was a dead giveaway. James pulled it off and found two supermarket carrier bags stuffed with more cocaine, and a few thousand pounds in scrunched-up cash. James stuffed the drugs into the carrier bags on top of the money and carried the lot into the living room.

"Shall we take all this?" James asked.

"Why not?" Kerry said, smiling. "He made us suffer."

"We better not hang around here," James said.

"You kids are in way over your heads," Joe gasped.

Kerry bunched up her fist. "Did I ask for your opinion?"

She grabbed a wad of serviettes out of a greasy pizza box and forced them in Joe's mouth.

"Are we gonna call a cab, or what?" James asked.

Kerry pointed at a picture on the wall. "Is that parked around here somewhere?"

James looked over his shoulder at a framed photo of a slimmer, younger Joe, standing in front of an American car. It was a fancy two-seater, with mad-looking air scoops on the bonnet and a two-tone orange paint job. James read the little gold plaque stuck on the frame: 1971 FORD MUSTANG MACH I. TUNED TO 496 HORSEPOWER.

"They look like car keys on the coffee table," Kerry said.

Joe wriggled his arms and furiously tried to shout something through the serviettes plugging his mouth.

James grinned as he picked up the keys. "Sure beats hanging around for a minicab to turn up. Where's it parked?"

"You wouldn't leave that on the street around here. It

must be in one of the garages out the back." Kerry pulled the soggy wad of tissue out of Joe's mouth. "What's your garage number?"

"If you *touch* my car," Joe gasped, spitting bits of white fluff off his tongue, "you're both dead."

Kerry smashed her trainer into Joe's guts.

"Next time it'll be your balls. . . ." Kerry shouted, as Joe groaned in agony. "What's your garage number?"

"No way," Joe grunted.

"James," Kerry said sweetly, "hand me the gun, please."

James passed it across. Kerry pulled down on the stock to load it and pointed the sawn-off barrel at Joe's knees.

"The next word out of your mouth had better be the garage number," Kerry snarled. "Or it's gonna take a miracle to get the bloodstain out of this carpet."

James knew Kerry wouldn't pull the trigger, but she put on a good act and Joe wasn't so confident.

"Forty-two," Joe said.

"How hard was that?" Kerry said. "And if you're lying, I'll come back here in a minute and blow off your foot before I ask again."

"OK, OK," Joe gasped. "I lied. . . . It's in number eighteen. Why don't you call a cab? It's a very powerful car. Do you kids even know how to drive?"

"Don't you worry yourself about that," James said.

All CHERUB agents are taught to drive. It's essential to be able to escape on wheels if things turn nasty.

"Why don't you take a pair of Joe's trainers?" Kerry asked.

"Too big," James said. "They'd be like clown shoes on me."

"We better rip the phones out," Kerry said. "We don't want him calling his pals before we're well on our way."

She pulled the phone out and kicked the socket off the wall with her heel. James pocketed Joe's mobile and demolished the extension in the bedroom.

Kerry grabbed both packs.

"Ready to go?" she asked.

James got the carrier bags with the money, pistol, and Joe's drugs. They went out of the front door and walked briskly along the balcony, down the stairs, and around to the garages at the back. Kerry's head was spinning so fast, she never noticed that she still had the shotgun in her hand.

The padlock sprang open and James noisily rolled up the metal door of garage number eighteen. The Mustang looked better than the day it had come out of the showroom, thirty-five years earlier. Crazy Joe had spent serious money on it.

"Bags I'm driving," James said, unlocking the driver's door and lowering himself into the leather seat. Kerry didn't care, she wasn't into cars.

James moved the seat as far forward as it would go so he could reach the pedals. He'd learned on the private roads around campus in a little car with an engine the size of a thimble. He wasn't prepared for the thunderstorm when the tuned V-8 blasted to life, juddering through the pedals into his socked feet.

"Hoooooooly mother!" James grinned, searching for the headlight control.

The road ahead lit up and the dials on the dashboard turned electric blue. James put the automatic gearbox in drive and rolled the gargling beast out of its pen.

The first couple of kilometers were dodgy. The car had big acceleration, but the brakes had much less bite than on a modern car. It caught James out when he nearly went into the back of someone at the first set of traffic lights. Once they were a few kilometers clear, he parked. Kerry found a road atlas under her seat and worked out the route home. By the time they got on to the motorway, James was feeling confident. When the road ahead was clear, he couldn't resist slamming the accelerator and taking it up to 110 mph.

The trim inside the car started to shake and Kerry started going bananas.

"Really sensible, James," she shouted. "Two kids in a stolen car carrying guns and drugs. I tell you what: Why don't we attract lots of attention by slaughtering the speed limit?"

After seeing the way she dealt with Joe, James decided it might be best if he slowed down.

They parked the stolen Mustang at the back of a DIY store about a kilometer from Thornton. It was gone eleven o'clock and, now the adrenalin rush had worn off, James and Kerry felt like they could sleep for twenty hours.

"We could leave the keys in the door and someone will nick it," James said.

"It's got our fingerprints all over," Kerry said. "Joyriders usually burn cars out. If we don't want it to look suspicious, that's what we'll have to do."

James gave the car an admiring glance. "Seems a shame to kill it."

Kerry leaned inside and flipped open the glove box.

She found Joe's cigarettes and lighter, then tore pages out of the road atlas and screwed them up into loose balls. When there was a mound of paper on the passenger seat, she flicked the lighter and set the edges alight. The left the passenger door open so the fire could breathe, then ducked into some trees and waited until they were sure the flames had taken hold.

The front seats were quickly ablaze. Once the roof lining caught, the flames flashed into the back. The whole interior glowed orange and smoke started curling out from under the hood.

"Better run," James said. "There's bound to be a security guard round here somewhere."

They'd only gone a hundred meters when the heat blew out one of the back tires. A few seconds later, the fuel caught and the back end of the car went up in a fireball.

It was less than a kilometer home, but they were feeling their injuries and the walk seemed to take forever. James had a pounding headache. When they staggered through to the kitchen, Ewart jumped up from the table, surprised by the state they were in. He made them both hot drinks and sandwiches while Zara and Nicole cleaned up their cuts and bruises.

"Shower and go to bed," Zara said, after they'd explained what had happened. "Don't bother getting up for school in the morning. You both need a good day's rest."

"I better ring Kelvin first," James said.

"OK," Ewart said. "Do that while Kerry's in the shower, then go straight to bed."

CHAPTER 18

RISKS

James was out as soon as he hit the pillow and the next thing he knew it was 10 a.m. the following morning. He had six huge bruises, a couple of grazes, and a giant scab on his bottom lip. When he stood up, his thigh muscle felt tight and he could only manage short steps.

Down in the kitchen, Joshua was on the floor playing with some magnets he'd pulled off the fridge door and Kerry was at the table in her nightshirt. She looked shell-shocked.

"Sleep OK?" James asked.

"Not bad," Kerry said. "Zara just made a pot of tea if you want some."

James poured a mug and got a bowl of cereal.

"I can't believe all we went through last night," Kerry grinned. "If I didn't hurt in ten places, I might believe it was all a dream."

"Same here," James smiled. "You were so tough on Crazy Joe when you had him tied up. I know you've got a temper, but I've never seen you juiced-up like that before."

"I was so angry," Kerry said. "I mean, what kind of scuzzball pays skinheads to beat up kids?"

"At least Kelvin seemed cool when I explained how we got the drugs back; and we saved the mission."

Zara stepped in from the garden and threw an empty laundry basket down beside the washing machine. She'd heard James's last line.

"You know," she said, "sometimes a mission isn't worth saving."

"What?" James gasped.

Kerry looked surprised as well.

"I respect what you two did last night," Zara said. "You made a decision under tricky circumstances and it came off. But Ewart and I both feel you should have come home. It was an unacceptable risk going up against a man with a gun."

James and Kerry both looked wounded.

"There's no need for those faces," Zara said.

She picked Joshua up off the floor and sat him on her lap at the table.

"CHERUB is one of the most secret organizations in the world," Zara explained. "Only two people in the British government know it exists: the Intelligence Minister and the Prime Minister. When politicians first find out about CHERUB, they're usually queasy about putting kids in danger. Then Mac explains about all the useful work cherubs do and the lengths we go to make you guys safe.

"Imagine if you two had been hurt, or even killed, last night. Mac would have had to go to London to explain the facts: two kids got mugged and went chasing after an armed drug dealer. At the least, Mac and the senior people within CHERUB would be sacked for letting something so irresponsible happen. The politicians might even decide they can't stomach what CHERUB does and shut the whole show down."

Kerry nodded. "When you put it like that, I can see it wasn't worth it."

"Sorry," James said.

"You've got nothing to be sorry for," Zara smiled. "Just try to be less gung ho from now on."

Kelvin rang James's mobile around midday.

"I've been making calls about what happened," he said. "Can you meet us down here at the boxing club and bring everything you got off Crazy Joe with you?"

"I'm not in shit, am I?" James asked.

"No, no way," Kelvin said. "I just want you to fetch the stuff down and we'll see you right. And that bird you had with you."

"Kerry," James said.

"Yeah, bring her as well."

Kerry had never been up to the boxing club. The gym was quiet at this time of day, just a few of the more serious boxers putting themselves through punishing workouts. Ken, as always, sat in his chair holding a mug of tea and watching everything that happened.

"They're using my office," he said. "Knock before you go in."

A gigantic man in a suit and tie stood guard at the door of the dingy office. James did a double take when he got inside. Crazy Joe was leaning against a back wall; he had a bloodstained dressing over a cut on his forehead. Kelvin sat on a cabinet off to one side and the big cheese himself was in the cracked leather chair at the desk.

"Take a seat," Keith Moore said.

He didn't look like anyone special. A smallish man, with cropped brown hair. He wore Levis and a white polo shirt. The only conspicuous sign of wealth was a chunky gold ring.

"I haven't had the pleasure before," Keith said, reaching over and shaking James's and Kerry's hands. "Have you brought everything you took off Joe?"

James rattled the carrier bags between his legs.

"It's all in there."

"I take it you know who I am?" Keith asked.

"Yeah," James said. "I've seen you at your house. I was on the PlayStation with Junior."

"My business runs itself these days," Keith said. "People go off to South America to buy stock, stock arrives, stock gets distributed."

James noticed that he never referred to drugs or cocaine, in case the room was bugged.

Keith continued, "Sometimes I go for weeks hearing the same message: 'All the usual problems, boss, but nothing we can't handle.' Then, just when you think nothing is ever going to excite you, something turns up like what you two did last night."

"It was a test, wasn't it?" Kerry asked.

"That's right," Keith smiled. "You won't last long in business without loyal people. The best way to find what they're made of is to give them some fake merchandise and put them in a situation like we put you two in last night. Some people get scared and turn hysterical. Those are the ones who'll cause problems if they get busted. We have to kick them out. Some people are sorry for losing the merchandise, but they tough it out and beg for another chance. That's what we're hoping for: guts and determination. Until last night, though, nobody ever showed enough guts to hunt down and get revenge on the guys we paid to rob them. What you two did was very impressive."

James and Kerry both smiled.

"This is all nice and cozy," Crazy Joe said bitterly. "But what about my stuff?"

"Yes," Keith said. "You'll have to return what you took from Joe."

"What about us?" James said. "I've lost my best trainers. We both lost our watches and mobiles and stuff."

"Joe can return them," Keith said.

Joe cleared his throat. "Actually, I said the two guys who duffed them up could keep what they took."

"OK," Keith said. "Take five hundred quid out of Joe's money, that'll cover it."

"That's a bit steep," Joe said tersely. "It's not my fault the brat was wearing expensive trainers."

Keith repeated himself. "Take five hundred quid out of Joe's money, that'll cover it."

He didn't change his tone or anything, but Joe knew his place and didn't push the argument. James took five hundred pounds and split it with Kerry. After that, he slid the carrier bags over to Joe.

"Is that everything you took?" Keith asked.

James nodded. "Everything."

"Where's my Mustang parked?" Joe asked.

James and Kerry looked awkwardly at each other.

"We were scared you'd report it stolen and our fingerprints were all over the inside," James said.

"You didn't clean them off with white spirit, did you?" Joe asked. "White spirit dries out the leather."

"No, we didn't," James said. "We, erm . . ."

He didn't have the bottle to say it.

"We burned the car out," Kerry blurted.

"You did *what*?" Crazy Joe shouted, lunging over the desk and grabbing James by his T-shirt.

"Let him go," Keith said, firmly.

"I'll kill these little pricks," Joe shouted, dragging James across the desk and trying to get his hands around his throat. James thrashed about, trying to push Joe off.

Joe had ignored Keith's order, so Keith gave Kelvin the nod. Joe was no match for the powerfully built boxer; Kelvin picked up the fat man like he weighed nothing, banged him against the wall, and slapped him around the face. Joe let out a high-pitched yowl that could have come from an eight-year-old girl.

"That car was my baby," he sobbed. "I spent months working on her."

Kelvin backed off with a stunned look on his face. Joe dabbed up tears with the end of his beard.

"Wasn't it insured?" Keith asked.

"That's not the point," Joe sniffled. "I invested love in that car. You'll never get that back."

Keith was killing himself laughing. "Joe, it's only a car. Get a grip on yourself."

"Those kids should pay damages, or something. They shouldn't get away with it."

"Joe," Keith said, looking a little angry. "It's not my fault you let yourself get outwitted by two twelve-year-olds. I've done what you wanted, now get out of here before I ask my minder to step inside and knock your head through the wall."

Joe grabbed his carrier bags and stumbled out of the office. He looked such a shambles James almost felt sorry for him. Keith got up from behind the desk, shaking his head.

"You know," Keith said, as Kelvin helped him into his overcoat, "if you two kids stay loyal and work hard, you're gonna make a lot of money."

James and Kerry both grinned. The bruises were worth it if they'd earned Keith Moore's respect.

"Actually," Kerry said, "I came along as a favor to James. All your deliveries are done by boys."

"I thought girls were soft until I met you," Keith said.

"I can set her up, if you like," Kelvin said.

"These two are really special," Keith said, grinning. "They've got brains and balls. Keep them busy and make sure they're properly rewarded."

"Thanks," Kerry said.

"And James," Keith said. "If you're over my house with Junior any time, be sure to stick your snout into my office and say hello."

Keith left with his minder like he was in a hurry. James looked at Kelvin, who was shaking his head in disbelief.

"I'm gonna have to treat you two right," Kelvin said. "With Keith singing your praises, I might just end up calling one of you boss someday."

CHAPTER 19

THIRTEEN

Friday before school, Kerry knocked on the boys' bed-room door.

"Are you decent in there?"

"I'm still in bed," James groaned, sounding knack-ered. "Come in if you want."

He'd been up until nearly midnight having a Play-Station competition with Kyle and a couple of Thornton kids. Kerry came through the door with Joshua in her arms and dumped him on James's bed.

"He wanted to wish you a happy birthday," she said.

James pulled his duvet over his face. Joshua tugged it back and giggled when James made a loud quacking noise.

"How come you didn't scream your head off when Kerry picked you up?" James asked.

"I think he's finally got used to me," Kerry smiled. "Can I leave him here while I get my books ready for school?"

Kerry went out. Joshua crawled up the bed and burrowed under a loose pillow near James's face. James moved in to blow a raspberry on Joshua's arm, but as he got close he recoiled from a powerful smell.

"Jeeeeeeesus," James shouted, covering his nose with his arm. "You smelly little . . ."

James jumped out of bed and picked up Joshua, holding him out at arm's length. He walked into the hallway, where Kerry and Nicole were wetting themselves laughing.

"I wondered when you'd smell it," Kerry said.

"You're evil," James grinned. "I'll get you two for this."

James carried Joshua downstairs to the kitchen. Zara was cooking a pan of sausages.

"Morning, teenager," Zara said. "There's presents and stuff on the table."

"This little monster filled his nappy," James said.

Zara grinned. "You know where the changing table is, James."

"Yes, I do, but you're not getting me anywhere near it."

"Think of it as a learning experience," Zara said. "An introduction to life as a young adult."

James knew Zara wasn't serious.

"Actually," he said, "a better introduction to young adulthood would be a crate of beer and some hot chicks."

Zara smiled. "I don't think so, somehow."

Ewart walked in behind James.

"You want to be careful," Ewart said, taking Joshua out of James's arms. "You start off with the hot chicks and before you know it you're leaning over a changing table with one of these little beasts peeing on you."

Ewart tickled his son's belly before taking him outside for a nappy change.

James sat at the table and started ripping into his cards. Because cherubs never have family, except brothers and sisters, they make a point of exchanging cards, even when they're away on missions. James had over thirty, including some with foreign postmarks redirected from campus. Gabrielle had sent one from South Africa. James's old training pals Callum and Connor had posted one from Texas, and Amy had sent a postcard with a picture of a giant pineapple on it from Australia. The tackiest-looking card was from Lauren.

"Here, Zara," James laughed. "Listen to what Lauren wrote. 'Dearest brother, you are an idiot. Sometimes you make me puke. I'll be in training by the time you read this and I wish you were doing it instead of me. P.S. Happy thirteenth birthday, I love U.' Then she's done a row of kisses."

James left opening his presents until Kyle and the girls had come down. The biggest box was from Ewart and Zara: a replacement for his stolen trainers. Nicole and Kerry had clubbed together and bought him a T-shirt he'd looked at the last time they went to the Reeve Center. He got a kiss from each of them when he said thanks. Kyle got him a pack of trendy men's toiletries. It included shampoo, conditioner, and a little bottle of aftershave. The label read, "Please use these regularly."

"This is all cool," James grinned. "Cheers."

He put his goodies aside and grabbed a sausage sandwich from the plate in the middle of the table. His mind wandered back a year to his twelfth birthday, just after his mum had died. He'd been living in a council home and wasn't allowed to see Lauren. It had been about the most desperate day of his life.

Then he thought about other birthdays, back when his mum was alive. Charging down the stairs to stacks of shoplifted toys and clothes, then racing to unwrap everything before school. When Lauren was tiny, she'd have to have a present as well, or she'd chuck a jealous fit.

Thinking back made James feel emotional and his eyes started glazing over. He didn't want to start bawling in front of everyone, so he scraped back his chair and bolted towards the stairs.

"Are you OK?" Zara shouted after him.

"Busting to pee," James lied.

He locked himself in the bathroom. He wasn't really miserable, it was just that thinking about his mum always made him feel empty. Even though there was loads of interesting stuff going on in his life, James often wished he could go back in time and spend a night in front of the TV with his mum.

After washing his eyes, James stared in the mirror at the same kid who'd been there the night before, only now he was a teenager. It didn't really make any difference, but it was a buzz all the same.

• • •

James, Junior, Nicole, and April arranged to meet at lunchtime, to bunk off and go to the cinema. They swapped uniform for casual clothes as soon as they got out of the school gate. James had loads of money, so he paid for tickets and popcorn and stuff.

It was a stupid thriller. Nicole started giggling every time this American actor spoke in a fake-sounding London accent. James and Junior started putting two fingers in their mouths and whistling noisily every time this fit actress came into shot.

The only other people in the cinema were a few pensioners. One bloke kept shushing them until Nicole turned back and waved her fist at him.

"Shut it, you old git."

The old man toddled off to make a complaint. The cinema manager came in and told them all to behave or else he'd chuck them out. James settled down to the film. He got a shock when he noticed Nicole and Junior had their arms around each other and an even bigger one a minute later when they started snogging.

They were all over each other. Nicole's leg was up in the air and James kept getting kicked. He got up and moved down two seats so he was sitting on the opposite side of April, away from any flailing limbs.

"They're getting on well," April grinned.

She grinned for a long time. James watched half a minute of the film and she was still grinning at him. He realized the girls had planned an ambush. Nicole already knew Junior fancied her because he'd asked her out before. James felt like he'd been hooked on a line and reeled in, but he checked April out and realized that as traps go, it wasn't a bad one.

April was decent-looking, with long brown hair and fit legs. James slid his hand under the armrest and put it on top of April's. She twisted in her seat, so she could rest her head on James's shoulder. James turned around, breathed April's smell and kissed her on the cheek while she grabbed a few of his Maltesers.

They stayed that way for a couple of minutes, until April moved away and blew chocolate breath over him.

"So," she whispered. "Are you gonna snog me or what?"

James figured, *"What the hell, it's my birthday."* They snogged for ten minutes, breaking up when the movie got near the end and turned into a big car chase and punch-up that was actually worth watching.

Nicole and Junior started messing around. They poured the dregs and melted ice from the Coke into one cup, then spat in chewed-up chocolate and bits of popcorn off the carpet. Nicole held the cup between James and April.

"Gob in that," Nicole said.

James and April obediently spat into the cup.

"That better not end up anywhere near me," James said.

Nicole grinned. "Don't you worry."

As soon as the titles came up, Nicole and Junior dashed over and caught up with the old man as he doddered up the aisle.

"Excuse me," Nicole said politely.

The old man turned suspiciously.

"What is it?"

"I just wanted to apologize for disturbing you," Nicole said. "I realize it was dreadfully inconsiderate of us."

The old man smiled. "That's OK, I suppose. Just don't do it again."

"Yeah," Junior said. "It's people like you that fought in hundreds of wars so that kids like us could be here today."

"We'd like you to have this as a token of our appreciation," Nicole giggled.

She chucked the contents of the cup at the old man, who wheezed in shock as the foul liquid drizzled inside his clothes. His jumper had massive stains and bits of popcorn stuck down the front.

"That'll teach you a lesson," Nicole shouted.

James looked stunned as Nicole and Junior broke into a run. He and April chased after them, knowing they'd get into trouble if they stuck around. When they got to the foyer, Junior launched himself into a rack of peanuts and snacks, spilling them over the floor. None of the cinema staff earned enough money to bother going after them.

They ran a few hundred meters from the cinema and cut into a side street. James was livid.

"Are you two retards or something?" he shouted. "What the hell did you do that for?"

"Who put a bug up your arse?" Nicole grinned.

Junior was laughing so hard he couldn't stand up straight.

"He was an old man," James stormed. "That was

totally out of order. You could have busted his hip or something."

April didn't say anything, but she stood beside James, showing she was on his side.

"I hope he *has* broken his hip," Nicole shouted bitterly. "I hope he drops dead."

"Nice," April said.

"I can't stand old people," Nicole said bluntly.

"You'll be old one day," James said.

"Nah," Nicole said. "Live fast, die young, that's my motto."

"Where are we going now?" Junior giggled. "Shall we get something to eat? I'm starving."

Being friends with Junior was part of James's mission, but sometimes your emotions take over no matter how hard you try.

"I'm going home," James said shortly. "I feel like a shower."

"You're not throwing a major strop, are you?" Junior asked. "You're still coming down the youth club tonight?"

"Sure," James said, half-heartedly. "Everyone's gonna be there."

"I'm smuggling some of my dad's beers in," Junior said. "Let's all get totally smashed."

Junior and Nicole wandered off towards a burger place with their arms around each other. James waited at the bus stop with April. When her bus came, he gave her a quick kiss.

"I'll see you at the youth club tonight," April said. "Don't let those two idiots spoil your birthday."

"I won't," James said.

But he couldn't help feeling it all the way home. There's a difference between mucking around and being nasty to someone. The thing with the old man had left a bad taste in his mouth.

CHAPTER 20

CELEBRATION

The incident with Crazy Joe was supposed to be kept quiet, but it was the kind of story that travels fast and gets wilder every time it's told. The story, combined with Keith Moore's seal of approval, had made James into a well-respected face.

He got a good vibe when he walked into the youth center alongside Kerry and Dinesh. Waves and smiles came from all directions. He sat at a table with Junior and Nicole, who looked like they'd already downed a few of the beers that were stashed under the table. Junior was in a good mood and James didn't want to make a big deal about what had happened at the cinema earlier.

"Beer?" Junior said, passing a can across the table.

Drinking was banned, but the youth club supervisor always just sat in the corner translating books into German. If there was a punch-up, he'd phone upstairs and get a couple of guys from the boxing club to sort it out; apart from that, you could get away with anything.

"Cheers," James said, cracking the can open.

April pulled up a chair next to James and they kissed. He felt awkward doing it with Kerry sitting a few meters away.

The next few hours passed in a blur. Kids came and went. Everyone was taking the mickey out of everyone else and drinking. Kerry and Dinesh only took sips, James and April had a couple of beers, while Nicole and Junior got completely trashed. One time, Nicole got the giggles so badly she fell off her chair.

The youth club closed at ten and James thought he'd better have a slash before they headed home. He was in a grand mood as he drifted downstairs to the foul-smelling basement toilets.

"You forgive me, don't you?"

James turned around and realized Junior was peeing beside him.

"For the old man?" Junior slurred. "Nicole's got a thing about old people. We got carried away."

"Course I forgive you," James said. "Don't sweat it."

"I've got something for you," Junior said. "Come outside."

They went into the space at the bottom of the stairs between the boys' and girls' toilets. Junior pulled a pillbox out of his jeans and popped off the lid. There was a stubby metal straw inside and a thin layer of white powder in the bottom.

"How long have you been snorting coke for?" James gasped.

"Since the cinema."

"No wonder you two have been acting like nutters," James said. He knew that coke gave you a high, but he'd never realized that it could make you act totally crazy.

"Give it a whirl," Junior said.

James had packets of cocaine in his locker at school and under his bed at home. He'd been tempted a couple of times, but it had never seemed quite this easy: a few centimeters from his face with a mate urging him to test it out.

"I'm not sure I want to get into that stuff," James said.

"You tart," Junior laughed. "What harm's one snort gonna do?"

Nicole came out of the girls' toilet and looked at James.

"The birthday boy doesn't want any," Junior giggled.

"Good," Nicole said. "More for me."

She shoved the metal straw up her nostril and vacuumed up half the coke left in the pot. Her head shot backwards and she wiped a tear off her cheek.

"You've *got* to, James," Nicole rasped, sounding like she was pinching her nose.

"It's not gonna blow your mind or nothing," Junior said. "It just makes the world seem a nicer place."

"Except inside your nose," Nicole giggled. "That goes like a chunk of rubber."

James looked into the dish. There was only a tiny bit left and he was curious to try it, just once. Nicole gave him the straw. James pushed it up his nose and leaned towards the white powder.

"Come on, you guys," Kelvin shouted. "I'm locking up."

He was at the top of the stairs. Junior pulled the coke out of sight before James had time to sniff. James spun around, hiding the metal straw in his hand.

"Give us a second," Junior shouted.

"*Now,*" Kelvin shouted. "Don't mess me about."

The three of them staggered upstairs, through the youth club and on to the pavement out front. The nights were starting to turn cold. Kerry, April, and a big bunch of other kids were standing around shivering. James found April.

"You want to come round to our house?" James asked. "It's only ten minutes' walk."

April shook her head. "Kelvin's giving me, Junior, and Dinesh a lift home. I'll have to smuggle Junior in round the back. If our dad sees him in that state, he'll go bonkers."

"OK," James said, leaning forward and giving April a kiss. "I'll speak to you tomorrow. Maybe we can go to the Reeve Center or something."

"Cool," April smiled. "It looks like you've got your own set of problems over there."

James turned around in time to see Nicole hurl up in the gutter.

Kerry went in first and checked the coast was clear. Ewart and Zara had gone up to bed early, which was a relief. James and Kyle dragged Nicole into the kitchen and draped her over a dining chair.

"I'm gonna die," Nicole sobbed, resting her elbows on the dining table. "I feel so ill."

Kerry ran her a glass of water. "Drink that," she said. "Alcohol dehydrates you. The water will stop you getting a hangover."

James hadn't drunk anywhere near as much as Nicole, but he decided a drop of water would do no harm and ran a glass for himself.

"I think I'm gonna be sick again," Nicole moaned.

Kyle got one of the buckets from under the sink and stood it on the table. Nicole leaned into it, her sobs echoing into the plastic.

"Get us a tissue," she groaned. "My nose is running."

James ripped off a square of kitchen towel and handed it over. When Nicole took the bucket away from her face, they all saw her nose bleeding.

"Oh, my God," Kerry gasped. "I think we should wake Zara up."

"No," Nicole begged. "I'll get into trouble. Take me to bed and I'll sleep it off."

Kerry grabbed the roll of kitchen towel and the bucket, and took them upstairs to the girls' bedroom. James and Kyle each wrapped one of Nicole's arms around their back, picked her off the chair, and helped her stumble along the hallway.

"Nicole," Kyle said firmly. "We're at the bottom of the stairs. Lift your legs."

Nicole's head slumped forward and her legs gave way. A fresh wave of blood began streaking out of her nose.

"*Oh, Jesus,*" Kyle said desperately. "Put her down."

Kerry was coming back down the stairs to help them. When she saw Nicole's limp body on the hallway carpet, she spun around and burst into Ewart and Zara's room. Ewart raced downstairs in his boxers. Kyle was taking Nicole's pulse.

"Her heartbeat's all over the place," Kyle said.

"Shall I call 999?" James asked.

"There's no point hanging around for an ambulance," Ewart said. "I'll drive her."

Zara was running downstairs in her dressing gown, carrying clothes and trainers for Ewart. Ewart stepped into the clothes before scooping Nicole off the floor. Out on the driveway, Kyle had opened up the people carrier.

"She's taken some cocaine," James blurted.

He didn't want to grass, but it might save her life if the doctors knew what was in her system.

"Christ almighty," Ewart shouted, as Kyle helped him lay Nicole across the back seat. "That's all we need."

Ewart climbed into the driver's seat and slammed the door so hard James thought the glass might break. When the car was out of sight, James closed the front door and turned around to face Kerry and Zara, who were both in tears.

"I hope she's OK," Kerry sniffed.

"You're absolutely sure she took cocaine?" Zara asked.

James nodded, feeling a lump forming in his throat. "I saw it."

"Why didn't you stop her?" Kerry asked angrily.

"I tried to," James lied. "She wouldn't listen to me."

"What about you, James?" Zara asked. "Did you take any?"

"No way," James said. "I'd never go near it."

"That's a relief," Zara said. "If they find traces of cocaine in Nicole's urine, they'll expel her from CHERUB."

"Is that for certain?" James asked.

"You both know the rules," Zara said. "There's zero tolerance for class A drugs. We even put the reminder at the bottom of the mission briefing when you guys signed your names, in case you considered anything silly."

"Are you two going up to bed?" Kerry asked anxiously.

"I suppose," Zara said. "Unless you want a drink or something first."

"I don't think I'll sleep," Kerry said. "I don't want to be on my own wondering what's happening with Nicole."

Zara pulled Kerry into her chest and gave her a hug. "I'll sit up with you for a while," she said. "Don't worry."

James thought about Nicole. Imagining her being wheeled into hospital and having tubes pushed down her throat and needles under her skin. He wondered what it would be like to go into a coma and realized he didn't feel like being on his own either.

James and Kerry got their duvets and sat together in the living room with their feet on the coffee table. It was a weird feeling; anxious for news, being exhausted but not able to sleep. The hands on the clock seemed to be frozen.

Zara had to go upstairs to sort out Joshua when he started bawling.

"Did you really snort any coke?" Kerry whispered.

"No," James said indignantly. "I already told you."

"In front of Zara," Kerry said. "What about just between you and me?"

"I saw them doing it and got offered a snort, but I said no."

"I'm glad," Kerry smiled. "I'd have bet my life savings that if something as dumb as that was going down on your birthday, you'd be into it."

"I'm not a complete moron, you know," James said.

Kerry's mobile started ringing. James had changed her ring tone to the national anthem for a joke while she was in the toilet at the youth center, but that didn't matter now.

"Dinesh," Kerry said, surprised. "Are you crying? Calm down . . . Tell me what the matter is. What the hell are you doing at the police station?"

CHAPTER 21

BRAINDEAD

Three hours earlier, Dinesh had hitched a lift home in Kelvin's car with April and Junior. He lived with his mum and dad in a flash house a few doors down from Keith Moore. Mr. Singh was in his study, working on his laptop. Dinesh wasn't surprised to find him there, even though it was past eleven.

"Good tme at the youth club?"

"Nothing very exciting," Dinesh said. "Did Mum ring up?"

"She asked me to make sure you washed behind your ears and changed your underpants."

"Very funny, Dad," Dinesh said, grinning. "I'm off to bed. Don't sit up working all night."

Dinesh had brushed his teeth and was getting into bed when he heard a saloon car pull on to the driveway. Sometimes cars used the drive to turn around, but this one stopped and Dinesh watched two doors open. Another car stopped behind. It was white, with blue lights and cop markings on the roof.

"Dad!" Dinesh shouted.

The two cops from the first car were in plain clothes. The three out of the second wore uniform and carried rifles. Two cops split off and jogged around the house, covering the back exit. Dinesh quickly slid on his tracksuit bottoms and ran on to the landing.

"Dad!" Dinesh shouted again, nervously. "The police are outside."

The front door exploded into the hallway. Police never ring the doorbell when it's a drug bust, because it gives the suspect a chance to destroy evidence. Dinesh had never seen a gun outside of a museum before. Now two were aimed at his head.

"On the floor," the cop barked. "Hands where I can see 'em."

They ran up the stairs towards Dinesh, who was trying to stop himself shaking.

"Don't be frightened, son," the cop said. "Where's your old man?"

Mr. Singh opened the door of his study. The guns swung towards him.

"Hands in the air."

One of the plain-clothes cops bounded up the stairs. He pushed Mr. Singh against the wall and locked the handcuffs.

"You have the right to remain silent. Anything you do say can be taken down and used in evidence against you. . . ."

The armed cop looked down at Dinesh.

"Who else is home?"

"Nobody," Dinesh said.

"Where's your mum?"

"Barcelona. She's back tomorrow."

"How old are you?"

"Twelve."

"We can't leave you here on your own," the cop said. "You'll have to come with us."

A police car pulled up on the driveway. Dinesh looked nervous when Zara opened the door.

"You don't mind me staying, do you?" Dinesh asked. "They asked me to think of somewhere I could go until Mum gets home. Kerry was the first person I thought of."

"Don't worry," Zara said, putting her hand on Dinesh's shoulder. "There are so many kids coming in and out of this house, one more won't make any difference."

The cop gave Zara a custody form to sign, while Dinesh wandered into the living room. Kerry stood up and gave him a hug.

"I'm so sorry about your dad," Kerry said.

"I told you he was a crook," Dinesh said angrily. "It was bound to happen sooner or later." He looked at the duvets and pillows scattered around the living room.

"We couldn't sleep," Kerry explained. "They had to take Nicole to the hospital."

"Is it serious?"

"Kyle called from the hospital. They gave her an adrenalin shot to bring her round. Then they pumped her stomach."

"I saw that on TV once," Dinesh said. "It's so nasty. They force a rubber tube down your throat and right down into your stomach."

"They'll keep her in under observation for a few hours," James said. "But they reckon she'll be OK."

Dinesh managed a smile. "I wouldn't want to be in her shoes when she gets home."

It was gone 3 a.m. when a cab dropped Kyle home from the hospital. Zara told them all to go upstairs and try to get some rest. Dinesh slept on Nicole's bed.

While the mission was going smoothly, Ewart had been acting calm, but when he shook James awake at eleven o'clock that Saturday morning, he looked rabid.

"In the bathroom, *now,*" Ewart barked.

"Uh?" James said, still half-asleep.

Ewart grabbed James by his wrist and practically dislocated his shoulder as he yanked him out of bed. He shoved James towards the bathroom, bolted the door, and pushed him up to the wall.

"We've got to keep the noise down while Dinesh is in the house," Ewart whispered. "But you better start giving me straight answers about last night, or I'm gonna make you sorry."

"I haven't done anything," James said.

"So what's *this* then?" Ewart asked, producing the metal straw that had come out of Junior's cocaine. There were still specks of white powder stuck on one end.

"It's not mine," James said.

"Liar," Ewart snarled. "I was checking inside the pockets before I put the washing on. It was in your jeans."

James realized he must have pocketed it when Kelvin had surprised them.

"I swear I never took coke," James said frantically. "That belongs to Junior. I must have picked it up by mistake."

Ewart opened the medicine cabinet and took out a plastic sample bottle.

"We'll see, won't we? I got three of these at the hospital last night," Ewart said. "Pee in that. I'm gonna have your, Kyle's, and Kerry's urine samples tested and if there's cocaine in there, you'll be out on your arse with Nicole."

James was pleased to see the sample bottle. The test would clear up any argument.

"Give it here," he said, smirking confidently. "How much do you want to bet that I'm clean? Fifty quid, a hundred?"

"Cut the smart mouth," Ewart said. "And piss."

James angrily snatched the bottle off Ewart, flipped up the plastic lid, and stood over the toilet. He was usually busting when he woke up, but he couldn't go with Ewart standing behind him.

"Can't you wait outside?" James asked.

"You might tamper with it," Ewart said. "Try thinking about waterfalls or something."

When he'd finished, James handed the bottle to Ewart.

"Any money you'd like," he said cockily.

His air of confidence had taken the edge off Ewart's anger. "Go back to your room and tell Kyle to get over here."

After Kyle had gone, James slumped on his bed feeling pleased with himself. Ewart would look like an idiot when the drug test came back. Then he had a horrible thought: if Kelvin had called down the stairs a couple of seconds later . . .

James relived the drunken instant when the dish of white powder was just centimeters from his face. He felt sick when he realized how close he'd come to snorting a dangerous drug—and getting himself booted out of CHERUB.

CHAPTER 22

NICOLE

Junior called James on his mobile.

"Dude."

"You sound happy," James said. "What's up?"

"It's pandemonium here," Junior said. "I've got a killer hangover and the pigs arrested over eighty KMG people last night. My dad thinks he's about to get busted. He keeps running up to the curtain every time a bird flies past the window."

"Mr. Singh got nabbed," James said. "Dinesh spent the night here. Ewart's taken him to the airport to meet his mum."

"They nicked Uncle George and Uncle Pete," Junior said. "They're not my real uncles, but they've been working for Dad since before I was born."

"So how come you're in a good mood?" James asked.

"Nicole, of course," Junior said. "I had my hands *everywhere*. No offense, James, I know she's your sister and everything."

"She's in hospital," James said. 'The coke did her in."

"No way," Junior gasped. "That explains why I couldn't get her mobile. Is she OK?"

"Yeah, but I wouldn't get your hopes up about seeing her any time soon. She overdosed once before," James said, repeating Zara's latest cover story. "Ewart and Zara are terrified that she's gonna end up killing herself. They've arranged for her to go back to a care home in London for a psychiatric assessment."

"Oh, my God," Junior blurted. "I'm really sorry, man. I'd never have offered her coke if I'd known she had a problem. How long will she be gone for?"

"Um," James said, scratching for an answer, "it all depends on the assessment, I suppose. . . . She might not be back at all . . . Anyway, I just heard Zara pulling up with a carload of shopping. She goes loopy if I don't help her unload."

"I'll see you then," Junior said. "April asked if you fancied coming round for Sunday lunch?"

"Maybe," James said. "I don't know what's going on at the moment, with Nicole and that. I'll ring you later."

James ended the call. There really was a car pulling up, but it was John Jones. Zara made tea while John Jones explained what had been going on over the last twenty-four hours.

"It all came out of the production facility you kids

found at Thunderfoods. KMG imports and distributes cocaine through lots of different channels, but you guys uncovered the weakest link in the chain. Almost every gram was being packaged in the automated plant at Thunderfoods.

"We wired the place with cameras and bugs and watched everybody who came and went through binoculars. I've been on drug investigations where you go months without finding a good lead. Once we had Thunderfoods under surveillance, we started getting so much information we had to bring in extra staff to handle it.

"You'd get a couple of guys coming in to mix and package a few kilos of coke. It's boring work, so they'd usually start gossiping. They were off guard and the quality of information was unbelievable. Names, dates, phone numbers, flight numbers. 'What are you doing next week? Where's your next shipment coming in? What deal is old so-and-so working on at the moment?'

"We've made a hundred arrests already, but we're not even scratching the surface. We're sending information to police stations all over the country and another two or three hundred guys are gonna get pulled over the next few days. By the time we're done, KMG will be lucky if it can sell a bag of sweets in a school playground."

"I just spoke to Junior," James said. "Keith Moore still hasn't been arrested."

"That's politics," John said. "Us MI5 guys wanted to keep the undercover work going until we had enough evidence to get Keith, but the police wouldn't hold out. They've got hundreds of people working on Operation Snout. Not just police officers, but the administration and back-up staff that go with them. It's costing over a million pounds a month and there was talk of shutting it down if they didn't start getting results."

"So Keith Moore might get off?" Kerry asked.

John smiled uneasily. "I hope not, Kerry. I'd say out of the top ten people in KMG, we've got enough evidence to put eight in prison. We're gonna try and flip a couple of those guys. We're offering total immunity from prosecution. Given a choice between twenty years in prison and walking home to your wife and kids, we reckon a few people might start tattling on Keith Moore."

"So is there anything special we should be looking out for?" Kyle asked.

"I'd be amazed if you kids make another breakthrough to match the one you've already made," John said. "Just keep in with the bad guys and we'll see if anything else turns up."

"Actually, kids," Zara said, "I had to phone Mac and explain what happened with Nicole. He seems to think we've achieved most of what we set out to do. He's not impressed by what happened to Nicole and he wants the rest of you out of harm's way. I expect we'll be heading back to campus in a few weeks, so you might want to start dropping hints to your friends. Suggest that Ewart has gone for a job interview and there's a chance you might be moving back to London."

John Jones did his routine of shaking everyone's hands before he left.

"Of course," he said, holding on to Kerry's hand after he'd shaken it, "this young lady is the biggest hero of the lot."

Kerry still had an ear-to-ear grin five minutes after John Jones had driven away. James got sick of looking at it and chucked Joshua's furry cement mixer at her head. Kerry chucked it back and they ended up chasing each other around the dining table, along the hallway, and into the living room.

"I'm a hero," Kerry sang as she ran. "Hero, hero, hero. Hero, hero, hero."

James chucked a couple of sofa cushions at her. Kerry pushed James on to the floor and pinned him down. She grabbed his ankle and started tickling the bottom of his foot. It was James's weakest spot. Within thirty seconds she'd reduced him to a drooling wreck.

"OK," James gasped. "You're a hero. You're a hero."

Kerry stood up sharply and straightened her expression. Ewart and Nicole stood in the doorway, stone-faced. James got off the floor and wiped his lips on his sleeve.

"They tested your samples at the hospital," Ewart said. "You two are both clean for drugs, though they found higher levels of alcohol than I'd like to have seen, especially you, James. I know you're allowed to drink if you're in a situation where the kids around you are drinking, but that's not a license to go crazy."

"So you're glad you didn't bet me fifty quid?" James grinned.

Ewart gave James a vicious look. He definitely wasn't in the mood for joking.

"Go help Nicole pack and say your good-byes," Ewart said. "I'm driving her back to campus in half an hour. Where's Kyle?"

"He's in the kitchen," Kerry said.

"Right," Ewart said angrily. "Let's go and sort him out."

Ewart stormed off and slammed the kitchen door.

"What's Kyle done?" Kerry asked, looking at Nicole.

"Don't know, don't care," Nicole said bitterly. "I suppose he failed his drug test."

"No way," James said.

"He wasn't doing coke with me and Junior," Nicole said. "But he's been going to loads of parties. Who knows what he gets up to?"

"Oh, my God," Kerry said, cupping her hands over her face. "This is so sad."

Nicole started up the stairs. Kerry and James followed her.

"How do you feel?" Kerry asked.

"Not bad, except my stomach's agony and I feel like I've got an elephant standing on my head."

"I'm really sorry what happened to you," James said, as they stepped into the girls' bedroom. "It could have been any one of us."

Nicole smiled. "By the skin of your teeth, James."

"How's that?" Kerry asked.

"He was ready to snort a line," Nicole explained. "But he got distracted."

"You moron," Kerry said, giving James a shove. "You told me you tried to stop Nicole."

"That's not what I said," James squirmed.

"That's *exactly* what you said, James."

"So, anyone who takes drugs is a moron?" Nicole asked. "Eh, Kerry?"

"Nicole," Kerry said angrily, "if you'd passed out when you were in bed instead of on the stairs, nobody would have realized until morning. You might have *died*."

"You're so sly, Kerry," Nicole stormed. "You and your prissy 'I'm a good girl' act."

"What do you want me to do?" Kerry asked. "Congratulate you on getting expelled?"

"I don't care about any of this CHERUB stuff," Nicole said defiantly. "It's just a bunch of dumb kids getting hot under the collar over who wears what color T-shirt and what stupid missions they've been on. Who cares about any of that anyway? They're gonna set me up with a foster family and a place in a nice public school. I can have a boyfriend, chill out, and lead a normal life."

"Don't you get it, dumbo?" Kerry said, tapping her head with her finger. "You nearly died last night."

"You don't know what you're talking about," Nicole said, shoving Kerry backwards.

"Don't dare touch me," Kerry said, rearing up on the balls of her feet. "I could kick your butt so easily, but you're such a worthless tramp I can't even be bothered."

Kerry spun around and stormed towards the door. James went to follow her, but Nicole called him back.

"Stay and help me pack, James."

There was a desperate touch in Nicole's voice that made him turn back.

"Go ahead, help her," Kerry said. "You can make sure she doesn't rip off my stuff."

Kerry banged the door and stomped downstairs to the living room. Nicole dragged a sports bag from under her bed and started filling it.

"You know, James," Nicole said, "you're a good laugh, you don't belong at CHERUB either."

"You've no idea how badly I need CHERUB," James said. "Sometimes all the work and training does my head in, but my life was a nightmare before I came here. I was in some crummy council home and I kept getting in trouble. If CHERUB hadn't picked me, I probably would have ended up in prison."

"I'm glad I'm out of it," Nicole said, zipping up her bag. "As long as my new foster parents don't turn out to be old farts."

"What is it you've got against old people?" James asked.

Nicole sat on the edge of her bed. "You know my family died in a car crash?"

"I'd heard."

"They were crossing a road in broad daylight. This stupid old fool sailed his car through a red light and smashed into them. They tested his eyes after the accident and it turned out he could barely see past the end of his nose."

"That's so bad," James said. "I'm sorry."

"If it had been a young guy, they would at least have locked him away. But no, because it was some old fart, they took pity and let him off. My mum, my dad, and my little brothers were killed and he totally got away with it. Then everyone goes around telling me I should have respect for old people. Well, they can shove that idea right up their arse."

Ewart leaned in the door and looked at Nicole.

"Are you packed?"

"Just finishing off," Nicole said.

"OK," Ewart said. "I'm going to the toilet. I'll see you at the bottom of the stairs in five minutes."

"Wish me luck?" Nicole asked, looking at James.

"Sure," James said, wrapping his arms around her and giving her a squeeze. She had a tear rolling down her cheek.

James carried one of Nicole's bags out to the people carrier. Kerry stood in the living room doorway with folded arms and a frosty expression. James thought it was a shame Kerry and Nicole had fallen out. They'd got on well up to now.

Zara came out from the kitchen, gave Nicole a hug, and wished her good luck with whatever life she chose to lead. When the car started pulling off the driveway, Kerry had a change of heart and ran on to the doorstep. She stood between James and Zara, and waved Nicole off.

"I hope she sorts herself out," Kerry said.

"We'll set her up with a good family," Zara said. "I think she'll be better off in the long run. Not everyone is cut out to be a cherub."

"Oh," James said, suddenly remembering, "what happened with Kyle?"

"It's his business," Zara said. "It's up to him whether he wants you guys to know or not."

James and Kerry found Kyle face down on his bunk, having a sulk.

"Why was Ewart having a go at you?" James asked.

"They found traces of cannabis in my urine sample," Kyle said. "Almost every drug you could name passes through your body in a day or so. Unfortunately for me, cannabis lingers in your system for up to three weeks."

"But you *did* take some?" Kerry said, sounding outraged.

"It's not some massive deal, Kerry," Kyle said defensively. "I had a few puffs of a joint that was going around at some kid's house two Saturdays ago."

"So how come you're not expelled?" Kerry asked.

"Cannabis is a class C drug," Kyle explained. "I would have been sent back to campus, but they could hardly send me and Nicole away on the same day without it looking suspicious."

"So you're gonna get your botty spanked when we go back to campus?" James grinned.

"That's how it looks," Kyle said. "Probably a few weeks scrubbing floors, followed by a few months suspended from missions."

CHAPTER 29

LUCK

Sunday morning, James was in the living room on his PlayStation. Ewart came in and pushed his feet off the coffee table.

"You just gonna sit around doing nothing all day?" he asked.

"That was plan A," James grinned. He'd missed a lot of sleep over the last couple of weeks. It was nice to bum around indoors for a change.

"What about deliveries?" Ewart asked.

"Kelvin called me," James said, reluctantly pausing his game. "The nice lady who calls me with my deliveries has been busted. Not that it matters, because there aren't any customers. Everyone's heard about the arrests and they're scared that if they ring up for a drug delivery, they'll have PC Plod turning up on their doorstep rather than the likes of me."

"Does Kelvin think KMG is ruined?"

"He says it'll take at least a month to get new supplies of coke and set up distribution. Even then, customers will be wary. Other gangs will move in and snatch a lot of the business, but Kelvin thinks KMG has the clout to get back on top of things, provided Keith Moore doesn't get nicked."

"What about Junior and April? Have you heard from them?"

"I've spoken to both of them. I got invited to lunch, but I can't be arsed."

Ewart sounded slightly annoyed. "Why aren't you going?"

"What's the point?" James shrugged. "The mission's as good as over. We'll all be back at campus in a week or two."

"James, the mission carries on either until Keith Moore is caught, or we officially get told to come home. You're our closest link to the Moore kids now Nicole is gone. I'd be interested to know what Keith is up to at the moment."

James reached forward and switched off the PlayStation, looking thoroughly put-out.

"Fine," he huffed. "I'll call Junior and reinvite myself."

Ewart left James at the Moore house, then drove on a few hundred meters to drop Kerry at Dinesh's.

James thought there might be a bad atmosphere, but

when Keith opened the door he was in swimming shorts with a big grin on his face. The house was huge and even though they had a cleaner, you could tell four kids lived there the second you walked through the door. There were trainers and cushions chucked everywhere, dirty cups and plates. James thought it was cool. He hated it when you go round some kid's house and the mother goes hysterical when you put your cup down in the wrong place.

"Come in," Keith said, dripping over the floor tiles. "April and Junior are swimming."

"I never realized you'd be in the pool."

"Don't worry. Go up to Junior's room. He's got about ten pairs of swimming shorts in his middle drawer."

"Cheers," James said.

Junior had a massive room with a big screen TV and video, a wardrobe full of decent clothes, and a gumball machine. It wasn't a bad spread for a kid who claimed to be hard done by.

James stripped off and came down in a pair of orange shorts with seahorses on them. The indoor pool was about fifteen meters long, with palms and flowerbeds along one side. Ringo and Keith were swimming laps. April and Junior were at the far end in a whirlpool tub. James stepped into the steaming water, gave April a kiss, and sat beside her. She looked fit in her swimming suit.

Once he was in the tub, James was glad Ewart had made him get out of the house. The warm jets of water made him feel relaxed and having April cuddled up close was a bonus. He took his hand off her back when Keith wandered up.

"I'm ordering take-away," Keith said, raising his voice

above the bubbling water. "What do you guys want?"

"Indian," April said.

"Pizza," Junior said.

Keith looked at James. "Deadlock. The guest gets the casting vote."

James didn't like Indian much, but April had a cute grin on her face and she started sliding her toes up his leg.

"Indian," he said.

"Traitor," Junior said, slicing his hand through the water and giving James a soaking.

James, Junior, and April had a splashing battle, then toweled off and put on robes before the food arrived. Ringo and Keith sat on the sofa while James, April, and Junior arranged themselves on cushions around the coffee table will all the boxes of food on it.

Keith found the remote between two sofa cushions and switched the TV hanging on the wall to News 24. They all concentrated on stuffing their faces until the TV cut to a policeman. The title up on screen said: "Superintendent Carlisle, Operation Snort." He started speaking to the camera.

"We've made over one hundred and fifty arrests in the last three days and believe we have taken a major step against illegal drugs in this country. . . ."

A lump of prawn vindaloo smacked Superintendent Carlisle in the forehead and began sliding down the screen.

". . . This represents a giant stride forward in our war against illegal drugs in the U.K. . . ."

"Try and catch me, Superintendent," Keith shouted, chucking another prawn.

Keith's kids joined in, hurling lumps of curry and

handfuls of rice until the screen was a blurry mess. Everyone laughed, but it had a hollow ring, like they were really scared by the arrests.

Junior turned and looked at his dad. "Did you ask James about Miami?"

"No," Keith said.

"Miami?" James asked.

"I usually take the boys to my place in Miami for half-term," Keith explained. "But Ringo says he's got a lot of homework and doesn't want to go this year."

"He's having a party," April explained. "I expect we'll come home and find this house razed to the ground."

"Who says I'm having a party?" Ringo said defensively.

"It'll be boring without Ringo," Junior said. "And the plane ticket's paid for, so Dad suggested I take a mate."

"Cool," James said, bursting into a grin. "I'll have to check with my parents, but it should be OK. Are you going, April?"

"No," April said. "Me and Erin are skiing with our mum."

"It's a family tradition," Keith explained. "We all used to go on holiday together, but I'd always be strangling my wife, Junior and April usually end up rolling around the floor if they're together for more than a few hours, and Erin . . ."

"We think the real Erin was abducted at birth and replaced by an alien from Neptune," Junior explained.

"I've been here about ten times and I've still never met Erin," James said.

Keith shook his head and smiled. "That girl may be

my daughter, but I haven't got a clue what goes on inside that little head of hers."

"You'll love Miami," Junior said. "It's boiling hot and our house is right on the beach. You can crawl out of bed, run down the beach, and be in the sea within thirty seconds."

"I'll ring Zara up right now," James said.

"Is Kyle home?" Ringo asked.

"Probably," James said. "Did you want a word with him?"

Ringo gave his dad a mischievous grin as he spoke. "Just tell Kyle there's a big party going down here, Friday after next."

Keith burst out laughing. James thought Keith was a really cool dad, especially considering the stress he was under.

"You can have your party," Keith said. "But Kelvin and a couple of other guys from the boxing club are gonna chaperone it, in case any of your pals decide to start peeing on the carpets or stubbing out ciggies on my Egyptian rug."

"What?" Ringo asked. "I don't want some crew of muscle heads bossing my mates around. I'll be totally embarrassed."

"Don't worry," Keith said. "I'll tell them to keep a low profile."

James gave Zara a call. She was surprised, but she said it was OK to travel.

It was already turning dark when James got home. He recognized John Jones's Toyota on the driveway. He was in the living room, with Zara, Ewart, Kerry, and Kyle.

"What's this in aid of?" James asked.

John Jones explained. "As soon as Zara heard about your little holiday, she contacted me and I rushed over here."

"Why is me going on holiday such a big deal?" James asked.

"Miami is the center of the world drug trade," John explained. "It's no coincidence that Keith Moore has a home there. The saying goes: 'If you want a gram of cocaine, stand on any street corner. If you want a ton of cocaine, stand on any street corner in Miami.'

"There are twenty smaller gangs snapping at the heels of KMG. Keith has to get his hands on fresh supplies of cocaine and get KMG working again. A lot of his top people have been arrested and he won't know who he can trust, so he'll be brokering the deal himself."

"So what can I do?" James asked.

"We know KMG has a long-standing relationship with a Peruvian drug cartel called Lambayeke," John explained. "To pay Lambayeke, Keith will have to transfer millions from his overseas bank accounts. If we can find out what bank and country Keith's money is coming from, we'll have a lead that could help us unravel the whole financial structure of KMG and maybe even Lambayeke as well.

"Keith can't keep every detail of his business in his head. He'll be going to Miami carrying some piece of information that links him to his money. It might be a bank account number, or the phone number of a bank, or a file on the hard drive of his laptop. Whatever it is, you're going to be in Keith Moore's house for seven days. You're never going to get a better opportunity to grab information than that."

James smiled. "So much for bumming around on the beach all day."

"As soon as this meeting is over, I'm driving you back to campus for two days' emergency training," Ewart said. "There's a lot you need to learn, but we don't want you away from the Moore family for more than a few days."

"What excuse will we use for me not being at school?"

"We'll tell everyone you were planning to visit your aunt and cousin Lauren during half-term, but we brought it forward because of your trip to Miami."

CHAPTER 24

FACTS

James slept better than he had for ages. His bed in Luton was cramped and had springs that jammed into your back; plus on campus there was no Kyle squirming in the top bunk and no 300-seater jets whizzing overhead. The plumbing worked better as well. James put on a Metallica CD and rocked out in his shower, without having to worry about getting scalded every time someone touched the tap in the kitchen.

When he was clean, he put on his CHERUB uniform. The rooms and corridors in the main building reminded James of a hotel. As he waited for the lift down to the dining room, he reflected that the only thing lacking was room service.

He loaded up a plate with bacon and hash brown and ate bits with his fingers while one of the staff cooked him a mushroom omelette. Most kids had gone off to first lesson, but Amy was sitting at a table dipping a finger of toast into a soft-boiled egg.

"You're wearing a white T-shirt," James said, taken aback.

You got the white shirt when you retired as a cherub.

"My undercover days are over," Amy said.

James looked sad. "But . . ."

"I'm seventeen, James," Amy said. "I took my A-levels in the summer. I'm working here as an assistant dogsbody to earn some cash, then I'm off to see the world before I start university in January."

"Where are you going?"

"Cairns, Australia. My big brother lives there."

"That's the other side of the world," James said miserably. "I'll probably never see you again."

"You've only got to hop on an airplane. My brother set up a diving school when he finished university. He took me up to the Great Barrier Reef a couple of weeks ago. It's so beautiful there."

"So you're training me up for my Miami trip?" James asked.

Amy nodded. "And you better behave. Now I'm staff, I'm allowed to dish out punishments."

"Cool," James grinned. "Who have you nailed?"

"Only one kid," Amy said. "I was covering for one of the judo instructors. This horrible little red-shirt boy kept giving me lip. He got a week cleaning up the changing room near the cross country trail."

"It always gets really muddy in there," James smiled. "How old was this kid?"

"Eight," Amy said. "He started bawling his eyes out, but I didn't back down. After that, all I got from the other kids in the class was, 'Yes Miss, No Miss, Of course Miss.'"

"So what have I got?" James asked.

Amy slid a heap of books across the table. They were all weighty. One was called *The Ultimate Hacker's Reference* and was over ten centimeters thick.

"It's gonna be a busy couple of days," Amy said. "I'll try and get you through techniques for hacking Keith's computer by this afternoon. Then we'll make a start on international banking."

"What's that in aid of?" James asked.

"Suppose Keith was on the telephone and he mentioned a euro CD and an order party. Unless you know about banking, you wouldn't be able to tell whether Keith is on the phone to a Russian money laundering syndicate, or organizing a disco."

"Sounds like this is gonna be a real riot," James said, flipping through one of the giant books as he tucked in a fork-load of bacon.

Amy ignored him. "MI5 are preparing a dossier on the Lambayeke cartel. They'll e-mail it here and we'll work on that tomorrow morning. Tomorrow afternoon we'll finish up by testing out your hacking skills on real computers."

James and Amy studied into the evening. You normally got at least two weeks on the background material for a mission, but everything had to be crammed into a couple of days. When it got to eight o'clock, Amy finally let him off.

"I feel like a swim," she said. "Coming?"

CHERUB had four pools. The learners' pool was the smallest and least attractive, but Amy had taught James to swim there before and they both wanted to go back for old times' sake. There was nobody else around. Most kids preferred using the main pool, which had diving boards and water slides.

They had a ten-lap race. James kept up with Amy until they made the last turn, when she blasted off into the distance. They got out and sat on the edge. James felt like his lungs were about to burst.

"You're getting stronger," Amy grinned, not even short of breath. "You might be able to give me a real race when you grow a bit bigger and shed the puppy fat."

James's heart sank when he realized Amy had been toying with him.

"I'll definitely come and visit you in Australia when I'm older," he said, circling his big toe through the water. "If that's all right."

Amy smiled. "Of course it's all right. My brother has mates from his CHERUB years turning up all the time."

"It's weird," James said. "I never even think about the kids I knew before I came to CHERUB, but I feel really close to the kids I know here."

"It's a defined psychological phenomenon," Amy said.

James looked mystified. "You what?"

"All humans have a basic need to share their lives

with someone," Amy explained. "Children with their parents, adults with their wives, husbands, or whoever. Because the kids at CHERUB have no parents, they make very strong bonds with each other. There's a big reunion on campus every couple of years. You'd be amazed how many cherubs end up marrying each other."

"Sometimes it really gets on my nerves how smart-assed everyone at CHERUB is," James grinned. "I mean, how come you know stuff like that?"

"I'm doing psychology at university," Amy said. "They gave us a list of books to read before the course starts. Besides, James, you're not exactly dumb yourself. CHERUB wouldn't even sniff at a kid who wasn't way above average."

"When I'm at a normal school, I'm always one of the cleverest," James said. "But I'm just kind of ordinary here."

"So anyway," Amy said. "When you arrived at CHERUB a few months after your mum died, it was natural that you formed a strong attachment to any girl who played a big part in your life."

"Like you, because you were teaching me how to swim."

Amy nodded. "And Kerry, because she was your partner in basic training. Have you asked her out yet?"

"God! Don't you start," James moaned. "It's bad enough Kyle was always going on about it."

"But you and Kerry are always *so* sweet together. I love the way you two pick at one another like some old married couple."

James didn't want to hear it. He slipped off the side of the pool and began swimming towards the deep end.

The dossier that arrived from MI5 on the Lambayeke cartel ran to over three hundred pages, though a lot of it was photos and maps. James and Amy spent Tuesday morning in one of the mission preparation rooms, skimming through the chapters and marking the most relevant stuff with highlighter pens. James could take the books on computer-hacking back to Luton for study, but the Lambayeke dossier wasn't allowed off campus.

After they'd worked through the dossier, Amy got five laptop PCs out of a storage room and lined them up on a desk. She set an ancient wind-up timing clock to count down from fifteen minutes.

"Each of these PCs has a list of stolen credit card numbers hidden on the hard drive," Amy explained. "You've got to hack each one inside the time limit, without leaving any footprints behind."

"Which one first?" James asked.

"Doesn't matter," Amy said, leaning over and starting the timer. "Go."

James had a mini heart attack before grabbing a laptop, flipping up the screen and tapping a couple of keys.

"What do I do?" he said to himself, drumming his hands on the desk in front of him.

"Turning it on would be a good start," Amy smirked. "Don't forget to read the BIOS screen before Windows starts."

James read the figures aloud. "Two-fifty-six meg of memory. Windows ME. The hard drive isn't partitioned.

If it's ME it uses a FAT32 file system, so if I press F8 and enter DOS, I'll be able to open any file, even if it's password protected."

James hunted around the desk for a floppy disk. He waved it at Amy.

"This is the disk with the utility on that lists every file on the PC, isn't it?"

Amy nodded. "I'm not supposed to be helping you."

James looked around the side of the PC for somewhere to slot the floppy disk.

"Oh . . . This bloody thing doesn't have a floppy drive. Is there an external drive for this somewhere?"

Amy shook her head.

"Well, what do I do?"

Amy shrugged and looked at the timer. "You've got twelve minutes left to figure it out."

James fiddled hopelessly with the laptop for another three minutes. He could have happily chucked the clicking timer out the window.

"Nine minutes left."

"Tell us, Amy," James begged. "I'm totally stuck. How can I get this floppy running?"

"The computer has a network interface on the back," Amy said. "You could wire it up to one of the other laptops that has a floppy drive. Then you could go into the network properties on the second laptop and change it to a networkable floppy drive. Then the floppy drive on the second PC will work as if it's attached to the first one."

"I'm never gonna get all that done in nine minutes," James gasped.

"You might if you hurried. But why not try something much simpler?"

"Like what?" James asked.

"What's the first thing I taught you about computer hacking? The first golden rule?"

"'The weakest link is the human link,'" James said.

Amy nodded. "You're trying to find a back door into the operating system before you've tried the front door. Never assume the information you're looking for is encrypted or hidden. For all you know, you can open the document you want just by clicking on it."

"You're telling me I've just wasted six minutes?"

"Nearer to seven now," Amy said, smirking.

James switched off the computer and started from scratch. The computer only had a few programs installed and the documents were all in one folder. James opened up the list and spotted one called "Card Numbers." He double-clicked the mouse to open the file. A single line of text popped up on the screen: YOU DIDN'T THINK IT WAS GOING TO BE THAT EASY, DID YOU?

James was in too much of a state to see the funny side. He looked at the long list of documents on the screen in front of him. There wasn't time to open every one, but James realized he was looking for a list of numbers, which meant the file would be fairly small. He changed the view, so the computer showed him the size and format of each file. He skipped down the list, opening any text file that looked likely to be the list of numbers.

"Three minutes left," Amy said. "Better get your skates on, cowboy."

James started opening up files as fast as he could.

A few demanded a password before they'd open. James dragged these into a separate folder. When he ran out of documents that didn't need a password, he decided to try and guess the password of the encrypted ones.

A password can be any combination of letter and numbers, but James knew the golden rule of computer hacking: OVER 75% OF PASSWORDS ARE EASILY GUESSED. He started working down the list of most commonly used passwords that Amy had made him memorize the day before. Things like "password" "open," and "security."

After these failed, James tried to find personal details about the man who owned the laptop. He remembered that one of the documents he'd opened had been a letter to a school. He clicked on the file and skimmed through it. It was signed off by a man called Julian Stipe and mentioned the names of his three children. James tried the name "Julian" in the password box, then "Stipe." Then "Julian Stipe" with and without a space in between.

"Ninety seconds," Amy said.

He started trying the names of Mr. Stipe's kids and hit the jackpot when he typed "Jennifer." The document opened, only it wasn't the credit card numbers. The other protected documents opened with the same password and James got a massive rush when a sheet of sixteen-digit credit card numbers popped up on a screen.

"Bingo," James shouted.

"Fifteen seconds," Amy said.

"I've got them," James said. "What are you on about?"

"Time's up," Amy said. "Better luck next time."

"But I got them," James said tetchily.

"I know," Amy said. "But you weren't supposed to leave any traces behind. It was a good idea to move the password-protected documents, but you should have put them all back where they belonged and deleted the new folder you created. . . . Ready for the next one?"

"My head's spinning," James said. "Can't I have five minutes' break?"

Amy gave him an evil grin. "You don't deserve a break after that sorry performance."

She tapped the reset button on top of the clock, then flipped up the lever to set it ticking.

CHAPTER 25

DIGGING

James made such a hash of the laptop-hacking test, Amy kept him upstairs in the mission preparation room until gone nine o'clock for extra tuition. He got ratty with her as his brain stubbornly refused to accept any more information.

When they got downstairs to the dining hall, the kitchen had finished serving. There was a fridge stocked up with sandwiches and microwave meals, but James had been looking forward to a proper dinner before his return to Luton and Zara's dodgy cooking.

James slammed the door of his bedroom. He was in a stinking mood. He packed his hacking textbooks and some odd bits in a backpack, then stripped to his boxers and went to take a pee before getting in bed. There was a muggy smell as he got near his bathroom, like the smell trainers get after a couple of hours on a muddy football field. It spooked him a bit. His imagination toyed with dead rats and leaking sewage as he leaned in warily and flipped on the light.

"What the hell . . ."

It was Lauren, propped on the toilet lid in her filthy training clothes. Her hair was cropped, she had a nasty scab down her face, and all the cuts and bruises you'd expect after a month of basic training.

"What's going on?" James asked.

"I messed up," Lauren said miserably. "And I'm in so much trouble."

She did a massive sniff, followed by a howling noise. Then she broke into five minutes of the most desperate bawling James had ever heard. He tried to give her a hug, but she wouldn't let him anywhere near her.

"Lauren," James pleaded, "I want to help you, but I can't until you tell me what's happened."

"I . . . I . . . hit," she sniffled, unable to control herself.

She stood up and draped her filthy arms around James's back. Her clothes stank of mud and sweat.

He stepped backwards out of the bathroom, with Lauren flopped over him. It felt like dancing with a drunk. When he got near his bed, James peeled off Lauren's arms and she slumped on to the corner of his mattress.

"I hit him," Lauren sniffed.

"Who?" James asked.

"Mr. Large."

James sat down beside her. "I doubt he even felt it, Lauren. He's ten times your size."

"He felt it all right," Lauren said, salvaging a touch of composure.

James reached over to his beside table and got her a tissue.

"Bethany injured her back yesterday morning," Lauren explained. "We were on the assault course. I was helping her as much as I could, but she was still slow. We finished the course miles behind the other kids. Mr. Large started shouting his head off! 'You two are worthless. You're not even fit to be cherubs. You're not even fit to eat your own puke.' He got two spades and told us to start digging our own graves."

It was a standard torture from Mr. Large's repertoire. James and Kerry had got it a couple of times when they were in basic training. Large made you dig a massive hole, then fill it in. If he decided you weren't fast enough, he'd make you do it again.

"It's so tough," Lauren said. "I managed, but my back and shoulders were killing me. Bethany had a bad back to start with, so you can imagine how she was after two hours' digging. Large made me stand to attention at the edge of my grave until Bethany had finished. She kept slowing down, until she could barely drag her shovel. She begged Mr. Large for a drink, so he got that massive fire hose and drenched her with it. But the time he'd finished, the water was up to her knees. She was crying and sobbing, covered from head to toe in really thick mud. Then he started kicking the mud she'd already dug up back into the hole.

"It was hitting her in the face and he screamed at the top of his voice: 'You're too weak, little girl. You'll never make it. Why don't you quit?' It made me so angry. I was so sick of his stupid voice. I just got this urge to make him shut up. Then I realized I still had my spade on the ground, right in front of me."

"You didn't," James gasped.

"When Mr. Large turned around, I took this massive swing with it and whacked him behind the knees to knock him over. The first time only made him go wobbly. He started running towards me and I was *so* scared. I thought he was gonna kill me, so I whacked him again. As he went down, he caught his head on a rock and got knocked out."

James couldn't help smiling. "You knocked out Mr. Large! That's pure class."

"It's not funny, James," Lauren moped. "I'm probably gonna get expelled. I thought I'd killed him for a minute. There was all blood coming out of his head. I was so afraid, I ran out of the training compound and didn't stop. I wanted to speak to you before anyone else, so I went to my room and phoned you. Zara said you were on campus, but I'm not allowed upstairs to mission preparation, so I waited for you in here."

James pondered for a few moments.

"First things first," he said. "You better wash up, then we'll have to find Mac and sort this whole mess out."

"Do you think they'll boot me out?" Lauren asked.

"I hope not," James shrugged. "But laying out a teacher . . . Let's just say it's not gonna go down too well."

• • •

James found some of his smaller clothes for Lauren to wear after she got out of the shower. When they got down to the ground floor, Mac's office was locked. They asked the receptionist on the front desk.

"Mac usually heads home at about eight," he explained. "But one of the training instructors got injured and I think he's still over at the medical unit. I can ring his mobile if it's urgent."

"I think you'd better," James said.

The receptionist had a short conversation before putting down the receiver.

"Mac's coming over ASAP," the receptionist said. "I don't know what you two have done, but judging by the tone of his voice, I wouldn't want to switch shoes with you at the moment."

A few minutes later, Mac rolled up the gravel driveway outside in one of the golf buggies the staff used to move around campus.

"This way," he said stiffly, striding through reception.

He pulled a great bunch of keys out of his jacket and unlocked his door.

"Sit at the desk."

James nervously sank into one of the leather chairs at the big oak desk. Lauren looked ready to start crying again.

"So, young lady," Mac snapped. "Would you be so kind as to tell me why my senior training instructor is lying in the medical unit with a serious concussion and eight stitches in the side of his head?"

"I'm really, really sorry," Lauren groveled. "He made

me so mad. Poor Bethany could hardly stand up and Mr. Large wouldn't leave her alone."

"If Bethany was injured, she should have quit," Mac said. "It wasn't your business to interfere."

"So what are you gonna do to her?" James asked.

"I don't like expelling people," Mac said. "But if I don't expel a cherub for a serious assault on a member of staff, then what exactly *do* you get expelled for?"

"I know what Lauren did was wrong," James said. "But it's not like she walked into a classroom and belted a teacher for no reason. She was knackered and she was watching one of her friends get tortured by a raving lunatic. Everyone wants to take a swing at Mr. Large at some point during basic training. It's just unlucky Lauren happened to have a spade nearby when the thought crossed her mind."

"Hmm," Mac said, covering a tiny smile with his fingers. "I suppose there's an element of truth in that. If I did expel Lauren, though, we'd send her to a good school and set her up with a foster family near campus so that you could visit her at weekends."

"I don't care if she only lives across the street," James said. "If she goes, I'm going with her. We were separated after our mum died and I don't ever want that again."

"Recruiting cherubs is tricky," Mac said, "and I don't want to lose either of you two. But if I allow Lauren to stay, she'll have to accept a stiff punishment; otherwise, we'll have every kid on campus taking pot shots at the training staff."

"Please let me stay," Lauren begged. "I'll do whatever you want and I'll be so good, I swear."

"James," Mac said. "Do you have any thoughts on how we should make Lauren suffer?"

James looked uneasily at his sister.

"It's obviously got to be the worst punishment going," he said. "And it'll have to last the whole two and a bit months until she can restart basic training."

"Agreed," Mac nodded.

"What about cleaning toilets and changing rooms?" James said. "Everyone always says that's really horrible."

"Not hard enough," Mac said, sweeping the idea away with his hand. "Kids get toilets and changing rooms for swearing or skipping lessons. It's unpleasant, but all it boils down to is pushing a mop and squirting disinfectant."

"Worse than toilets, then," James said, trying to work out how Mac had twisted the situation around so that he was trying to think up some awful punishment for the person he was supposed to be helping out.

"Well," Mac grinned. "It just so happens, I did have an idea. There's a drainage problem in the wooded area on the far side of campus. The fields keep flooding because the ditches have gradually become blocked with silt. I reckon someone Lauren's size would take a couple of months to clean them all out. She'll have to work hard, every day before and after school, plus all days on Saturdays and Sundays. How do you like the sound of that, Lauren?"

"I've got to be punished," Lauren said, nodding meekly. "If that's what you want, I'll do it."

"Ditches it is," Mac said, clapping his hands together.

"And I'll be putting you on final warning, Lauren. That means if you do one more thing wrong, you'll get kicked out. And I mean *every* tiny thing. Run in the corridor, you're out. Miss a homework assignment, you're out. For the next three months, you're walking on eggshells. Your behavior must be immaculate. Is that understood?"

Lauren nodded.

"And there's one more condition," Mac said. "For you, James."

"For me?" James gasped.

Mac nodded. "You've talked me into giving Lauren a final chance. In return, I want something from you. If Lauren breaches her final warning, I want you to promise that you'll stay at CHERUB."

James thought for a couple of seconds. "But you'll put her with a family nearby so I can still see her when I'm not on missions?"

Mac nodded. "That seems reasonable."

"I suppose, then," James said.

It seemed pretty convenient, the way Mac had found the perfect punishment for Lauren. James suspected Mac had worked everything out in advance. The expulsion threat was a ploy to make him and Lauren squirm.

"And of course, Lauren," Mac grinned, "once you've cleaned out those ditches and start your second attempt at basic training, I'm sure Mr. Large will wreak his own special revenge."

Lauren slept in James's room. The bed was a double, but the two of them cuddled up in the middle. Lauren woke early and didn't seem too miserable, considering that the next five months of her life looked like being a living hell.

"Have you got a diary?" she asked.

"It's in my desk," James said, still buried under his duvet.

Lauren used the diary to work out that it was one hundred and seventy-four days until she finished her punishment and basic training. She took a sheet of paper and began writing the numbers from 174 down to zero in her neatest writing.

James poked his head out of his covers. "What are you doing, Lauren?"

"Making a countdown chart. For the next hundred and seventy-four days, I'm not gonna whinge or cry about anything. I'll take this piece of paper everywhere I go. However bad it gets, all I'm going to think about is how many hours it is until I can tick off the next number. In one hundred and seventy-four days I *will* pass basic training. I swear it, on our mum's grave."

James scrambled out of bed.

"No way," he said angrily. "You can't swear something like that on Mum's grave. Some things are out of your control. What if you get injured, or sick?"

"I won't," Lauren said sternly. "If something hurts, I'll close my eyes and think about the piece of paper in my pocket."

"It's a good idea to focus your mind," James said, sliding his legs into a pair of tracksuit bottoms. "But try and be realistic. There are quite a few kids who've taken three or more attempts to get through basic training. You could be setting yourself up for a big disappointment."

Lauren stood in front of James and barked an order. "Slap my face."

"Yeah, I'm really gonna hit you," James said, shaking his head with contempt.

"I'll show you I can take it," Lauren said. "As hard as you like."

"Give us a break, Lauren. You realize we could have lain in bed for at least another half hour?"

Lauren lunged forward, grabbed hold of James's nipple and gave it a savage twist. James rolled backwards on to his bed, howling in pain.

"What the *hell* did you do that for?" he shouted.

"Slap my damn face," Lauren shouted back.

"You really want to see you tough you are?" James raged. "Fine. Maybe I'll knock some sense into you."

There was a sharp *crack* as his hand hit her face. It was more painful than Lauren had expected, but she stifled her groan and toughed it out with a thin-lipped smile.

"One hundred and seventy-four days," Lauren said. "Believe it."

James grinned. "Will you be coming down to breakfast with me, or are you too tough for food as well?"

There were about sixty cherubs in the dining-hall when James and Lauren arrived. It took a couple of seconds for the room to go quiet, then chairs grated backwards and everyone stood up and started clapping and banging cutlery on the table. There were shouts of "Lauren" and whistles as well.

Shakeel was standing nearby; James looked over at him.

"What's this all about?"

"Your sister," he said, as if James was some kind of idiot. "She's the biggest hero in the history of CHERUB. Everyone dreams of getting revenge on Mr. Large, but I never imagined any kid would really have the guts to do it."

Kids piled in from all directions, until Lauren stood in an ocean of hugs and handshakes. A couple of stocky teenager boys hoisted Lauren off the ground, balanced her on their shoulders, and took her on a victory parade around the dining room. She had a mixture of emotions on her face; happy, freaked out, and afraid of getting her head smacked on a light fitting. As Lauren was galloped around the room, the kids at the dining tables were all pledging to help her dig.

"Dig what?" James asked.

"We heard Lauren's got to clean out the ditches at the back end of campus," Shakeel explained. "Everyone is putting on their wellies and going up there Saturday morning to help her out. We reckon with a hundred or more kids on the job, we'll get the whole lot cleared away in a day."

"Cool," James said. "That's really great of everyone."

"It's what she deserves," Shakeel said. "I wish I'd belted Mr. Large one. There's a collection going around as well. Everyone's putting money in and we're gonna get her something from that shop in town that does trophies."

Amy came up to James as Lauren was on her third circuit of the dining room.

"We had a whip round up on my floor," Amy said. "We got seventy quid. What's Lauren's favorite shop?"

"She gets a lot of stuff from Gap Kids," James said. "Why?"

"There's already more than enough for the engraved tankard," Amy explained. "We were thinking of getting her some gift vouchers, or maybe a humongous teddy bear. . . ."

CHAPTER 26

SOCKS

"You're such a jammy little git," Kerry said. "You realize me and Kyle are stuck here on Thornton until this mission is finished?"

It was Friday night. They were in the boys' bedroom and James was packing a hold-all for his flight to Miami in the morning.

"That's the wrong attitude," James said, grinning. "We're all equally important members of a team. It's just that my role is toasting on some beach in Florida, while you get to spend half-term here. If you're lucky, someone might start a fire and you can watch one of the derelict houses burn out."

"You're *such* a funny guy," Kerry sneered.

"How many socks do you reckon?" James asked.

"At least one pair for each day."

James looked in his underwear drawer and realized he only had two clean pairs. He started hunting around the floor and balling odd socks together.

"Aren't those dirty?" Kerry asked.

"A bit," James said. "But I've only worn most of them once. They don't smell that bad." He put one of them under Kerry's nose. "See."

"For *God's* sake," Kerry said angrily, pushing James's arm away. "They're appalling."

James gave them a sniff.

"*Phew,*" he gasped. "Those ones are a bit ripe. I think they're what I wore to boxing club last night. But most of these are OK."

Kerry shook her head. "You're an animal, James."

She slid off the bed and walked across the hallway to her own room. James's mobile rang.

"Hey, April," James said. "Where are you?"

"I'm at the airport with Erin and my mum," April said. "We're sitting here waiting to board the plane and I thought I'd say hi."

"I only saw you a few hours ago," James said.

"Don't you want to talk to me?" April said, with a hint of acid in her voice.

"Of course I want to talk to you," James lied. "It's just . . . I'm really busy, packing and stuff."

"I'm wearing your Nike watch," April giggled. "So I can think about you whenever I look at the time."

"Don't forget to give that back," James said. "It's my only good one."

"Blow me a kiss," April said.

James shook his head before doing a couple of quick smooches into his phone.

"I think Zara's calling me downstairs, April. I've got to hang up. Have a wonderful trip, bye."

"James. I—"

"Gotta go, April, sorry."

James ended the call and tutted. Kerry had walked back in behind him. She was holding four pairs of clean sports socks.

"Girl trouble?" she inquired.

"Don't ask," James said.

"Borrow these," Kerry said. "My feet aren't much smaller than yours. Just make sure you wash them before you give them back."

"Cheers," James said, tucking the socks into his hold-all. "You know, April's driving me round the bend."

"Why?" Kerry asked. "She seems like a really nice girl."

"She is," James said. "But she's too intense. She phones me *all* the time. She follows me everywhere at school and starts putting her arm around me. If I'm talking to someone else, she pulls me away and whispers stuff in my ear."

"She's got a crush on you," Kerry said. "You should be flattered."

"It's more than a crush," James said. "I bet she's already picked out the wedding dress, and now she's working out the names of our kids."

"Typical man," Kerry said indignantly. "You like having a girl draped off your arm, but only so you can snog her and impress your stupid mates."

"Give over," James said. "It's just, April is a lot keener on me than I am on her. It's not my fault girls can't resist me."

"In your dreams," Kerry grinned. "I suppose you'll dump April and leave her in a state, like you did with Nicole."

"Nicole?" James said, looking mystified. "I only kissed her once, for about two seconds."

"Nicole asked if you liked her," Kerry said. "So you snogged her, then you dumped her."

"I just didn't snog her again," James said. "I don't know why you're turning it into some big deal."

"But you didn't have the decency to face her. You just skulked around the house avoiding her for the next couple of days. Nicole was really upset."

"Well . . ." James said. "I didn't mean to hurt her feelings."

"Yeah, right."

"Look, Kerry, I don't deliberately treat girls like that. To tell the truth, there's someone else I really like."

"You mean Amy?" Kerry said. "You can practically see the drool run out of your mouth every time she comes near you, but get over it, she's seventeen years old."

"That shows how much you know," James said tersely. "Every boy on campus fancies Amy, but it's not her I'm talking about."

"Who is it then?"

"None of your business."

"Huh," Kerry sneered. "You're making it up so I don't think you're a pig."

"No," James said.

"Do I know her?" Kerry asked.

"Yes."

"It's not Gabrielle, is it?"

James laughed. "No."

"You're such a plonker," Kerry said. "I don't know why I'm even bothering to talk to you."

James loved the way she reared up on the balls of her feet whenever she got ratty.

"You really want to know who I like?" James said.

"I don't care," Kerry said, folding her arms.

"Fine, I won't tell you then."

But James had piqued Kerry's curiosity and she quickly changed her tack. "Oh . . . go on then."

James toyed with the idea of making someone up, or saying something stupid, but he realized he was never going to have a better opportunity to tell Kerry how he really felt. He couldn't carry on bottling it for the rest of his life. He took a deep breath.

"I . . ."

His mouth dried up. He felt like his head was about to explode.

Kerry shook her head. "I knew you were lying."

"No, I like *you,*" James blurted.

He stared at Kerry for what felt like a trillion years, studying her face for some kind of reaction.

"Are you winding me up?" Kerry asked, suspiciously.

"Ever since basic training," James rambled. "Even when we were covered in mud doing combat practice and you were battering me, there was something about you that I really liked. I mean . . . We're always really good together, because you're kind of stuffy and do everything by the book and I'm kind of . . . Well . . . I suppose you could say I'm an idiot at times."

"You really like me?" Kerry grinned.

James felt like he wanted to die. "Yes."

"So you're serious?" Kerry asked. "Because if you're messing with me, I'll punch every single tooth out of your dumb head."

"I swear," James said. "So, you know . . . Am I wasting my time? . . . Or?"

Kerry smiled a bit. "Everyone we know has been going on about us having a thing for each other. I never thought you really liked me though. You're always going on about tits and I've hardly got any."

"Yeah, well," James said. "I'm not perfect either. But you do like me?"

Kerry nodded. "When you're not driving me insane, you're just about my favorite boy on campus."

James leaned forward to kiss her, but the hold-all was stuck in the middle of the tiny room and they had to shuffle around it. It was only a quick peck on the lips, but James got a massive rush.

"I wish you were coming to Miami with me," he said.

"It's only a week," Kerry smiled. "And there's one condition if I'm gonna be your girlfriend."

"What?" James asked.

"From now on, your underwear only gets worn once."

CHAPTER 27

MIAMI

James and Junior touched down in Miami on Saturday evening. Keith had changed his plans and flown out a couple of days earlier with his minder, George. The beefy ex-heavyweight met the boys at immigration and drove them to Keith's house in a Range Rover.

James spent the whole drive with his face stuck up against the window like a five-year-old. He loved the differences that make you know you're in a different country: traffic lights strung over the road on wires, billboards with prices marked in dollars, the huge double-trailer trucks that looked like they'd roll over your car without the man in the cab feeling so much as a jolt.

Automatic gates parted obediently when the car got

near Keith's house. The pastel blue building sprawled out behind a mass of palm trees. There were two stories, with balconies overlooking the ocean and lush terraces planted with palm trees and flowering cacti.

"Your dad is *so* loaded," James said as he stepped out of the car, shaking his head in disbelief.

"Come and check out his cars," Junior said.

There was a separate garage, the size of which reminded James of a fire station. The boys wandered in as George dealt with their bags. There was a row of everyday modern BMWs and Mercedes, but the exciting stuff was parked behind: the outlines of seven Porsches, clad in protective blankets. Junior pulled up a corner of one, revealing a headlamp.

"This ran in the Le Mans twenty-four-hour race," Junior said. "My dad had it taken up to Daytona for a track day. He got it up to three hundred kph on the straight."

"Class," James said.

"Like my motors, James?" Keith asked.

James turned around to see Keith standing in the doorway, wearing pool shoes and an unbuttoned Hawaiian shirt.

"You've got a different Porsche for every day of the week," James grinned.

"I'll take you for a cruise down South Beach in one of them tomorrow night," Keith said. "It's all lit up with neon signs after dark and there's heaps of great restaurants. Did you see anything else you wanted to do in that guidebook?"

"Is it too far to go up to Orlando?" James asked. "Junior said Universal Studios is cool."

"It's a few hundred kilometers," Keith said. "But it's no hassle driving out there. We can stay overnight and get a couple of theme parks in if you want. I've got some business to sort out, but that should be wrapped up in a day or two. Was there anywhere else?"

James shrugged. "I dunno, don't put yourself out or anything. Me and Junior can hang out on the beach, go shopping and stuff."

"The fan boats over the everglades are good fun," Keith said. "And how are you fixed for spending money?" He pulled a roll of dollars from the back of his shorts.

"I can't take money off you as well," James said. "You've already paid for my flight and everything."

Keith handed James three hundred-dollar bills and gave the same to Junior.

"Buy something for April at the mall," Keith said. "She's sweet on you."

"Cheers," James said. "Is it all right if I use the phone to tell Zara I've arrived?"

"Sure," Keith said, spreading his arms out wide. "With a house this size, the phone bill is the least of my worries."

After a quick call home, the two boys stripped to their boxers, jumped off the wooden decking at the back of the house and sprinted across the deserted white beach towards the ocean. James was feeling grotty after eight hours crammed on an airplane, but all that washed away as he curled his toes in the mushy sand and let the sea water spew over his chest.

"I'm so glad you came instead of Ringo," Junior said,

raising his voice above the waves. "This week is gonna be such a laugh."

James slept in one of the guest bedrooms. He had a four-poster bed, plus an en-suite bathroom with a giant marble tub. When he woke up, he slid on shorts and a T-shirt and opened up a set of glass doors that led on to a balcony overlooking the ocean. He took some lungfuls of sea air and leaned against the metal railing, letting the sun toast his skin.

The coastline was dotted with yachts and motor launches out for a Sunday morning cruise. An elderly Hispanic gardener was hosing the terraces below. The man nodded politely when their eyes met. It made James wonder where he'd end up in life. Would he have the $10 million oceanfront house, or would he be like the crinkled old guy who watered the flowers?

"Yo," Junior shouted.

He came strolling through James's bedroom and stepped on to the balcony.

"What you doing out here?" Junior asked.

James shrugged. "Just thinking."

"Dumb idea," Junior said. "Thinking wears out your brain. My dad wants us downstairs. We're going to IHOP for breakfast."

"You what?"

"It's a pancake place," Junior explained. "I'm getting a stack of strawberry whipped cream pancakes. They give you so many you can barely move when you finish. Dad and George are going into town for some business meeting, so they're dropping us at the mega-mall.

It's about twenty times the size of the Reeve Center. We can spill some dosh on shopping, then there's a sixteen-screen cinema and a rollercoaster if we get bored."

"Sounds good," James grinned.

James bought himself new jeans and swimming shorts and a couple of CDs, including one as a present for Kerry; then they caught a movie and waited around until George arrived to collect them. It was mid-afternoon when they got back to the house.

"How was the meeting?" James asked.

"Good," Keith grinned. "Very, very good."

"Does that mean I'll be able to go back to making money from deliveries?"

"I don't know about that," Keith said awkwardly. "Everything is gonna be different. Do you fancy going for a swim now the sun's lower?"

"Actually," James said, "do you mind if I use your laptop to e-mail my family?"

"No worries," Keith said.

George, Keith, and Junior put on swimming shorts and walked down to the sea. Once they were out of sight, James raced up to his room and got a couple of USB memory sticks and a hacker's toolkit CD-ROM out of the bottom of his bag. He climbed on to one of the metal stools at the breakfast bar in the kitchen, turned on Keith's laptop and connected to the Internet.

James clicked on Hotmail and checked the e-mails in an account he'd set up for his James Beckett alias. He had three messages from April, including one that contained a blurry photo of April and Erin in their ski suits with the message "Miss U already, April, XXX." James replied insincerely with "Miss U2," before writing a longer message to Kerry, gloating about the weather and the beautiful house he was staying in.

When he'd finished typing his e-mails, James stood up and peeked out the window, making sure Keith, George, and Junior were well clear of the house. As he flipped confidently through the files on the laptop, he realized that his marathon training sessions with Amy had been worth the brain-ache.

He clicked on Keith's documents folder. There were a couple of hundred files inside. Most had a little padlock symbol next to them, meaning they were encrypted. James decided it was too risky trying to read stuff with Keith just down on the beach. Instead, he plugged a memory card into the USB socket on the side of the laptop. The card was only the size of a pen top, but it held as much data as six CDs.

A gray box popped up on the screen: NEW USB DEVICE DETECTED. James checked the size of Keith's documents folder and realized there was enough space on the memory card to copy the whole lot over. He waited a couple of anxious minutes while the computer copied Keith's files. Then he switched off the laptop and walked back to his bedroom. He got his mobile out of his luggage and set it to search for an American network. When it found a connection, James speed-dialed the number of a local Drug Enforcement Agency office he'd been given before he left.

John Jones answered. "James?"

"Hi."

"Settled in OK?" John asked.

"Not bad," James said. "You?"

"My flight was fine, but the heat out here does me in. I'm more of a fish-and-chip-supper-on-a-cold-winter-night kind of guy."

"I can't talk for long," James said. "But I've been through Keith's laptop."

"Anything exciting?"

"Dunno," James said. "I checked for fancy stuff, like hidden partitions on the hard drive, but there's none of that. All Keith's documents are encrypted. I didn't want to fiddle about trying to open them. I've copied the whole lot on to a memory card for you guys to deal with."

"Good work," John said.

"The only thing is, how do I get the card to you?"

"We can schedule an unscheduled rubbish collection for this evening. Have you got something you want to throw out that you can hide the memory card inside?"

James looked around the room.

"There's a half-eaten box of Milk Duds I got at the cinema," he said. "I can stick the memory card inside that then throw it out."

"Perfect," John said. "Scrunch the box up, so the card doesn't fall out. Then make sure you put your rubbish in the main bins out by the road. We'll send a dust-cart along to pick them up."

"Will you guys be able to break the encryption?" James asked.

"Depends on what software Keith's using," John said. "But probably. Is there anything else you'd like to report?"

"One thing Keith said struck me as odd," James said. "I asked him when I'd be able to go back to making deliveries. Keith goes, 'I don't know, everything's gonna be different.'"

"Hmm," John said. "I've no idea why he'd say that, but it's certainly interesting."

"I better go anyway," James said. "They'll be wondering what I'm doing."

"OK then," John said. "Keep up the good work and watch out for yourself."

CHAPTER 28

ORLANDO

James was having one of the best weeks of his life. Monday he went out on a fishing boat with Junior. He'd never fished out in the ocean, but the crew showed him the basics and helped him reel his first catch.

He called John Jones from the beach that evening with some snippets he'd picked up from Keith's telephone conversations. John told James that American drug enforcement agents had retrieved his Milk Duds box and MI5 specialists had managed to read most of the files. They contained details of several foreign bank accounts with transactions linking Keith to a money-laundering operation whose specialty was collecting your cash, bouncing it around the world banking system until it was untraceable, and finally depositing it in an anonymous foreign bank account—minus their 25 percent commission.

John didn't think it was enough information to get Keith convicted, but he reckoned it was a useful piece of the jigsaw.

The next day, James, Junior, and Keith set off early for the 350-kilometer drive up to Orlando. It was low season, so the boys had a great time at Islands of Adventure, scaring themselves witless on all the roller coasters and simulator rides, without wasting too much time queuing. James went nuts in the gift shop, buying T-shirts for Kyle and Kerry, and a little bib and shorts for Joshua. When he went to pay at the till, Keith put the whole lot on his credit card.

By mid-afternoon, they were all knackered and sunburnt, so they checked into a hotel and showered before heading down to the restaurant. They got an outdoor table at the edge of a man-made lake with ducks and fountains in the middle. Keith ordered tagliatelle, while James and Junior got half-pound burgers and fries. The waitress brought walnut bread and olive oil to the table while they waited for their food.

"I think I'm safe to talk here," Keith said. "Unless a bunch of cops follow me here and they're pointing a parabolic microphone at me from the other side of the lake."

James looked away from the ducks, which were scrapping over a handful of bread he'd thrown into the pond a second before he noticed the PLEASE DO NOT FEED THE DUCKS sign.

"Talk about what?" Junior asked.

"Anything," Keith said.

"Do you think the cops are listening to you most of the time?" James asked.

"The cops have microphones everywhere," Keith said. "The house in Luton, the house in Miami, my cars, my offices. I don't even know what people I can trust any more. I've even got the secret service after me."

"MI5?" James asked.

"They've been after me ever since the corruption allegations inside Operation Snort." Keith nodded. "One of my better sources told me George is working for the cops. I don't think it's true, but you can never be sure. He's a family man with a couple of kids. If the cops threatened him with a long stretch in prison, who knows what he'd be prepared to do?"

"Are you gonna have him whacked?" Junior asked.

Keith burst out laughing. "Son, if I had somebody killed every time I head a rumor about an informant, I'd be a mass murderer. The cops plant most of these rumors, hoping it will create friction inside KMG. We get our own back by dropping rumors that straight cops are taking bribes."

"Have you ever had anyone killed?" Junior asked.

"I get problems and I tell people to make them go away," Keith said. "It's not my business to know whether they tickle the guy's feet until he promises to be a good boy, or chuck him off a tenth-floor balcony."

"Cool," Junior said, grinning.

"You know that scene in the movies, where the car's heading for the edge of the cliff, and the cop cars are chasing?" Keith asked. "That's where everyone thinks I'm at, but the cops don't realize something."

"What?" Junior said.

"I've bailed out of the car," Keith said. "Everyone thinks I'm out here buying drugs, trying to get KMG up and running again. I've made a few noises in that direction, but all I'm really doing is settling debts and sorting out finances. I'll be staying in America for a few months, until things die down back home, then I'm gonna rest of my laurels. How many millions does a man need anyway?"

"That's cool, Dad," Junior smiled. "I don't ever want you going to prison."

"What will happen to KMG without you?" James asked.

"I expect it'll break up into a thousand pieces," Keith said. "Some people will go to prison. Some of the ones left on the outside will make contacts with my overseas suppliers and start importing cocaine themselves. In a year or two, nobody will even remember me. The same guys will be making deliveries and selling coke on the street; it'll just be new faces supplying them and stacking the big money into foreign bank accounts. Give it four or five years and you'll probably find one group has become dominant; a new KMG. The police will set up another Operation Snort type deal; they'll break it up. Then the whole cycle will start again."

"Stopping KMG must have some effect on the cocaine trade," James said.

"The police have budget cuts and efficiency targets, the drug dealers have got billions of pounds," Keith said. "It's like the weediest kid in Year Seven picking a fight with the entire Year Twelve rugby team. The police might land the odd punch, but they're always gonna get their arses kicked at the end of the day."

"Do you think you'll stay out of prison?" James asked.

"I'm shelling out enough in bribes and legal fees," Keith said. "So let's hope for the best, eh?"

The waitress came over with the three plates of food.

"Anyway," Keith said, shovelling down his first mouthful of pasta, "all this serious talk's gonna spoil my appetite. You boys want to go see a movie or something tonight?"

James waited until Junior was asleep before slipping out of the hotel room. He made his nightly call to John Jones from an alcove down the corridor that had an ice dispenser and a couple of Pepsi machines in it. James explained about Keith's retirement plans.

"We've tracked down more of Keith's money with the information you copied off the computer," John said. "I was starting to suspect Keith wasn't in Miami to do a drug deal and what you said confirms this. But I still don't think he's told you the whole truth."

"Why's that?" James asked.

"We traced a transaction from one of Keith's bank accounts in Trinidad. Keith just purchased half a million dollars' worth of U.S. treasury bonds in the name of Erin Moore. We contacted the bank and asked for details. Keith Moore has handed the bonds over to the bank, with instructions to sell them on Erin Moore's eighteenth birthday and pay her the money. Keith has made similar transactions for Junior, April, and Ringo. He's also set up a trust fund for his ex-wife. He's paid off the mortgages for the two houses in England and sold the house in Miami for a lot less than it's worth, to raise fast cash."

"But Keith told me he's planning to stay in Miami until the heat dies down back in England."

"There's a new owner moving into the Miami house in three weeks," John said. "And we can't find any trace of the eleven million dollars he got from the sale."

"Do you think he's using the money to buy drugs?" James asked.

"I don't think so."

"What then?"

"How many boats have you seen since you got to Miami?" John asked.

"Millions," James said. "They're everywhere."

"Once he's set up the arrangements to provide for his family, I think Keith is going to sneak out of the house, climb aboard one of those boats, and vanish like a puff of smoke."

"How come?" James asked.

"Keith can feel the net closing in. He has informants inside Operation Snort, so he knows we're close to having enough evidence to put him behind bars for a seriously long stretch."

"Where will he go?" James asked.

"Eleven million bucks will go a long way in South America. My money would be on Brazil. It's easy to disappear in a country with two hundred million people. He can buy a new identity off some corrupt government official, maybe even have a spot of plastic surgery to change his appearance."

"What about his kids and stuff?"

"They'll be set for life financially," John said. "Keith will have made double sure that the money set aside for his family can never be traced back to drug dealing."

"But he'll never be able to see them again."

"He won't see much of them from inside a jail cell, either," John said. "You keep telling me Keith is in a good mood, but that's all front. He's got to make decisions and none of his options are easy."

"So what are you doing to stop him disappearing?" James asked.

"We have a big problem. We've asked the Americans to put a twenty-four-hour watch on Keith, but they're only prepared to spare us one DEA agent. We've even offered to pay their costs, but they're short-staffed and they've got their own bad guys to catch. We're having more meetings with the Yanks to try and sort out a deal, but for at least the next few days, there's nothing to stop Keith Moore slipping off into the night."

"Except me," James said.

"Remember you're undercover," John said. "And you're supposed to be a regular kid, so don't interfere. All you can do is call me if you think he's about to leg it."

James heard someone coming along the corridor and quickly hung up his phone. It was Keith, wearing a hotel gown and carrying the ice bucket from his room. James was in a T-shirt and boxers, so he had nowhere to hide his phone.

"Trouble sleeping?" Keith asked. "Who are you ringing at this time of night?"

CHERUB training teaches you to always have an excuse ready.

"Zara," James said. "It's morning back home and Joshua always wakes her up early."

"Most mobiles don't work in America," Keith said. "You must have a tri-band."

James's mobile phone had been modified by the intelligence service so it worked on just about any network in the world, but he couldn't tell Keith that.

"I've got no idea," James said, shrugging. "I just turned the thing on and it worked. I stepped out here because I didn't want to wake Junior up."

"You know it's about four quid a minute using your mobile from America?" Keith said.

"Is it?" James gasped, acting like he was really worried. "Ewart will murder me when he gets the bill."

Keith filled his ice bucket from the dispenser and put quarters in the Pepsi machine.

"I must have got dehydrated walking about in the sun all day," he said. "I woke up with a raging thirst. Do you want one?"

James nodded. "Yeah, I wouldn't mind."

Keith fed in more quarters until a second can dropped out of the machine. He handed it to James and they both pulled back the tabs and swallowed a couple of gassy mouthfuls.

"I'm really grateful you brought me out here on holiday," James said. "Ewart and Zara could never afford to take me abroad."

"That's OK," Keith said, smiling. "When Ringo dropped out, it was me who suggested you came instead."

"Really?" James said. "Why?"

"You're the only one of Junior's mates I thought I

could rely on to look after him if something bad happens," Keith said.

"Bad like what?" James asked.

"They could arrest me at any time, James. I know Junior likes to think he's the big man, but he's led a pretty sheltered life and I'm a lot happier knowing there's a guy like you with him."

"You've got George back in Miami," James said.

"George is good for two things," Keith laughed. "Breaking heads and polishing cars. I've known the man since infant school and I love him, but frankly, it's a miracle he can tie his own shoe laces."

"Who knows?" James said. "Maybe you'll never get arrested."

"Life is certainly full of surprises," Keith said. "I'll tell you that for nothing."

He ripped off a monster belch that echoed down the corridor. James giggled and responded with a tiny burp.

"Pathetic," Keith said. "Check this out."

Keith tipped back his head to drain his can, then rolled out the longest, loudest belch James had ever heard. An elderly American was toddling along the corridor. She had giant rectangular sunglasses and the wrinkled face of somebody who'd spent too much of her life in the sun.

"Why don't you mind your damn manners?" she said furiously.

"Don't worry, ma'am," Keith said, giggling as he gently cuffed James around the back of the head. "I'm make sure the boy doesn't do it again."

"It wasn't me," James gasped, struggling to keep a straight face.

The woman shuffled a few more steps and stopped outside her room. As she rummaged through her handbag for the plastic card that unlocked her door, Keith stepped into the corridor and belched again. It wasn't as big as the first two, but it was still loud. James couldn't control himself and started howling with laughter. The woman scowled so hard, he half expected laser beams to shoot out of her eyes.

"This hotel used to attract decent people," she shouted. "Why don't you act your age?"

Her door slammed. James and Keith stood there laughing for about ten minutes. James got it so bad his sides started hurting.

Keith looked at his watch. "You better get back to bed, it's gone midnight and we're doing another theme part tomorrow."

James crept back into his room, being careful not to wake up Junior. He took a quick pee before sliding between his sheets. He was tired, but his brain kept churning over as he lay away, listening to Junior's gentle breathing.

James wondered if Keith really was planning to do a runner. It seemed sad that a guy who'd been showing him the time of his life was facing a choice between twenty years in prison and running off and never seeing his family again. James asked himself what he'd do if he saw Keith making a run for it. Would he grab his mobile the second he realized, or give Keith time to get away?

They left the hotel early next morning and went to DisneyWorld, then spent the afternoon cooling off at a water park. It was getting dark by the time they left Orlando for the five-hour drive back to Miami.

James woke up late Thursday morning on his four-poster bed in the Miami house. He was on top of his duvet, wearing the trainers and clothes he'd had on the day before. The last thing he could remember was falling asleep in the backseat of the car. He needed a shower and his mouth tasted like a sewer, but before any of that, he scrambled downstairs to see if Keith was still around.

George, Keith, and Junior sat at the breakfast bar in the kitchen, wearing swimming shorts and watching a daytime talk show.

"Here's sleeping beauty," Keith said.

Junior started to laugh.

"What?" James asked.

"I pinched your cheek and everything," Keith said, "but you didn't bat an eyelid. I had to get George to carry you upstairs and dump you on your bed."

"All red-faced and tired-out," Junior giggled. "You looked like a little angel."

"I can't remember a thing," James gasped. "God . . . That's so embarrassing."

"It's all those midnight phone calls," Keith said. "You're not getting enough sleep."

James had a mental jolt. He'd missed his nightly call and John Jones might be worried.

"I better go freshen up," James said.

As soon as he got to his room, he found the overnight bag he'd taken to Orlando and grabbed his mobile. He tried to switch it on, but the battery was dead. He hunted around the room until he found his charger and his American socket adapter. The phone bleeped to life as soon as it was plugged in.

"Rip Van Winkle," John Jones said. "How you feeling?"

"Don't you start," James said. "How did you know about that?"

"When it got to one in the morning and I still hadn't heard from you, I got worried. We got a track on your mobile phone signal and realized you were driving back from Orlando. Then your mobile stopped transmitting."

"It went flat," James explained. "I forgot to take my charger with me."

"Pretty basic operational mistake, James," John said, tutting. "But I guess we have to make allowances for the fact you're thirteen years old."

"I'm glad *you* make allowances at MI5," James laughed. "Nobody from CHERUB ever does."

"Anyway, I thought I'd better check you were OK, so I hid in the bushes out back and watched George carry you out of the car. You looked like you were six years old, all bundled up in his big fat arms."

"I'm never gonna live this down," James said. "So, apart from me making an idiot of myself, nothing much happened yesterday. What about your end?"

"The Yanks want to help us watch Keith, but they don't have the manpower. We think we've got enough evidence to convict Keith on tax evasion and money-laundering charges, but that's only worth a two- to five-year sentence. We wanted to wait until we could bust him on drug charges, but with no twenty-four-hour surveillance and the risk of Keith running off for good, we've decided to move now."

"Extradition?" James asked.

"That's right, James. Bedfordshire Police will be contacting the DEA later today, asking them to arrest Keith on money-laundering charges and send him back to Britain. We have to present evidence to an American judge before they issue an arrest warrant. It'll take a day or so to get the paperwork together and organize the hearing."

"So you're hoping Keith doesn't leg it in the meantime."

"Exactly," John said. "And one final thing. I got a message from Zara. Dr. McAfferty has decided to pull the CHERUB side of this operation whether or not Keith Moore is in jail. Tell Junior and Keith that Ewart's been offered a better job and you're all moving back to London."

CHAPTER 29
NIGHT

That night James ended up in Junior's room watching a horror film on DVD. James got up to go back to his room when it finished.

"That sofa pulls out," Junior said. "You can sleep in here if you want."

James smiled. "Scared of being on your own? Think that guy with the bloody ax might come bursting through your window?"

"No," Junior said defensively. "I just thought we could talk and stuff."

James fetched his duvet and pillows while Junior pulled out the sofa bed. They switched the light off and lay in the dark talking. "If you could have any car in the world, what would it be? What if you could live anywhere you wanted?"

"Would you stick your tongue up a dog's arse for a million pounds?" Junior asked.

James thought for a couple of seconds. "Yes."

Junior started rolling about laughing. "EUGHH, James. You filthy animal."

"It's OK for you," James said, laughing. "Your dad's loaded already. But a million pounds would change my life. I'd never have to go to work. I could have a decent house and a cool car and stuff."

"What if you had to do it on TV and everyone knew about it?"

"Doesn't make any difference," James said. "A million would set you up for life."

"OK," Junior said. "What's the *least* amount? Would you do it for ten thousand?"

"No way."

"What then?"

"I dunno," James said. "Half a million, maybe . . ."

An arc of light burst into the room and Keith's head appeared in the doorway.

"Come on, guys," Keith said. "Be sensible. It's one in the morning. We're going out early tomorrow and you two are gonna be wasted. Calm down and go to sleep."

Both boys struggled to stop laughing.

"Good night, Dad," Junior said.

"Get some sleep," Keith said firmly.

He closed the door. The boys waited until they were fairly sure Keith was in his bedroom.

Junior sounded sad. "You know," he whispered, "if

you're moving back to London, I'll probably never see you or Nicole again."

"I'll miss you as well," James said. "You're one of the best mates I've ever had."

"Maybe we could visit each other in the holidays," Junior said.

"Maybe," James said, although he knew it could never happen. "It's only half an hour on the train to London. You know what else?"

"What?" Junior asked.

"I was looking forward to boxing against you."

Junior thought for a second. "Do you want to fight right now?"

"Your dad will go psycho," James said.

"There's gloves that go with the punchbag downstairs in the gym. We can fight on the beach in the moonlight. You can't see from the house if you stay down near the sea."

"OK," James said, sitting up on the sofa bed and smiling. "Just don't start bawling to Daddy when I punch the snot out of you."

Junior sneered. "You talk pretty big for someone who's only ever done sparring."

Junior flicked on the lamp beside his bed and put on his watch. Both boys slipped on shorts and trainers. They sneaked downstairs and got the gloves. James was surprised when he saw how small they were.

"These are pro-weight," Junior whispered. "Much less padding than for amateur boxing. You really feel a sting if you get hit with one of these."

"Are there head guards?" James asked.

"We're fighting like men," Junior said. "No finger tape, no head guards, no gum shields, pro-gloves. Not chicken, are you?"

James was starting to wonder if fighting was a good idea. The CHERUB staff wouldn't be impressed if he got himself injured in an unnecessary midnight boxing match, but he was too proud to back down.

They walked through to the living room and got a fright when George let out a loud snore. He'd fallen asleep in front of the TV. Junior quietly slid one of the French doors open and they jumped off the decking onto the beach.

The tide was on its way out. The moon was bright and the wet sand near the sea squelched under their trainers. Junior used a stick to draw the outline of a lopsided boxing ring, before setting his watch to do a three-minute countdown.

"Three rounds, lasting three minutes each," Junior said. "If you go down three times you're out of the fight."

James felt nervous as he pulled his second glove on with his teeth.

"Go to your corner," Junior said.

When Junior's stopwatch bleeped, the two boys charged forward and started throwing punches. With amateur gloves, even a full-force punch barely hurts, but Junior's first barrage with the professional gloves connected hard. One punch knocked James off balance. He couldn't catch his breath as he stumbled backwards. Junior sunk a blow below the elastic of James's shorts, doubling him over. Junior's next punch caught James in the side of the head. He splattered helplessly into the damp sand.

"Low blow," James wheezed, clutching his abdomen.

The fight had only been going a few seconds, but it was a warm night and both boys were pouring sweat.

"It wasn't low," Junior said. "That counts as my first knockdown."

James clambered to his feet. He usually loved the rush you got during a fight, but Junior was fast and strong. James had a nasty feeling he'd bitten off more than he could chew.

"So we're fighting dirty, are we?" he said, holding back a burst of anger. "That's fine by me."

He threw a fast punch. Junior wasn't ready and the thinly padded glove smashed into his nose. James's next shot was an uppercut that snapped back Junior's head.

"Stop," Junior shouted, groaning in pain as he wrapped his arms over his face. "Jesus Christ . . . You idiot."

"What?" James asked.

"You've got sand in your gloves. It's gone in my eye."

Junior tore off a glove and started rubbing his eye.

"Sorry," James said. "I never realized. Are you OK?"

Junior broke into an uneasy smile as he blinked out the sand.

"You know what?" he said. "I blame the idiot who thought up this stupid idea in the first place."

James laughed. "That would be you."

"Call it a draw, eh, James?"

"Fair enough," James said. "Now we know why they don't have beach boxing."

"I'm going for a swim," Junior said, kicking off his trainers. "I need to wash all this sweat off."

James thought he heard a banging sound as he pulled off his gloves.

"Did you hear that?"

"What?" Junior asked.

"I thought I heard something up in the house."

Junior smiled. "Maybe George woke up and fell off the sofa."

"Yeah," James laughed. "Either that or they've set loose the ax-wielding maniac from that movie."

Junior waded into the sea and dived forward, turning a somersault underwater. James pushed off backwards and let a wave wash him back towards the beach.

"You ever had a nightmare after watching a scary movie?" Junior asked.

"You know the film *Seven*?" James asked as he bobbed in the surf.

"I love that movie," Junior said. "It's totally sick."

"When my mum was alive, I showed off until she let me watch the video. I woke up in a state and climbed in her bed. My sister, Lauren, heard about it and didn't stop ribbing me for about a week."

"Your sister?" Junior said, surprised.

"I mean cousin," James said, nervously covering his mistake. "It was the summer holidays and Lauren was staying at our house."

"Ringo used to tease me when I was little," Junior said. "I'd ask him to put on my *Pingu* video and he'd stick on *The Terminator* to scare me."

"We better go to bed," James said, as he picked his

boxing gloves off the sand and slid his wet feet inside his trainers. "I'm looking forward to the air-boat ride tomorrow."

"We never usually do half the cool stuff we've done this week," Junior said. "My dad really likes you for some reason."

James thought Keith was spoiling them because he was planning to disappear in a few days and would most likely never see Junior again. As they walked towards the house in their dripping shorts, Junior turned around and started walking backwards, staring at the moonlit sea.

"Just think," he said, spreading his arms out wide. "If you count the time difference between here and London, in less than three days' time we'll be getting up for another miserable Monday at Gray Park School."

"Cheer us up, why don't you?" James said. "Is your eye OK now?"

"Stings a bit," Junior said. "I wish we could have had a proper fight."

James clambered onto the wooden decking at the back door of the house and put his foot inside the sliding door. His trainer slipped in something wet. He rested his palm on the wall to steady himself. The light was on in the kitchen and George's body had rolled off the sofa on the floor.

"Something's going on," James said edgily.

Junior grinned. "What is it, the ax murderer?"

"I'm serious," James said, lifting his trainer out of the sticky liquid.

He felt like his head was going to explode when he realized it was blood.

"Give over, James," Junior said. "You're not scaring me."

Junior stepped through the door and noticed George on the floor.

"He really did fall off the sofa," Junior laughed.

James crouched down and clicked on a table lamp. Junior saw George was dead, realized his trainers were planted in a puddle of blood, and let out a massive scream.

CHAPTER 30

BODY

James was still haunted by the cold touch of his mother's fingers the night he found her dead in front of the TV. George's body didn't affect him the same way, though the sight was more horrible. There was blood seeping from a bullet wound under his shirt. It was draining down a hanging arm and along the joins in the floor tiles, creating a grid of red lines leading to the pool of blood by the sliding doors.

James felt like everything was happening in slow motion. He could feel every vibration in Junior's screams and watch the droplets of saliva spraying out of his mouth.

James had a theory: Keith had shot George for betraying

him, then disappeared. But the theory sprang apart as he crept across the room and stared down the hallway through the half-open kitchen door. Three armed men had Keith Moore pinned on a stool at the breakfast bar. It looked like they'd roughed him up.

"Leave the boys," Keith shouted when he heard Junior scream. "I'll tell you everything."

James knew he had only milliseconds before one of the men beating up Keith came out of the kitchen pointing a gun at him and Junior. He turned back to Junior, who stood rigid in the doorway, staring at George's body.

"Run!" James shouted. "Get help."

Junior snapped out of his panic long enough to hear the order. He jumped off the wooden decking and began sprinting down the beach. James hoped he'd have the sense to run to one of the neighboring houses and call the police.

James planned to follow Junior, but a thuggish-looking guy emerged from the kitchen before he got the chance. James could see tattoos through the sweat-drenched vest clinging to his skin.

"Get here, kid!" he shouted, sliding out the pistol tucked into his jeans.

James burst through the nearest door, into the front living room where Keith kept his hi-fi and record collection.

"Hey!" the man shouted furiously. "You wanna mess with me? I'll kill you before you reach the door."

He sounded Mexican or something. James didn't know what the men wanted from Keith, but they'd shown they were prepared to kill and he didn't fancy being their next victim. He thought about climbing out of the window, but the room only had a long narrow window up near the ceiling. He'd never get through before the man shot him.

There was a key inside the door. Turning the lock bought James a few seconds. He pushed an armchair against the door as the gunman rattled the handle on the outside. James desperately needed some kind of weapon.

"Unlock this or I'll shoot you to pieces," the man shouted, as he pounded the door with his fist.

James slid one of Keith's LPs off its rack. He'd learned in weapons training that you can make a dagger by shattering any object made out of hard plastic. He leaned the record sleeve against the wall and stamped on it with his bloody trainer.

The gunman shoulder-charged the door.

One of his colleagues shouted after him from the kitchen. "You need a hand?"

The gunman didn't sound worried. "It's just some smartass kid who's gonna be feeling a lot of pain real soon."

Three deafening shots fired into the door, blasting away the lock. James tipped the pieces of the album out of its sleeve and grabbed the longest shard of what, until a few moments earlier, had been a valuable purple vinyl edition of Led Zeppelin IV.

The gunman kicked the door twice, barging the armchair out of the way. James backed up to the wall beside the door, with the shard of purple vinyl clutched tightly in his hand. His heart drummed like it was set to burst.

If he got this wrong, he'd end up with a bullet through his head.

The second he saw the pistol coming through his door, James grabbed the muzzle with one hand while plunging the sharp piece of plastic into the gunman's wrist. The man screamed out. His fingers sprang apart and James snatched the gun, before backing up to the opposite wall and turning it around so that his finger was on the trigger.

The man tugged the plastic out of his arm as he stumbled over the armchair. He faced James off with a self-assured grin.

"Big gun for a little boy, eh?" he said, showing off a rack of yellow teeth. "Are you really going to shoot me?"

Some sort of commotion broke out in the kitchen. Keith Moore screamed in pain.

"Get on your knees and put your hands behind your head," James stuttered.

The man edged closer. James remembered his firearms training: from a safe position you can shoot to wound, but if you're in mortal danger you can't risk missing. You have to aim for the biggest target: the chest.

"Don't make me shoot you," James said desperately.

The gun weighed a billion tons in his trembling hands. The man ignored the threat and kept moving closer. James didn't want to shoot, but what choice was there? He held his breath to steady the gun.

"You ain't gonna kill *noooooo*body," the man sneered, as he lifted his shoe off the carpet, preparing to take a step that would bring James into reach.

A shockwave ripped through the room. The bullet

slammed into the gunman's chest from less than two meters. His feet lifted off the floor as his body crashed backwards into the upturned armchair. Stunned by the fact that he'd just fired a bullet into a real human being, James felt sick as he scrambled over his bleeding victim and out into the hallway.

James ran into the front living room, planning to escape via the beach, but another gunman was frog-marching Junior across the sand towards the house. He ducked back into the hallway, hoping the man walking up the beach hadn't spotted him. It could only be a matter of seconds before the men in the kitchen came out to investigate the gunshot. The only way out of the front of the house was by walking past the kitchen door, which would be suicidal. That only left one option.

Still holding the pistol, James ran upstairs. He went into his room, grabbed his mobile phone off the bedside table, and called John Jones. A woman answered.

"Is John Jones there?"

"I'm Beverly Shapiro," the woman said. "Is that James Beckett?"

"Yeah," James said. "Where's John?"

"He's in the restroom. You sound worried, James. You can talk to me. I'm the Drug Enforcement Agency officer working with John."

James gasped with relief. "Thank God. Listen, I'm at Keith Moore's house. There's a whole bunch of gunmen downstairs. They're beating up Keith, trying to get some kind of information out of him."

"I'll call the local cops out," Beverly said. "Can you make it out of the house?"

"They caught Junior running down the beach. I think they've got guys watching the outside."

"I'm calling the cops right now," Beverly said. "You find yourself a good place to hide and keep this line open."

James thought about hiding, but he didn't think he'd be safe for more than a few minutes. The cops would take longer than that to arrive and even when they did, they'd be unlikely to come charging straight into the house and risk getting shot. James considered hiding out at the top of the stairs and shooting at anyone who tried to come up. It might have worked in a house with one staircase, but Keith's Miami home had three. Four if you counted the metal walkway that led across to the garage.

The garage.

James realized that was his best chance. He leaned out into the corridor as Beverly said something into the phone.

"What?" James asked.

"I said, the police are on their way. Have you found a safe place to hide?"

"I don't think it's safe up here," James said. "Someone's gonna come up looking for me any second."

"I *told* you to hide," Beverly said stiffly. "Keep calm and wait for the police."

"No way," James said. "I've got to bust out."

He tucked the phone into the waistband of his soggy shorts, without ending the call. He sprinted down the hallway to the master bedroom and found Keith's trousers on the floor. He grabbed a bunch of keys from the pocket and rapidly flipped through them. There were keys to a couple of the Porsches and Mercedes, but James thought the huge four-wheel-drive Range Rover would give him his best chance of escape.

When he got back into the hallway, he heard footsteps on the staircase. He fired a shot towards the stairs, knowing it would make the men stay back for a minute or two.

James cautiously opened the door at the end of the hallway. He checked no one was around outside, before stepping on to the metal steps that linked the house to the garage. He opened the door into the garage and walked down a set of spiral stairs to ground level, before unlocking the Range Rover and sliding on to the driver's seat.

He put the key in the steering column and started the engine. Clipping on his seatbelt to cut off the annoying bing-bong noise, he pressed the button on the dashboard that opened the garage doors and the iron gates at the front of the house.

The wooden doors, less than a meter from the front of the car, began parting slowly. James knew someone would hear them if he just sat waiting. He put the car in drive, floored the accelerator pedal, and ploughed through. He had to slam on the brake to avoid a brick wall as chunks of wood sprayed in all directions around the car.

As he put on full steering lock and turned towards the gate, James's heart sank. The front gates were still closed. The button on the dashboard hadn't worked. James realized the gunmen must have short-circuited the automatic gate when they broke into the house. The

Range Rover might have been able to break them open, but the gunmen had their two cars parked in front of the gates, ready for a quick getaway.

As James looked around, frantically trying to work out an alternative escape, a bullet came out of the first-floor window, ripping through the roof of the car, and punching a neat hole through the front passenger seat. James floored the accelerator and spun the car around. He pointed the Range Rover at the thickly planted terraces around the house, hoping the car was powerful enough to punch through a hundred meters of plants and trees. If it was, he'd be able to escape onto the beach at the back of the house.

The chunky front tires reared onto a set of narrow steps. The car crawled up a gentle slope, rocking from side to side as it trampled bushes and tore a couple of small trees out of the ground. Chunks of stone and wood clattered against the underside of the car, then it hit a massive palm tree and ground to a halt.

The car slipped backwards as a second bullet ripped through the tailgate. The noise made James's eardrums pop. He thought he might have to bail out and run for it, but the car's automatic gearbox slipped into its lowest ratio. The rear tires dug into the soft ground. James dabbed the accelerator. After a touch of wheelspin, the car toppled the palm tree and bounced over its thick trunk.

At the top of the slope, the ground leveled off onto a tiled patio. James swerved around Keith's brick barbecue and picked up speed as he rolled downhill. It was much easier navigating through the low bushes and flowerbeds on the windswept ocean side of the house. At the bottom, James swerved to avoid Keith's fishpond, then floored the accelerator. He needed speed to break through the fence at the back of the house.

A thin concrete post shattered as the front of the car ripped a hole through a tangle of plastic mesh and barbed wire. The car nose-dived off a meter-high wall. The back wheels spun in free air until the front wheels burrowed into the soft sand and pulled the front of the car forward. Once all four wheels were firmly planted on level ground, James hit the accelerator and began tearing along the sand, dragging a ten-meter section of chain-link fence behind him. He nudged the steering wheel left to right until the wire disentangled itself from the rear bumper.

Once the wire was gone, everything seemed eerily calm; just the gentle whoosh of the air-conditioning and a few hundred meters of level sand lit up by the headlamps. James looked back in the mirror. Nobody seemed to be coming after him. He reached into his shorts and grabbed his mobile.

"Beverly, are you still there?"

"What the hell was that noise?" John Jones asked, sounding like he was in a bit of a state. "Did I hear gunshots? Are you OK?"

"I'm OK, but I might have just killed some maniac and now they've got hold of Junior. I'm driving along the beach in Keith's Range Rover. When I see a gap between the houses, I'm gonna pull up on to the road."

"OK," John said. "You're sure nobody's following?"

"Not so far as I can tell."

"Do you know how to drive to the IHOP from where you are at the moment?"

"Sure," James said. "It's only a couple of kilometers."

"I'll meet you there in fifteen minutes. Beverly will be with me. She knows you're my informant, but she doesn't know anything about CHERUB, so watch what you say."

"No worries," James said.

"Get off the beach as quickly as you can and drive sensibly. You don't want to get picked up by the cops."

The pancake place was closed, so they ended up in a twenty-four-hour McDonald's across the street. John sat across the table from James, while Beverly got apple pies and coffees at the counter. James looked between his legs at his blood-stained trainers.

"A hundred and nineteen ninety-nine," James said bitterly. "The first lot got stolen, now this lot are ruined."

John Jones laughed. "Maybe it's God's way of telling you that a hundred and twenty pounds is an obscene amount of money to pay for a pair of plimsolls."

Beverly put the tray of coffee on the table and squeezed up next to James on the plastic bench. She was small, about twenty-five, with long chestnut hair and freckles. She didn't look hard enough to be a drug enforcement agent.

"I spoke to the local units," Beverly said. "The bad guys got rattled when you escaped. They tried to take Keith Moore away in their car. The police spotted them and there was a shoot-out. Keith Moore took a bullet through his shoulder. It's early days, but they think he'll be OK."

"What about Junior?" James asked.

"The guys knocked him around quite badly. He's been taken to hospital, but it's too early to say what kind of state he's in."

"I hope he's OK," James said anxiously. He took a sip from his steaming polystyrene cup. "So who were those guys? What did they want with Keith?"

"They're probably linked to the Lambayeke cartel," John said. "I'd bet my last dollar bill that they were after the numbers of Keith's secret bank accounts."

"I thought Keith dealt with the Lambayeke," James said. "Weren't they friendly?"

"Keith dealt with the Lambayeke cartel for twenty years," John said. "But they're not the kind of people you invite round to your house for a dinner party. As long as Keith was buying drugs from Lambayeke and making them money, they left him alone. Then KMG collapsed around Keith's ears. He's not going to buy any more drugs, he doesn't know who he can trust, and he's sitting on a big pile of money."

"So they decided to rob him?" James said.

"That's right," John nodded. "Keith Moore has millions stashed away in illegal bank accounts. So they send some thugs in to take Keith hostage and smack him around until he gives them all the bank account details and transfers all his money over to them."

"Keith would have had no comeback," Beverly added. "You can hardly go to your local precinct and complain that the money you made selling drugs that's stashed away in illegal overseas bank accounts has been stolen."

"It's almost the perfect crime," John said. "Except

the guys they sent in were so incompetent they forgot to check upstairs and get you and Junior out of bed."

"Actually," James said, "we weren't in bed. Me and Junior sneaked out and went down the beach for a midnight swim."

He thought it was best not to mention the boxing match.

"Well, it's a good job you did," John said, breaking into a smile. "Otherwise you'd have woken up with a gun pointing at your head."

CHAPTER 91

CATCH

James grabbed a few hours' sleep in Beverly Shapiro's office at the DEA's Miami headquarters. She woke him up at ten the following morning and dumped clean clothes and trainers on the desk in front of him.

"We got those from the house," Beverly said. "There are showers down the hall if you want to clean up. We're going to speak to Keith Moore in about forty minutes. John said you can sit in the observation room and watch if you want to."

"I thought Keith had been shot," James said.

"Only in the shoulder. It'll heal up."

"How's Junior?" James asked.

Beverly sighed. "The bad guys didn't think Keith was

telling them everything about his bank accounts, so they stopped hurting Keith and started on Junior. He's got a broken nose, broken collar bone, and some serious internal injuries."

James felt sick when he tried to imagine what Junior must have gone through. "I should have done something to help him," he said.

"What could you have done against eight armed men?" Beverly asked, smiling sympathetically.

"So is Junior going to be OK?"

"He won't be able to fly home for a while. He's asked to see you, but you don't exist anymore."

"What do you mean?" James asked.

"The United States has no immigration record for James Beckett. You're booked on a flight to London this evening. We want you to disappear before people start asking questions about you and the guy you shot in the chest."

"Oh," James said. "I kept having these creepy dreams about the gun going off and the room where it happened. Is he dead?"

"Yes."

"He wouldn't stop coming closer," James said, feeling tense as he replayed the scene in his mind. "I tried getting him to back down. I thought about shooting him in the leg, but I was taught to go straight for the chest."

"I would have done the same," Beverly said. "You can't take chances, especially when it's not your own weapon. You didn't know how many bullets you had, or if the gun was some rusty piece of junk that'd jam up the second the barrel gets hot."

"I just can't believe I killed someone."

• • •

James showered in the men's locker room. There was paraphernalia everywhere—police radios, holsters, body armor. James stared at his hands while the water rushed over his body, studying the finger that had killed someone a few hours earlier. He didn't exactly feel guilty about killing a man who was going to kill him, but it did make him a bit sad. The guy probably had a mother, or a kid, or something.

"Hey, boy, what you doing?"

James looked up to see a couple of muscular cops stripping off their clothes.

"Beverly Shapiro said it was OK to clean up in here."

"You sound English."

James nodded. "I'm from London."

"Cool," the cop said. "You ever met one of the royal family?"

"Sure," James said, laughing. "I hang out with them all the time."

James stepped out of the shower and started toweling off. He looked at the cops' guns lying on the slatted wooden bench and wondered if they'd ever been used to kill anyone. Then he wondered what it would be like to die. He hadn't given it a thought while he was trying to escape, but there were the two bullet holes in the Range Rover, less than a meter from where he'd sat.

Beverly took James to the canteen. She told him to put his bacon and scrambled eggs in a polystyrene box so he could eat it in the observation suite. It was a narrow room, with a row of plastic chairs and black and white monitors. There was a giant one-way mirror in one wall that looked into an interrogation room. Keith Moore was in there. He stared into space, nervously drumming his fingers on the table in front of him. His T-shirt was bulked out by the dressing wrapped around his shoulder.

"You'll have to keep quiet in here," Beverly said. "It's quite a thin partition."

She walked out, leaving James with the eerie sound of Keith's breathing, amplified through the tinny loudspeakers in the ceiling.

Seconds later, Beverly walked into the interrogation room behind John Jones.

"Good morning," John said, pulling out a chair opposite Keith and sitting down. "My name is John Jones. I'm here to help you out."

"I want a lawyer," Keith said. "I've been shot. I've no sleep. You can't question me like this."

"I'm with British Intelligence," John smiled. "I have no authority here in the United States. All we're doing is having an informal chat."

"I don't care if you're the grand wizard of the Ku Klux Klan," Keith said. "I'm not saying one word until I see a lawyer."

"The local cops found a deceased member of the Lambayeke cartel and a bunch of unlicensed firearms in your house," John said. "Somebody killed him, and unless the bad guys decided to start shooting one another, you're the main suspect."

"I want a lawyer," Keith said sourly.

John turned and looked at Beverly. "What's the standard sentence for a drug-related murder in Florida?" he asked.

"Life without parole, on a good day," Beverly said, smiling. "Though if the judge doesn't like the look of you, he might bump that up to death by lethal injection."

"What if Keith claims self-defense and puts in a guilty plea to a charge of manslaughter?" John asked.

"Between twenty and fifty years in prison," Beverly said.

"Man," John Jones laughed. "They're certainly tough down here in Florida. Keith Moore, I believe you're in a big heap of trouble."

"I've got money," Keith said, trying to sound confident. "I can afford a very smart lawyer."

"You reckon this case will ever make it anywhere near a courtroom?" John asked.

"Why shouldn't it?" Keith asked.

"You'll be charged with murdering a member of the Lambayeke cartel," John said. "You're a foreign citizen on a murder charge, so there's not a hope in hell you'll get bail. You'll be banged up on remand, awaiting trial, in a Florida prison stuffed with members of the Lambayeke cartel. How long do you think you'll last before one of them sticks a knife in your back?"

Keith looked a lot less sure of himself when he thought about this. John theatrically slammed his mobile phone on the desk.

"There's my phone, Keith. Go ahead, call your big-shot lawyer if you want to. The Florida legal system will take you under its wing and you'll be a dead man by Christmas."

"So what's my alternative?" Keith asked.

"You'll have to sign a deal," John explained. "The DEA will grant you immunity from prosecution in the United States, if you give a full and accurate account of your dealings with the Lambayeke cartel over the last twenty-whatever years. And you'll have to agree never to set foot in the United States again.

"The DEA will pass all the information you give to the British police. I'm sure you'll have given them enough to prosecute you. You'll face the full weight of British justice, which will probably be a twenty to twenty-five year prison sentence. With remission for good behavior, you could be a free man inside fifteen years."

"Why not leave me out here to rot?" Keith asked.

"This deal makes everyone happy," John said. "The Americans get lots of valuable information on the Lambayeke cartel, rather than a big bill for prosecuting you and trying to keep you alive in prison. Back in Britain, the home secretary gets to stand up in parliament and mouth off about the success of Operation Snort and his big crackdown on drugs. And most importantly, you'll still be alive this time next year."

"What if the Lambayeke cartel comes after me in Britain?" Keith asked.

"They might try to get at you," John said, shrugging. "But Lambayeke members are thin on the ground in British prisons, whereas you'll be on home turf. I expect a man with your resources will be able to find plenty of friends to protect you."

"You've got it all worked out," Keith said, shifting uneasily in his chair.

"This is a once in a lifetime deal," John said. "There

won't be any negotiation. You've got one hour to make a decision."

Keith leaned back in his chair and ran a hand through his sweaty hair. "You know what?" he said. "I reckon I've been in business long enough to know when someone's got you by the balls."

He reached his arm across the table to shake John Jones by the hand.

"I think you've got yourself a deal, Mr. Jones."

When the interview was over, James went back to Beverly's office and called the house in Luton.

"Kyle?" James asked. "Is that you?"

"James, what's happening?"

"John Jones just nailed Keith Moore," James said. "They arrested him last night and he's cut a deal to save his butt."

"Excellent," Kyle said. "We're just packing up here. We've had to tell everyone we're moving back to London."

"How was half-term?"

"Ringo's party was nuts. Kids were smashing up furniture, puking on the stairs. I met this cool kid called Dave, he's really cute and—"

"Stop, stop, *stop,*" James said sharply. "I can just about get my head around you being gay, Kyle. That doesn't mean I want graphic details . . . What about Kelvin and that? I thought they were supposed to be looking after Keith's house."

"Didn't you hear?" Kyle said. "The police raided the boxing club on Tuesday night. They arrested Kelvin, Marcus, Ken, and that tall kid in your class."

"Del?"

"Yeah, Del, and loads of other guys. The cops found the contact diary of the woman who used to organize the deliveries. They nabbed all the young couriers. You probably would have got busted if you'd been there."

"So is Kerry in?" James asked. "Can I have a quick word?"

"She's with Max Power."

"Who?" James gasped.

"This new kid turned up in her class on Monday. They're all over each other, snogging morning, noon and night."

James realized it was a wind-up. "Yeah, right, Kyle."

"I had you going for a second." Kyle giggled. "Kerry . . . it's your new beau. He wants to talk to you."

Kerry came to the phone.

"We busted Keith," James said. "He's looking at twenty-five years."

Kerry let out a big shriek. James had to move the phone away from his ear.

"Brilliant," she said. "We're heading back to campus tomorrow morning. When will you be home?"

"I'm flying out of here this evening," James said. "I'll probably get to campus about the same time as you guys."

"You *were* serious about the boyfriend-girlfriend thing, weren't you?" Kerry asked.

James smiled. "Oh, yeah. I can't wait to see you."

CHAPTER 32

LAST

James walked into Meryl Spencer's office, which overlooked the athletic track on CHERUB campus. Even though the window was open, you still got a hint of the damp smell from the changing room across the hallway.

"Ewart is impressed," Meryl said. "Zara's impressed and even Mr. Jones from MI5 is impressed. I have to say it, James, *I'm* impressed."

James smiled at his handler as he placed a blank bin liner on the desk and sat down opposite her. Meryl tipped out the contents. There were clothes, trainers, CDs, an envelope with over five hundred pounds in cash, and the five PlayStation games he'd stolen from the Reeve Center.

"I trust there's nothing else hidden up in your room?" Meryl asked.

"No," James said. "That's everything I either stole, or earned from selling drugs. Except for money I spent on food and going out, some presents I got for Joshua, and Lauren's birthday money."

"Which charity do you want me to give it to?"

"Me and Kerry looked on the Internet. She found this hostel near Luton that helps young people with drug problems. Gets them off drugs, finds them jobs, and gets them places at college and stuff."

"That sounds excellent," Meryl said. "You're due over thirty pounds' pocket money for the time you were away, and the clothes won't go for much in charity shops. If you want, I'll put the pocket money in the envelope and you can keep the clothes and trainers."

"Cool," James said. "I'll go for that."

"You know, James," Meryl said. "It must be Kerry's influence, I could almost mistake you for a reformed character."

James couldn't help smiling at the compliment. "I've been at CHERUB for exactly a year," he said. "I reckon I've spend too much of that time scrubbing corridors, peeling vegetables, and running punishment laps to mess you around any more."

Meryl burst out laughing. "That's what I like to hear," she giggled, "total obedience . . . But seriously, James, your performance on this mission shows that the training and hard work have paid off. When Keith Moore was being held hostage a few nights ago, you kept your head in a very nasty situation and thought your way out of it. If you'd found yourself in that position before you came here, I'm sure your reaction would have been very different."

James nodded. "I probably would have freaked out, like Junior did."

"And the bond you made with Keith Moore was tremendous."

"Keith's really nice guy," James said. "I know he's a drug dealer, but I almost feel sad that he's gonna go to prison."

"Well, *don't,*" Meryl said sharply. "Keith had enough money and power to keep his distance from the nasty side of the drug business. He might have spent his days swanning around his pool acting like a cool guy, but he knew what was going on. KMG was a ruthless organization that didn't hesitate to use violence and intimidation to get what it wanted. For every person KMG made rich, there's probably a thousand more who messed up their lives with drugs. Either by taking them, or getting caught selling them."

"Keith said breaking up KMG wouldn't even make a difference to the amount of cocaine being sold on the streets."

"Maybe there's some truth in that," Meryl said. "But you can't stop fighting against something just because it's difficult. That's like saying there's no point having doctors and hospitals because everyone eventually dies."

"So when's my next mission?" James asked.

"Ah," Meryl said, "bad news on that score, I'm afraid. You've been on two long missions already this year and you've missed a lot of school. We're not looking to send you off campus again until the new year."

"That's not so bad, actually," James said. "Missions are hard work. It'll be nice to go a few months without waking up every morning wondering what my name is and if I'm gonna get shot at."

"I heard about the man you killed. We do all we can to keep our agents out of situations like this, but it's an unfortunate fact that drug dealers and guns are inextricably linked. Have you thought about it at all since you got back?"

"A bit," James said. "But I get more freaked-out wondering what would have happened if me and Junior hadn't decided to go down the beach for a boxing—erm . . . For a swim, that night."

"Have you had trouble sleeping, or nightmares?"

"I was lying awake thinking about the car chase on the plane home," James said. "The woman sitting next to me said I looked pale. She got me a little tub of mineral water."

"I'll arrange some sessions with a counselor," Meryl said. "You've been through a traumatic experience and it's important that you talk about your feelings with someone."

Kerry was sitting on a bench for the athletics track waiting for James when he got out of Meryl's office. He gave her a quick kiss and sat next to her.

"How many punishment laps did Meryl give you?" Kerry asked.

"None," James said.

"That's got to be a first."

"I didn't do anything bad."

Kerry started giggling. "Another first."

"They don't want to send me on another mission until the new year. It'll be cool if we can just chill out on campus together. Watch movies, do homework and stuff."

"That's OK for you to say, James. You've already fluked into the lead role on two major missions and earned your navy T-shirt. I'm still a nobody."

"It's not such a big deal," James said casually. "It's just a T-shirt."

Kerry huffed. "If there's one thing I really hate, it's people who have something and say that it doesn't matter. It's like those rock stars on MTV who go on about how their millions and supermodel girlfriends haven't made them any happier. But you never see them giving it all away and going back to live in Mummy's trailer home, do you?"

James thought it was best to change the subject before Kerry got into one of her moods. "Do you fancy taking a stroll over to the back of campus?"

"That would be nice," Kerry said, breaking into a smile. "The leaves are pretty colors at this time of year. I never thought you had a romantic side, James."

"Actually, Kyle and Lauren are up there cleaning out ditches. I thought we could go over and wind them up a bit."

Kerry gave James a gentle shove. "I might have known you *didn't* have a romantic side. . . . What happened about Lauren, anyway? The last I heard, everyone was gonna go up there and help her out."

"Mac said Lauren had to be punished and that anyone caught helping her dig would have to run thirty laps every day for a month. Everyone's making her life easier in other ways though: doing her laundry, letting her jump the queue in the canteen, copying homework, that kind of stuff.

"It was so funny when Kyle got back from ditch-clearing last night," James continued. "You know how he's always immaculate? His uniform was plastered in mud and it smelled *so* bad. A lot of the water in those ditches runs off the farms around here. It's all full of cow and pig manure, and God knows what else."

"Serves him right for taking drugs," Kerry said.

"Give over, Kerry, all he did was take a puff on a joint. He would never have got caught if Nicole hadn't collapsed."

"I don't care," Kerry said. "If something's against the law, you shouldn't do it. Especially drugs."

James started to laugh.

"What's so funny?"

"You," James said. "You're always *such* a Goody Two-shoes."

Kerry jabbed a finger in James's ribs.

"What was that for?"

"I'm not a Goody Two-shoes."

James grinned. "Little Miss Perfect."

"Take that back or I'll make you sorry."

James mocked her voice. "Take that back or I'll make you sorry."

"Don't start repeating what I say."

"Don't start repeating what I say."

"That's *it,* James," Kerry said angrily.

"That's *it,* James." James leaned forward and planted

a cheeky kiss on Kerry's face. She broke into a smile.

"I knew you weren't really mad at me," James giggled. "I'm too delightful."

He stopped giggling when he realized it wasn't Kerry's nice smile. It was her evil smile. She jabbed James in the ribs again, then used the moment while he was in spasm to wrap her arm around the back of his neck and wedge him into a headlock under her arm.

"Still Goody Two-shoes, am I?" Kerry grinned as she tightened her grip.

"No," James croaked.

"Quite sure?"

"You're not a Goody, Kerry," James squirmed. "Just . . . Please . . . Let me go."

Kerry let James loose. As he straightened up, James couldn't but help see the funny side of being effortlessly humiliated by a twelve-year-old girl wearing pink and white striped socks with penguins embroidered over the ankle.

Kerry got off the bench.

"Where are you going?" James asked.

"Romantic stroll," she explained, as she marched towards the trees. "Are you coming or not?"

After their walk, James, Kerry, and a big bunch of other kids spent Sunday evening at the bowling alley in the nearest town. They got beaten three games to two by the identical twins Callum and Connor. James and Kerry had a total laugh. James had never felt so relaxed with a girl before. Now he'd asked Kerry out, it seemed dumb that he'd spent so long finding excuses not to.

James lay awake until gone midnight. His body was still running on Miami time and it was early evening over there. He tucked his hands under his head and stared at the shadows on the ceiling.

He wondered how Junior was doing in hospital and got pissed off when he remembered that April still had his Nike watch. But the KMG mission already seemed distant, like part of some other kid's life. James Beckett was no more. James Adams felt warm and comfortable under his duvet. He realized he was the happiest he'd been since his mum died.

James thought about life on campus. He knew the quickest routes around every building. He knew everyone's names. Which kids not to start a conversation with in the lift because they'd bore you to tears. Which teachers would have a laugh with you and which ones would hammer you for the tiniest little thing.

James knew there would always be mornings when he woke up and didn't want to get out of bed for two hours' combat training, or a brain-numbing double history lesson. But when he pulled on his uniform and walked down to breakfast, he knew most other kids looked at him with respect. Whenever James got to the dining room and looked around for a seat, there were always a few tables where he could sit amongst friends, spreading the latest gossip and winding each other up.

A year earlier, CHERUB campus had been a bunch of strange faces, winding corridors, and scary teachers. Now it felt like home.

epilogue

KELVIN HOLMES was sentenced to three years' youth custody for conspiracy to supply drugs. Most of the younger boys who worked as delivery riders for KMG got off with police cautions and supervision orders. A few who had previous drug convictions received 3–6 months in youth custody.

Without funding from Keith Moore, the JT Martin youth center and boxing club closed its doors for the final time after the 2004 Christmas party. No charges were brought against KEN FOWLER, who died of a heart attack a few months later.

MADELINE BURROWS, the nice lady who called James with his deliveries, got a five-year prison sentence, as did her younger brother JOSEPH BURROWS (Crazy Joe). Over 130 other members of KMG received prison sentences as a direct result of the MI5 surveillance operation on Thunderfoods.

Dinesh's dad, PARVINDER SINGH, received a twelve-year prison sentence. DINESH SINGH and his mother moved away, to live near relatives in south London.

KEITH MOORE spent over a week being interviewed by DEA officials at their headquarters in Washington, D.C. Keith was bitter about the Lambayeke cartel's brutal attempt to steal his money and provided a mass of information that led to the immediate seizure of $130 million in drug money and the arrest of several senior figures within the Lambayeke organization.

Keith was later flown back to Britain, where he pleaded guilty to numerous charges relating to money-laundering and drug-trafficking. The judge sentenced Keith to eighteen years in prison and recommended that he should not be considered for early release until he had served at least ten.

The police have uncovered £12 million of Keith's personal fortune, but he is still believed to have at least another £40 million in secret bank accounts.

JUNIOR MOORE fully recovered from his injuries and flew back to Britain. Shortly afterwards, he was expelled from Gray Park school for persistent truancy. His mother said she was "sick of his behavior" and didn't want him ending up like his father. She found him a place at a tough boarding school that specializes in dealing with difficult boys.

APRIL MOORE quickly grew tired of James Beckett not responding to her text messages and e-mails. She returned James's best watch to the address where the Beckett family had supposedly moved and it was eventually forwarded to CHERUB campus. When James opened the envelope, he found his watch had been hammered into a dozen pieces. It was accompanied by a note reading: "You could at least have had the decency to dump me to my face. Hope you die slowly, April."

JOHN JONES announced he was leaving MI5 after nineteen years' service. He has accepted a new job as a CHERUB mission controller.

EWART & ZARA ASKER are expecting their second child in April 2005.

NICOLE EDDISON now lives with two retired cherubs on a farm in Shropshire. She has two young stepbrothers whom she adores and a boyfriend called James. She attends twice-weekly counseling sessions and is slowly coming to terms with the loss of her family.

Dr. McAfferty's beloved mission preparation building is on schedule to be completed in February 2005. He conducted a review of Nicole's recruitment to CHERUB, to see if any mistakes had been made. His report reached the following conclusion:

"If anything, the tests Nicole Eddison completed before

being asked to join CHERUB show that she had an above average chance of becoming a successful agent. Unfortunately, no recruitment test yet devised can account for all the complexities of human nature. It seems likely that a small number of unsuitable candidates will be recruited into CHERUB for as long as the organization exists. All we can do is remain vigilant and try to keep this number at a minimum."

A few weeks after James returned from Miami, AMY COLLINS left campus to live with her brother in Australia. James was part of the crowd that waved her through the departure gate at Heathrow airport.

It took KYLE BLUEMAN and LAUREN ADAMS two months to clean out all the ditches at the back of campus. Kyle was suspended from missions for another four months. Lauren re-entered basic training, with her daily countdown paper in her pocket and a grim determination to make it through no matter how tough Mr. Large tried to make it.

After a few weeks back on campus, KERRY CHANG was sent to Hong Kong on a mission that looked set to last several months. James and Kerry are exchanging daily e-mails and occasionally speak to each other on the phone.

JAMES ADAMS used his time on campus to catch up on schoolwork. He has recently started studying for GCSE exams in three of his strongest subjects, has begun regular weight training, and narrowly failed a second-dan black belt grading in karate class. He expects to be assigned to another undercover mission in early 2005.

CHERUB:
A HISTORY
(1941–1996)

1941 In the middle of the Second World War, Charles Henderson, a British agent working in occupied France, sent a report to his headquarters in London. It was full of praise for the way the French Resistance used children to sneak past Nazi checkpoints and wangle information out of German soldiers.

1942 Henderson formed a small undercover detachment of children, under the command of British Military Intelligence. Henderson's Boys were all thirteen or fourteen years old, mostly French refugees. They were given basic espionage training before being parachuted into occupied France. The boys gathered vital intelligence in the run-up to the D-Day invasions of 1944.

1946 Henderson's Boys disbanded at the end of the war. Most of them returned to France. Their existence has never been officially acknowledged.

Charles Henderson believed that children would make effective intelligence agents during peacetime. In May 1946, he was given permission to create CHERUB in a disused village school. The first twenty CHERUB recruits, all boys, lived in wooden huts at the back of the playground.

1951 For its first five years, CHERUB struggled along with limited resources. Its fortunes changed following its first major success: Two agents uncovered a ring of Russian spies who were stealing information on the British nuclear weapons program.

The government of the day was delighted. CHERUB was given funding to expand. Better facilities were built and the number of agents was increased from twenty to sixty.

1954 Two CHERUB agents, Jason Lennox and Johan Urminski, were killed while operating undercover in East Germany. Nobody knows how the boys died. The government considered shutting CHERUB down, but there were now over seventy active CHERUB agents performing vital missions around the world.

An inquiry into the boys' deaths led to the introduction of new safeguards:

(1) The creation of the ethics panel. From now on, every mission had to be approved by a three-person committee.

(2) Jason Lennox was only nine years old. A minimum mission age of ten years and four months was introduced.

(3) A more rigorous approach to training was brought in. A version of the 100-day basic training program began.

1956 Although many believed that girls would be unsuitable for intelligence work, CHERUB admitted five girls as an experiment. They were a huge success. The number of girls in CHERUB was upped to twenty the following year. Within ten years, the number of girls and boys was equal.

1957 CHERUB introduced its system of colored T-shirts.

1960 Following several successes, CHERUB was allowed to expand again, this time to 130 students. The farmland surrounding headquarters was purchased and fenced off, about a third of the area that is now known as CHERUB campus.

1967 Katherine Field became the third CHERUB agent to die on an operation. She was bitten by a snake on a mission in India. She reached hospital within half an hour, but tragically the snake species was wrongly identified and Katherine was given the wrong antivenom.

1973 Over the years, CHERUB had become a hotchpotch of small buildings. Construction began on a new nine-story headquarters.

1977 All CHERUBs are either orphans, or children who have been abandoned by their family. Max Weaver was one of the first CHERUB agents. He made a fortune building office blocks in London and New York. When he died in 1977, aged just forty-one, without a wife or children, Max Weaver left his fortune for the benefit of the children at CHERUB.

The Max Weaver Trust Fund has paid for many of the buildings on CHERUB campus. These include the indoor athletics facilities and library. The trust fund now holds assets worth over £1 billion.

1982 Thomas Webb was killed by a landmine on the Falkland Islands, becoming the fourth CHERUB to die on a mission. He was one of nine agents used in various roles during the Falklands conflict.

1986 The government gave CHERUB permission to expand up to four hundred pupils. Despite this, numbers have stalled some way below this. CHERUB requires intelligent, physically robust agents who have no family ties. Children who meet all these admission criteria are extremely hard to find.

1990 CHERUB purchased additional land, expanding both the size and security of campus. Campus is marked on all British maps as an army firing range. Surrounding roads are routed so that there is only one road onto campus. The perimeter walls cannot be seen from nearby roads. Helicopters are banned from the area and airplanes must stay above ten thousand meters. Anyone breaching the CHERUB perimeter faces life imprisonment under the State Secrets Act.

1996 CHERUB celebrated its fiftieth anniversary with the opening of a diving pool and an indoor shooting range.

Every retired member of CHERUB was invited to the celebration. No guests were allowed. Over nine hundred people made it, flying from all over the world. Among the retired agents were a former prime minister and a rock guitarist who had sold 80 million albums.

After a firework display, the guests pitched tents and slept on campus. Before leaving the following morning, everyone gathered outside the chapel and remembered the four children who had given CHERUB their lives.

Don't miss Mission 3:

MAXIMUM SECURITY

Before you entered basic training, you probably heard stories from qualified CHERUB agents about the nature of this one-hundred-day course. Although every basic training course is designed to teach the same core abilities of physical fitness and extreme mental endurance, you can expect your training to differ from that of your predecessors in order to retain the element of surprise.

(Excerpt from the CHERUB Basic Training Manual)

It looked the same in every direction. The sunlight blazing off the field of snow made it impossible for the two ten-year-old girls to see more than twenty meters into the distance, despite the heavily tinted snow goggles over their eyes.

"How far to the checkpoint?" Lauren Adams shouted, breaking her stride to stare at the global positioning unit strapped around her best friend's wrist.

"Only two and a half kilometers," Bethany Parker shouted back. "If the ground stays flat, we should be at the shelter in forty minutes."

The girls had to shout for their voices to override the howling wind and the three layers of clothing protecting their ears.

"That's cutting it close to sundown," Lauren yelled. "We'd better get a move on."

They'd set off at dawn, dragging lightweight sleds that could be hooked over their shoulders and carried as backpacks on difficult terrain. The good news was, the two CHERUB trainees had the whole day to trek fifteen kilometers across the Alaskan snowfield to their next checkpoint. The bad news was that at this time in April, the daylight lasted just four hours and wading through half a meter of powdery snow put enormous strain on their thighs and ankles. Every step was painful.

Lauren heard a howling noise rising up in the distance. "It's gonna to be another big one," she shouted.

The girls crouched down, pulled their sleds in close and wrapped their arms tightly around each other's waists. Just as you can hear waves approaching a beach, out here in the Alaskan snowfields you could hear a strong gust stirring up in the distance.

They were both dressed for extreme cold. Lauren's normal underwear was covered with a long-sleeved thermal vest and long johns. The next layer was a zip-up suit made from polar fleece that covered her whole body, except for a slit around the eyes. The second fleece was designed to trap body heat. It looked like a baggy Easter bunny suit, minus the pom-pom tail and sticking up ears. Then came more gloves, another balaclava, snow goggles, and waterproof outer gloves that went all the way up to Lauren's elbows, ending in a tightly fitting elastic cuff. Finally, on the outside was a thickly padded snowsuit and snow boots with spiked bottoms.

The clothing was enough to keep them comfortable as

they walked, despite the temperature being minus eighteen centigrade, but this dropped another fifteen degrees whenever a strong gust hit. The wind pushed the insulating layers of warm air between the girls' clothes into all the places where it wasn't needed, leaving nothing but a couple of centimeters of synthetic fiber between their skin and the ferociously cold air. Each blast ripped into their bodies, delivering searing pain to any exposed area.

Lauren and Bethany used their sleds as windbreaks when the gust hit. A spike of cold air punched through the tightly fitting rim of Lauren's goggles. She pushed her face against Bethany's suit and squeezed her eyes shut, as snow and ice pounded deafeningly against her hood.

When the gust passed and the snow had settled, Lauren brushed the dusting of powder off her suit and stumbled back to her feet.

"Everything OK?" Bethany shouted.

Lauren stuck up her thumbs. "Ninety-nine days down, one to go," she shouted.

Lauren and Bethany's home for the night was a metal container painted in a high visibility shade of orange. It was the kind of container you'd normally expect to pass on the motorway, mounted on the back of an articulated truck. There was a radio mast and a shattered flagpole lashed to the roof.

The girls had beaten the darkness. The sun's distant face was already touching the horizon and the light it sent through the mist of falling snow gave the whole landscape a powdery yellow hue. The girls were too exhausted to appreciate its beauty; all they cared about was getting warm.

It took a few minutes to dig out the snow from around the two metal doors that formed one end of the container. Once they were open, Lauren dragged the two sleds inside, while Bethany searched along a wooden shelf until she found a gas lamp. Lauren closed the metal doors, creating a boom that would have been deafening if the girls' ears hadn't been shielded by their outdoor clothes.

"We've got even less fuel tonight," Lauren shouted, as the lamp erupted in an unsteady blue glow. She looked at the single bottle of gas as she peeled off her goggles and outermost set of gloves. Her hands were freezing, but it was impossible to manipulate anything with three sets of gloves on.

On the first night of their week in the Alaskan wilderness, the girls had found two large bottles of gas in their shelter. They'd heated the room until it was toasty, cooked lavishly, and warmed up water to wash with. The fun ended abruptly when the gas ran out in the middle of the night and the indoor temperature rapidly dropped back below freezing. After this harsh lesson, the girls took pains to ration their energy supply.

Bethany fixed a hose from the gas bottle to a small heater and lit just one of its three chambers. This would slowly bring the temperature inside their container above freezing. Until it did, the girls would keep as many of their outdoor clothes on as the task at hand allowed.

They spent the next few minutes rummaging through the supplies that had been left for them. There were plenty of high-energy foods, such as tinned meats, flapjacks, instant noodles, chocolate bars, and glucose powder. They also found their mission briefings, clean underwear, fresh boot liners, and floor mats. Combined with the pots, utensils, and sleeping bags packed in their sleds, it would be enough to make the nineteen hours until the sun returned reasonably comfortable.

Once the girls had ensured that they had all the basics, Lauren couldn't help wondering what was under the tarpaulin at the back of the container.

"That's got to be something to do with our mission for tomorrow," Bethany said.

They stepped across and dragged the tarp off a giant cardboard box. It was over two meters long and almost up to Lauren's shoulders. Scraping at the layer of frost over the cardboard revealed a Yamaha logo and an outline drawing of a snowmobile.

"Cool," Bethany said. "I don't think my legs could handle another day trudging through that snow."

"Have you ever driven one?" Lauren asked.

"Nah," Bethany said, shaking her head excitedly. "But it can't be much different from the quad bikes we drove last summer at the hostel. . . . Let's open our briefings and work out what we've got to do tomorrow."

"We'd better take our temperatures and radio base camp first," Lauren said.

There was a radio set already linked up to the aerial on the roof. Its battery was cold and it took several seconds for the orange frequency display on the front panel to light up. While they waited, the girls took turns measuring their body temperatures with a small plastic strip that you tucked under your armpit.

The indicator lit up between the thirty-five and thirty-six degree marks on both of them. It meant the girls were running slightly below normal body temperature, which is exactly what you'd expect for two people who'd just spent several hours in extreme cold. Another hour would have been enough for them to develop early symptoms of hypothermia.

Lauren grabbed the microphone and keyed up. "This is unit three calling Instructor Large. Over."

"Instructor Large receiving . . . Greetings, my little sugar plums."

It was reassuring hearing a human voice other than Bethany's for the first time in twenty-four hours, even if it was that of Mr. Large, CHERUB's head training instructor. Large was a nasty piece of work. Pushing kids through tough training courses wasn't just part of his job; he actually enjoyed making them suffer.

"Just reporting in to say that everything is fine with me and unit four," Lauren said. "Over."

"Why aren't you using the coded frequency? Over," Mr. Large asked angrily.

Lauren realized her instructor was right and hurriedly flipped the scramble switch on the front of the receiver.

"Oh . . . Sorry. Over."

"You will be tomorrow morning when I get my hands on you," Large snapped. "Minus ten house points for Hufflepuff. Over and out."

"Over and out," Lauren said bitterly. She put down the microphone and kicked out at the side of the metal container. "God, I *really* hate that man's guts."

Bethany laughed a little. "Not as much as he hates you for knocking him head first into that muddy hole with a spade."

"True," Lauren said, allowing herself a grin as she

recalled the event that had brought her first attempt at basic training to an abrupt end. "I suppose we'd better get cracking. You start translating the briefing. I'll go outside and bring in some snow to melt for drinking water."

Lauren found a bucket and grabbed the torch out of her sled. She pushed the metal door of the container and squeezed herself and the bucket through a small gap, so as not to let out too much heat.

The sun was gone and only the tiny shaft of light from inside the container enabled Lauren to notice the giant white outline in the snow. Half convinced that she was overtired and imagining things, Lauren flicked on her torch.

What Lauren saw left her in no doubt. She screamed as she scrambled back inside the container and swiftly pulled up the metal door.

"What's the matter?" Bethany asked, turning sharply from her mission briefing.

"Polar bear!" Lauren gasped. "Lying in the snow right outside the door. Luckily it seemed to be resting; another few steps and I would have trodden on it."

"It *can't* be," Bethany said.

Lauren waved the torch in her training partner's face. "Here, take this. Stick your head out and look for yourself."

It only took the briefest of glances to confirm it. The mat of white fur, with plumes of hot breath steaming out of its nostrils, lay less than five meters from the entrance to the container.

Once Lauren recovered from her near-death experience, the girls thought things through and decided that the situation wasn't too serious.

They could get all the drinking water they needed by leaning out of the metal doors and scooping up the snow around the entrance. Once they'd got enough snow, they decided to leave the giant bear in peace. It seemed unlikely the animal would leave itself exposed to the cold all night. Surely it would move away to find shelter before the sun came back up.

The inside of the container had now warmed up enough for the girls not to be able to see their breath curling in front of their faces. After their day in the cold, it seemed toasty. They stepped out of their boots and outer suits, hanging them on a line in the warm air above the gas heater, so that the moisture in them would evaporate overnight.

The metal floor of the container was cold to touch, so they put on trainers and laid out insulating foam mats retrieved from their sleds. They turned the heater up and lined icy tins of corned beef and fruit in front of it, as Bethany melted a saucepan of snow over a portable stove.

It took an hour to read the briefings for the final twenty-four hours of their course, under the flickering light of two gas lamps. The briefings only ran to five pages, but were written in languages with non-European alphabets that the girls had only started learning at the beginning of the course: Russian for Bethany and Greek for Lauren.

The gist of the briefings was simple. The girls had to unpack the snowmobile from its shipping crate and prepare it for first use: a task that involved screwing various bits together, lubricating the drive track and engine, and filling the tank with petrol. From sunup, they'd have two hours to make a thirty-five-kilometer journey by snowmobile to a checkpoint where they would liaise with the four other trainees for something the briefing ominously described as the "*Ultimate test of physical courage in an extreme weather environment*."

"Well," Lauren said, as she dug her spoon into a can of corned beef that was warm and greasy on the outside but rock hard in the centre, "at least the instructions for the snowmobile are in English."

ABOUT THE AUTHOR

Robert Muchamore was born in London in 1972 and used to work as a private investigator. CHERUB is his first series and is published in more than twenty countries.

NEW SERIES. NEW WORLD.

LEVIATHAN

FROM

SCOTT WESTERFELD

THE BESTSELLING AUTHOR OF THE UGLIES SERIES

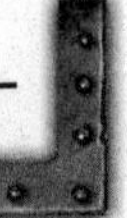

FROM SIMON PULSE
PUBLISHED BY SIMON & SCHUSTER

Exciting fiction from three-time Newbery Honor author GARY PAULSEN

Aladdin Paperbacks and Simon Pulse
Simon & Schuster Children's Publishing
www.SimonSays.com